SAVING GRACE

Reeling from her husband's betrayal and struggling to rebuild her marriage when he comes back to her, Grace finds her life is unravelling. Soon, however, she finds another life being woven around her. A book enters her life, one unlike any she has read, and after that, the man who wrote it, Richard Ortega, a man unlike any she has ever known. As she increasingly seeks strength and comfort not in Richard's books but his words, Grace finds herself becoming his muse. However, once the line between fiction and truth has blurred, she will find that his imagination can never let her go.

SAVING GRACE

SAVING GRACE

by

Penelope Evans

Magna Large Print Books
Long Preston, North Yorkshire,
BD23 4ND, England.

British Library Cataloguing in Publication Data.

Evans, Penelope
    Saving Grace.

    A catalogue record of this book is
    available from the British Library

    ISBN   978-0-7505-2791-0

First published in Great Britain in 2007 by Allison & Busby Ltd.

Published in Large Print 2007 by arrangement with
Allison & Busby Ltd.

Magna Large Print is an imprint of Library Magna Books Ltd.

Printed and bound in Great Britain by
T.J. (International) Ltd., Cornwall, PL28 8RW

Prologue

Author's introduction to Richard Ortega's thirteenth novel. (Untitled)

Sometimes a writer – if he is a true writer – is compelled to write true. True, that is, to his own experience, to the people and events that have overwhelmed him with the force of a tsunami. A personal tsunami, laying waste a personal horizon, destroying everything in its path, leaving only devastation. When such a force of nature strikes, everything may be lost, and a man left with nothing except what he is. A man.

But how much of a man?

He may, if strong, be left physically standing – as I am standing. But what else of him is there? What of his humanity, his trust? His ability to have faith? **His ability to love?**

These of course are the true qualities of a man, and if they are lost, then he must ask: can he, by his own measure, still call himself a man?

There is an answer. A writer's answer, and it can be found in the words of The Master. *For it was Henry James who said: 'try to be one of those writers on whom nothing is lost.'*

In this, as in so much else, I intend to follow his lead. This book has been written true to that

7

lead. *I have written true. Which means that these pages – though a work of fiction – will be the test of whether the qualities that Make the Man are indeed, even now, to be found.*

Is this writer still a man? The reader must be the judge. Is he a man still able to have faith in his fellow man? A man able to forgive? Is he, above all, still able – still willing – to love?

Out of the darkness has he, in truth, brought forth light?

Note to self # 1.
Maybe better to attach the above as introduction to *second* edition. Although, of course, before then Publicity (hopefully) will have done its job. Everyone will know the full history behind the book. Terrible traumas et cetera, et cetera. The chance meeting, the hounding that came after, the threats, the stalker who never goes away. The woman who never goes away. No need to dwell, not in the introduction. But v. important to make sure there's an *up* note. Goodness prevails and all that.

No, on second thoughts, attach to first edition. Reader's got to know there's light at the end of the tunnel. Don't want anyone to be put off buying the fucking thing.

Note to self # 2.
'*Tsunami*'. Like it. Never really used to hear it much. *Tidal wave* – that's the expression

we all grew up with. Sounds positively old-fashioned now. No, tsunami's good. Gets it across better, the damage it can do. Complete destruction.

Tsunami's good.

So where was I?

Damn. Lost the plot.

Chapter One

Grace. Gracie when young. By the Grace of God. *Dis*grace (rarely). Good Grace (often).

Grace had always tried to be good and happy, even when she was a little girl. And shut out bad thoughts.

But the thought hit her now, the way thoughts so often did hit her. That's to say with the force of an invisible hand thrust against her chest, stopping her, freezing her to the spot. This time it happened when she was halfway down the stairs with her husband's shirts in her hands, gathered out of the laundry basket. A week of them, all smelling of him. Familiar. Familiar as her own scent.

Was it something to be proud of? Knowing she could have divided an entire laundry-load of their clothes, with her eyes bound and her hands tied behind her back, just by

9

using her nose. Two piles. His and hers. Is this what it had done for her, being married so long to someone? Given her the talents of what? A sniffer hound?

Yet she had never scented anyone else on him, not in all those months.

It had never occurred to her: that she should have, could have, smelt anyone else lingering on her husband's shirts. It was only now, in retrospect, when it was all over, that she marvelled at how it was she had never lifted the scent of another woman off her husband's shirts and translated it as meaning to her brain. She had never smelt anything but him. Yet he had worn nothing else next to his skin. He had never been a vest man. And she had never guessed.

Now, motionless on the stairs, she knew why. It was because he hadn't been wearing his shirts. Not when it happened. He hadn't been wearing anything at all. He had been naked. Completely. With *her*, the other one. If Grace had been determined to seek the scent of another woman, she would have had to bury her face in her husband's skin, not his shirts.

The invisible hand pressed harder against her chest. She had to tell herself to breathe.

And so she did. Grace took a breath, pushed away the hand and carried on downstairs, through the kitchen, into the utility room, to the washing machine. On the way, she stepped past her son putting an empty bottle of milk back in the fridge, and her daughter frowning over the buttons of her mobile phone. Neither of them seemed to notice her and, still heading for the washing machine as if it were some distant goal, she had the feeling she had simply passed right through them like a cloud of particles through solid bodies.

Grace. Good Grace. How had it come to this?

She put the shirts into the washing machine, pushed the buttons and left them to drown.

Yet it was over. Simon had stayed with her. If she were to bury her nose in his skin now, she would smell nothing but Simon. Her friends had been gentle when she told them it was finished, and not one of them had said what Grace knew they were thinking. How did she know?

Well, she did know. Simon had taken weeks to make up his mind, mulled over his decision, weighed up the pros and cons. She had watched him – frowning, considering, comparing. He was an accountant and she had imagined his mind turned into a tally sheet, divided into columns of profit and loss. Her good points versus her bad. Life with Lucy versus life with her.

And when, almost embarrassed, she had

suggested that really such a decision could not be made while they still shared a bed, he had retreated to the loft conversion, to the empty but quite comfortable spaces beneath the eaves. There was a bathroom up there, and a kitchen. Even a small sitting room. All of it prepared for another kind of life, for when the children were grown up, but not quite ready to leave home. An in-between place.

All the same, he had seemed surprised that she had put him there. As if it had been one of the children that she had edged towards the outside of the family circle, before they were ready to go. It was that very surprise that had been the clue for her. In his – Simon's – ideal world, everything would have stayed the same. He wouldn't have had to make any choices. He could have carried on, safe in the centre, venturing every now and then into the outside like a teenager. In an ideal – no, make that a *perfect* – world, he would even have been able to bring Lucy home to meet her. The way he had brought Grace home to meet his mother.

So that's what I am, Grace had thought to herself. *His mother*. And deep down inside her, still there, sixteen-, eighteen-, twenty-year-old Gracie had giggled with shock.

But that's where he went to make up his mind, to the loft; ideal for a man not quite ready to leave. Not quite ready to stay.

One evening, late at night, he came down and called her name from the door. She had put down the book she was reading (tried to ignore the mental image of his mother putting down her sewing) and waited.

'I've decided to stay,' he said. 'With you. If you'll have me.'

She touched the pages of the book. 'Why?'

'Because of the children. I know they're older now, but they're still children. They still need me. And I need them. And because of *us*. All these years we've been together, all that history – I don't want to let it go, Grace. Not for something that's come out of the blue like this. And,' here he had hesitated. 'And I love you, of course. But you've always known that.'

He had stopped there, making no effort to elaborate, to explain the nature or the quality of that love. The depth or the shape of it. Nothing.

'I want to stay, Grace. And I won't see her again. Not in *that* way. It's over.'

Suddenly she was too tired to look at him. Instead her eyes had sunk to the book lying on her lap, to meet the eyes of the author staring out of the back cover. Dark eyes, quizzical and amused. Eyes older than Simon's, that seemed to understand exactly what was going on, and were asking her now: *is that all? Is that all he has to say to you?*

That was all. But if nothing else, she knew

Simon and his decisions. When he made up his mind, he meant it. If he had said it was over, then it was over. Finished. And so, slowly, she had nodded. He nodded in turn and stepped into the room, came and sat beside her on the sofa. For a moment neither of them said anything. Then he shifted in his seat, awkwardly, to remove something hard from under him, and came up with the remote control. He frowned at it and for a terrible moment she was afraid that he was about to turn on the television.

But he didn't. He put the remote down and felt for her hand, still not looking at her, and there they had sat for hours, hardly speaking, waiting for the world to settle back into its familiar places, like an animal home from the vet's.

But what had *she* done before and after the time Simon had been pointed to the loft to make up his mind, in those weeks when Simon was absent, but never in the way he should have been?

She had been able to hear his footsteps in the night, his voice murmuring through the ceiling as he talked to *her*, the other one, on his mobile phone. Still there, appearing for supper and breakfast, talking to the children, putting his shirts into the dirty wash. Still assuming he was part of the circle which included her.

What had she done? At first, in the very beginning, she had done nothing. Not for days, a whole week. Grace, good Grace, had been stunned as a female ox. Hardly human, she thought later. Her brain had ached from trying to make sense of it, and then shut down. Every night she had cried herself to sleep and woken heavy-eyed. Then she had got up to make breakfast and school boxes for the children.

The children. The next shock had been through them. Simon had left it to her to tell them, knowing she wouldn't paint him too hard. And she didn't. Robert, who was sixteen, had actually laughed. 'You mean, he's been ... you know, *doing it* ... at his age?'

'Shut up, Rob,' Anna, fifteen, had elbowed him. But even her face, pretty and peachy smooth, was uncreased. 'Must be terrible, Mum, really terrible.' She reached out a hand. 'Don't worry though. It's just a phase. You know what men are like. It doesn't mean anything, that sort of thing. It's you he loves. He'll realise it for himself, you watch. They all do, sooner or later.'

Grace had stared at her in wonder. *Where was she finding the words?* Then it came to her – it was all culled, syllable by syllable, from *EastEnders* or *Holby City*. Some soap where people were having to comfort each other all the time. Where couples were having TV weddings one week and slamming doors

15

against each other the next. Another week, and it would all be different again.

So Grace had nodded, just to keep within the script, and immediately felt better, more human, knowing there was a part she could play. Simon came home that night, and his relief was palpable when he looked at her. The smudged out, blank look had vanished from her face. She was wearing make-up. There was a proper supper in the oven. Everything was back to the way it was before the bomb had dropped, when weeping and drunk with guilt he had confessed all to Grace, unable to live with himself until it was off his chest – and loaded onto hers. The only thing not the same was that then she had pointed him upstairs, to the bed all made up in the loft, the in-between place.

The next evening they had even gone to a dinner party together and nobody guessed. Grace drank a little more, and Simon drank a little less and at least two people commented on how well they were both looking.

Home again that same night, with the sounds of Simon rolling over heavily in the bed above – the loft was proving to be anything but soundproof – Grace had stared at herself in the mirror. Forty years old. Slimmish. Darkish. Small breasts, still high. Small hands. Small feet...

Then she had started to cry. She couldn't see herself. Her face was a blank, her eyes

16

good for nothing except to stop her walking into doors. She could find not one distinguishing feature. She knew if she came across her double in a crowd she would walk straight on by without even noticing. Yet she remembered a time when she had been as vain as Anna was now, searching for and welcoming her reflection wherever she found it – in shop windows, car mirrors, even the reflecting lenses in the sunglasses of old boyfriends.

Not now. She could use the mirror as an inventory, ticking off the nose, the mouth – slightly too large, the curls – still brown, the fine lines above her brow. Put it all together, though, and it fell apart as if some necessary glue had stopped working. And the reason that she cried was because if *she* couldn't see herself, then how could she expect Simon to see her?

How long had she been invisible? She hadn't even noticed.

And then it was all over. Simon had come downstairs, she had put down her book, hiding the picture of the author with his quizzical stare, and they had held hands.

Lucy *(say the name)* was still there, working in the same company as Simon, his exact equal in position and pay; but even that wasn't anything to dwell upon. Simon had made up his mind, and he had told her

17

the reasons. Because of the children, because of all the history they shared. Because he loved her.

'I'm back, Grace,' he whispered to her that night as they climbed into bed. And he was. When he slept, which he did easily, Lucy's name never crept out of him in a dream. When they made love, which happened occasionally, rather formally, he looked directly into her eyes, so she knew she had all his attention. He bought her flowers, and left holiday brochures for her to browse through.

'You choose, Grace.'

Over. They were both agreed.

And that's what she had tried to believe at first, in those few days after he came down from the loft. But then, she was forced to acknowledge what she always knew. This wasn't the end; it was the beginning. The thoughts kept hitting her, even when she wasn't thinking. Stopping her, like now, halfway down the stairs with her arms full of shirts, because she had finally made the connection about why she had never smelt a woman on her husband's shirts. One thought after another, waiting in line to ambush her. How could it be the end, when the aftermath was worse than the actual event? Back when it was all happening, when Simon had still been maundering in his loft, she had had a kind of energy. After the first paralysis, there had arrived the adrenaline of shock to keep her moving. She had used the few close friends she needed to confide in – especially Tamsin the lawyer. She had signed up for an IT course. She had kept busy. She had even detected – in those rare nights when Simon was not overhead making his presence felt – a kind of shiver, a curiosity about what might happen next, where she would end up. A first ripple of excitement of a new life.

But most importantly, she had had the book, the one she had been reading (re-reading) when Simon came downstairs and told her he had decided to stay. The book with that face on the back cover, whose eyes had quizzed her own, and asked *is that all?* as if the eyes' owner had been the only person in the room who knew that she needed to hear more, so much more.

Not a book she would have picked up for herself. Deborah had pushed it into her hand one night. 'Give it a go, Grace. We read it in book group. The others hated it but that was all Tamsin's fault. You know how she always gets people thinking her way. But I thought it was brilliant. It's...' she searched for the word she wanted '...empowering.' She pronounced the word, triumphant. 'Completely empowering.'

Which was, Grace noticed, the very word printed down at the corner of the cover, a quote from *Cosmopolitan. Empowering.*

The cover itself was a study in light, with a naked, seated woman shown sideways in silhouette, arms wrapped around her legs. In the small triangle between her arms and her body the sun flared and blazed as if she was the channel.

'*The Maid And The Magician*,' she read the title aloud.

'Richard Ortega – he always uses titles like that,' sighed Deborah. 'Sort of mysterious. His first one was called *The Hierophant*. I didn't even know there was such a word until I read the book.'

'I see,' said Grace. And she thought she did. Deborah was one for the self-help books, for remedies. Deborah tried to comfort her with Indian head massages and made Tamsin snigger with her crystals. Deborah was kinder than anyone she knew.

'You know, it's a little hard to concentrate. Just at the moment.'

'Try it anyway, Grace.' Deborah was pleading with her, desperate to help.

She had picked the book up at three o'clock in the morning. Upstairs under the eaves, Simon's mobile phone had bleeped. Not that it had woken her. She hadn't been sleeping. Nobody was sleeping, it seemed to her – except Lucy's husband, which must be the reason she was phoning Grace's husband now.

She lay in bed, trying not to hear Simon's voice. Yet she couldn't help but see him, murmuring into the phone, propped up on pillows, his hair tousled. He was a man who had grown better looking as he had grown older. Probably Lucy would never have looked twice at him when he was twenty-five and fresh-faced and single. Middle age and marriage suited him. Football with his son had kept him sleek and muscled. His daughter's friends fancied him.

And now here he was, his voice rising and falling, filtered through the ceiling when he was supposed to be absent. Grace stuck her fingers in her ears, pictured herself stamping upstairs to demand that he not be talking to his mistress here, under this roof. Or any roof. And she pictured *her*, Lucy, smiling into her own phone at the sound of a jealous wife making demands. Enjoying every second, hands playing with the lace on her negligee.

She had to be wearing a negligee. Grace was wearing pyjamas.

That was the moment, the very moment in which to sink or swim, and Grace knew she was about to sink, dragged under by pyjamas and tiredness and betrayal, by the sheer weight of self. As if on a far bank she had a glimpse of other selves, images of sixteen-year-old Grace, twenty-year-old Grace, watching her go under, their firm young faces mystified that it had come to this, that here she was, sinking under nothing but her own weight.

Ashamed, Grace looked away, turning from the bank to what was closer to her. And her eyes fell on the book and the picture of the woman with the sun shining through her. As if it were a straw floating past she clutched at it and let her fingers find a page. Wild and dim, her eyes slid over the first sentence of the first chapter.

'There once was a man who looked at women. **Really** looked at women. When he gazed into their eyes, he saw the girl inside. Never mind how old a woman, never mind the years that greyed her hair and parched her flesh – never mind all that, he looked and he saw the girl, shut up like a captive princess behind the face that betrayed her. He looked at her and his glance was like a kiss, and set her free.

To see like that – it was both a blessing and a curse. When a woman feels a man's eyes, intuitively she knows what he is thinking, even if she cannot admit it to herself. This is the way of the world, the way of women. **This** man had only to look and instantly a woman would know: something magical was happening. Her soul would laugh and leap like a salmon inside her, waking up to the memory of being alive and being young. And so, naturally, women fell in love with him. All of them. Every woman that he looked at.

And here is how a gift can be a curse: when a woman falls in love with a man, she imposes on him a duty. A woman's love is a precious bind and when a man is thus bound, he must vow never to harm, never to hurt. But how can one man be so dutiful when all the women in the world are in love with him?

So he did the only thing he could honourably do. He looked away. He bound his eyes – not with scarves or ties but with careful sideways glances, guaranteed never to meet anybody's eye. Naturally people saw this and took him for cunning, untrustworthy and shunned him. And so it came about that the man who could have made every woman in the world love him was alone. Lonely and without comfort...'

Grace read this. She knew that if she had come across these lines at any other time, she would have tossed them aside. Even now she could imagine Tamsin with her dry laugh, snorting over *precious bind* and *captive princess*. Another time and Grace might have laughed too. But not this time. Not tonight, when her husband's voice continued to filter through the ceiling, and whose eyes next morning would glance at her and see only what she had become: invisible. With a mind's eye full of someone else, he wouldn't, couldn't, see the Grace inside.

Yet she was still there. Twenty-year-old Grace, who tried to be good but very often was attractively bad. Who, twenty years ago, had smiled at her reflection before walking over to the man standing at the edge of the party, and kissed him on the lips, simply to laugh at his surprise. Twenty-year-old Grace knew she could have kissed any man in the room. But then she had kissed him and smelt him. Smelt *him*, and she was lost. And Simon, well, he had been hers from that moment on. Young and fresh-faced and single – now he was bound to the girl who had unsingled him, rescued him from the party's edge and brought him into the centre, where he had stayed.

What had happened to that girl, to twenty-year-old Grace? *He'd* know, the man in these pages, the one who looked at women, really looked at women. He would have looked at Grace, wrapped up in pyjamas and years, and he would have seen *her*, the Grace inside. And here, Grace's aching heart almost burst. He would have honoured her love, with all its *precious bind*. He would not have hurt her.

And that was the reason she read on, page after page, hour after hour. Simon must have stopped talking into his phone, rolled over and gone back to sleep. But Grace didn't hear. The man who looked at women, *really* looked at women, worked his magic in the world, despite himself. Because a gift is a gift, even when it's a curse, and this was his destiny – to take a woman who had been betrayed and find the girl inside, curled up in a ball. And give her back to the woman who had lost her...

Dawn was staining the bedroom wall pink as Grace turned the last page. In the final paragraph a woman walked towards a town, her footsteps firm on the long straight road that lay in front of her. Behind her, in a monastery cell, a man lay exhausted, tended by monks, who murmured over their tasks and filled his ears with the sweet honey balm of prayers. He was blind and he would never have to look at another woman. Yet neither would he now be lonely or without comfort. For the road the woman walked, that seemed to take her further with every step, was in reality no more than a thread, binding them together so they would never fall apart. Grace put the book down. At the same moment the morning sun slid across the wall and touched her eyes. She sighed. And then sighed again with surprise, aware that something had changed. Wide awake, she felt touched by more than just light. She lay in bed and tested herself. The heaviness that had been set to drag her down and drown her – it had almost all gone. She felt different. She felt ... she felt... She felt like a girl again. That's what she felt. If only for that brief moment as the sun slid across her eyes and flooded them with light. Then, above her in the loft, she heard Simon snore, and she blinked as sense and memory hit her. A man who saw the girl inside – it was nonsense. The whole story was nonsense. No wonder Tamsin had laughed, and made every one else laugh at it too.

The heaviness descended harder than before. Tiredly, cynically, Grace turned over the book to look at the author. And saw *him* – Richard Ortega. Dark eyes, slightly hooded, looking out of a face where the lines were deeply etched. Warm eyes, watching and quizzical, with a hint of humour in them. A playfulness. Eyes that might meet your own and touch something deep within. Eyes that wanted to understand.

He was the one who had written about a man who could see. As if such a man could actually exist, in the same way that in olden days dragons and mermaids and dog-headed birds could exist, simply because someone had named them and thereby made them real. He was the one who made *him* possible – the man who could see the girl inside and give her back to the woman who had lost her.

Grace stared at those eyes. Then, instead of trying to snatch an hour of sleep before the house woke around her, she turned to the front of the book and started to read, all over again.

Of course, it couldn't last, the magic of the

dawn light coinciding with the ending of the book. But it had given her something that couldn't be taken away now. Not even when she caught Simon's eyes resting on her, puzzled, as if half wondering who she was, perhaps wondering if she was anyone at all. She had caught the children looking at her like this often, suddenly afflicted by the suspicion that she might be someone in her own right. Only to shake themselves out of it.

But the book had reassured her. Somewhere there was a man who knew that inside every woman was a girl, who was nobody's mother, not even her husband's. He, the author, might not have the gift of sight himself, but he had written about a man who did. He knew such a thing existed. Grace gave the book back to Deborah without saying much, but then quietly went and bought a copy of her own. And all the time Simon was in the loft, mulling over the direction of his future – and therefore her future – she kept it close to hand. She didn't even have to read it. There was the picture on the cover, with the author's eyes, playful and questioning, looking deep into her own.

It carried her through the dark days. Her rock. Her safe place.

But then Simon had come downstairs and suddenly the book couldn't help her, not any more. The affair was over and Simon was back. Yet nothing could stop the thoughts hitting her and freezing her. Thoughts of shirts and smells and things he had never said.

Simon was staying. She should have been happy, and she wasn't. Not remotely. He was staying because of the children, because of their history, because he loved her in some way that he knew better than to specify. And her one grand, overriding thought was she wanted him to stay for none of these reasons. She wanted him to stay because of *her*. Because of the woman she was now. But it was no good because Grace knew the truth. She didn't even have to put it into words; the truth hit her anyway, like a hand thrusting against her chest.

If Simon were to set eyes on her now, for the very first time – forty-year-old Grace – she knew that despite the slimmish figure, the small hands and feet, the brown curls, the still high breasts, despite the warmth she felt for him, and the (now shy) desire that reached out to him, none of it mattered. If he met her for the first time now, he wouldn't see her.

He wouldn't look twice at her.

The knowledge was there, it never left her. Even with her face pressed against his shoulder, breathing the warm, familiar, accountant smell that was his. Back in her bed, waking to the radio in the morning, turning off the light at night. He seemed more lost to her now than he had been when upstairs murmuring into his mobile phone to his mistress. She knew what he could see, and what he couldn't see.

Poor Grace. Good Grace. Trying to think good thoughts and block out the bad. And failing. Simon had made up his mind and now her energy had gone, the adrenaline was gone. There wasn't a book in the world that could help her. And this was only the beginning; she understood that now, better every day.

It would have been easier if he had died.

Chapter Two

Richard Ortega sat at a table with a wall of books behind him. None of them his own.

His books were stacked on the table in front of him and on the floor below; piles of them, as if anticipating a queue winding out of the shop and down the street. Countless eager people all waiting for him to sign his twelfth and latest book, *The Maid And The Magician*. It's how it used to be, and not so long ago actually. Like that time in Waterstones when an actual row had broken out between two women over the last copy of

29

The Mermaid's Tale.

Richard Ortega smiled as he remembered that. Later, in The Boho Club, he had described it as a nubile cat fight, a collision of nails and lipstick. And of course, in truth, it had just been two middle-aged biddies, tripping on HRT or whatever they took to keep their knees supple. But author's licence and so forth. It had made a good story, and that was the version repeated in the gossip pages of *Literary Lives*.

And it went to show, didn't it, what a success he had been. How he'd touched a chord, especially with women...

'That's good, Richard.'

The book shop photographer, aka the little teenage twerp nominally in charge of him for the day, flashed his digi camera. 'Nice smile, that was. Just what we want for our wall of fame. You can go right underneath Deborah Moggach.'

Richard opened his mouth to protest, then closed it wearily. He hadn't even seen the tiny camera appear. If he had, he would have used the face he preferred to be known for, the one that he could adopt at will and which graced all the covers of his books; thoughtful, quizzical, with a hint of humour. Playful even. Now, instead, *beneath* Deborah Moggach there was going to be an image of him gurning like an old man remembering the sea, when all he had been doing was smiling at the way things used to be. The way they should be.

The bookshop was empty. Bookshops always were empty nowadays when he turned up.

'Cup of tea?' said the little twerp brightly. Richard ignored him. But that was a mistake because now the little twerp, make that little *fucker*, was bent on revenge.

'Don't know where the punters could be. Last week we were heaving. You couldn't get through the door. Mind you, we had that Marcia Coyote. You know, the one that wrote the novel based on her childhood in a cult. The one where nobody wore any clothes and the kids had to watch their parents having sex. Or was that Alicia Milagro?'

Richard yawned.

'Then the week before we had a double signing. There was Seamus O'Connor and Miriam Rapko. Brilliant they were. They both gave a little speech about their childhoods and what they'd gone through. Makes you wonder how people survive, really. I suppose it's literature.' The little fucker looked pious. 'It's the saving grace. Like Marcia said, the writing saved her.'

'And made her a millionaire while she was at it.'

'Sorry Richard, didn't catch that.'

There was a silence. In the open doorway an elderly woman with a shopping basket on

31

wheels looked in, confused. 'I thought this used to be for vegetables,' she said, with the pent-up bewilderment of the very old.

'Not for a few years,' the little fucker smiled at her kindly. 'Go further down. There's a Tesco Express. You'll get your veggies there.'

Richard grunted.

The little fucker smiled at him now, kindly, patiently. Exactly the way he had smiled at the very old woman. 'Sure you don't want a cup of tea?'

It didn't used to be like this.

So what happened?

One moment he was there, face everywhere, books everywhere. Richard Ortega, best-seller, teller of fables for the twentieth century. *The true philosopher of love* – that's what *Cosmopolitan* had called him. A writer for the age, a new age, that is – or was. A golden age, Richard would have called it. The Nineties, when all that hard, black-chromed, Martin Amis inspired macho shit had hit a wall and left a vacuum for writers of the spirit. For writers like Richard, teller of tales. Who knew the value of allegory.

And people recognised it. *The poet of Philosophy, Britain's own Cuelho.* That's what they'd called him in *Marie Claire.* They knew a good thing when they saw it.

A man who understood that the world needed soothing with words. *Bedtime stories for grown-ups,* that's how the *London Review of Books* had described his work. On second thoughts, he hadn't liked that one so much. Or at all. Come to think of it, wasn't that when the rot set in? Some woman, her head flaky with Theory, had laid into him for being fey, for turning greetings card verses into entire slim volumes. Wrapping up philosophy-to-go for people who took their cue from the lyrics of pop anthems. It flayed him, that article, for not writing about what was real, the nitty gritty.

But that was the whole point, wasn't it? Forty years of hyper-real, of writers masturbating and smearing humanity all over the page like a dirty protest – readers had had enough. Richard knew that. He'd spent all the Eighties writing advertising copy; he knew what people wanted. Better still, he knew what *women* wanted and no one could ever say that about Martin Bloody Amis or Will Fucking Self. Or even Freud. How about that? Not even Fucking Freud knew what women wanted the way Richard Ortega knew.

Richard drew a breath. Had to. Sometimes thoughts hit him like a fist thrust into his chest, knocking the air out of him, and he had to remind himself to breathe.

Back in the Nineties, Richard knew what people didn't want was too much reality. So he had honoured that. *Honoured* being the operative word. He could have written like anyone else. Mean tales of excess, low-life characters with unbelievable vocabularies spraying polysyllables along with the bullets. He could have written about posh women with a taste for rough, darts players with a taste for world domination, children with hooks sunk deep, deep into their parents. He could have written all of that, and more. And better.

Instead he had written what people wanted, were crying out for. Tales of women redeemed by love, men redeemed by death. Children redeemed by teachers. Murderers redeemed by mermaids. Mermaids redeemed by philosophers...

'Richard?' The little twerp's voice was warning.

'What?'

'Someone's come into the shop. And ... well ... you were beginning to snore.'

Fucking ... fuck. Not snoring, but snarling.

Over by the door a woman had indeed sidled into the shop. Middle-aged. Therefore invisible. She had slipped in and headed straight for some shelves at the back as if she knew exactly what she was looking for. Yet more bloody self-help books probably. *Men Are From Planet Jupiter And Women From Alpha Centauri*, something like that. Richard Ortega despaired. Where was the poetry?

Because poetry was what he was about. Back in the Nineties poetry was what everyone had given up on. Allegory, fable, all gone. Magic realism – out the window. If you were a publisher looking for that sort of thing you needed to go to the Portuguese or the French, and then of course you had to pay for a translator, who quite honestly could have handed you any sort of crap. Then along had come Richard, homegrown teller of tales, writing in English, yet as universal as any South American. And that was it. His time had come. End of story.

Except it wasn't. Because the Nineties had turned into the Noughties and something else happened. People started writing about themselves. That's right, using their own lives as material. And not in any Hemingway, Patrick Hamilton kind of way. Richard Ortega could have respected that (mostly because Hemingway and Hamilton were dead). No bulls or rifles, no gaslit encounters between artists on smoky London streets. No star-crossed, Indo-French lost loves played out in Vietnamese bars. No revolution. No sex. No death. None of that. Just bad childhoods. Bad parents, bad schools, bad neighbourhoods. The odd vicious priest and nasty encounter...

Richard's upper lip curled. If it was nasty encounters that made a book, then he could write a series, based solely on his school days at the old alma mater, St Olave's of the Faint Hearted, and so could half the men he knew of his age and class. But fancy that – painting the best days of one's life as a portrait of unending, body-bending tortures that twisted the soul and...

Richard's lip stopped curling and twitched uncontrollably, assailed by sudden, unbidden memories swiftly suppressed.

It was cheating. That's how he saw it. No other way of looking at it. And that was why he sat with his back squarely turned against the wall of books behind him. Books by people like Alicia Milagro, Seamus O'Connor, Marcia Coyote. Books where every bad memory was used and worked and turned into art. At least that's what they called it. Hadn't anyone told them? Art. Short for artifice. Art was something you made up. Something out of nothing. That's what made it art. Duh.

'Writing about one's self is *not* art.'

'Sorry?' said the fucking twerp. 'Were you talking to me?'

And Richard shook his head, unaware that he had even spoken these last words aloud.

On the far side of the shop, in the section where philosophy merged shamelessly into psychology, Grace heard the sound of voices, and jumped because even though she knew every shop has a minder, she'd got the impression that she was completely alone. She had walked through the door without anyone acknowledging her or even seeming to know she was there. And this, nowadays, was all she had come to expect.

She put the book she was holding back on the shelf alongside the others with titles like *Happy With Hopi* and *Women Who Lie Down And Die Like Dogs.* After *The Maid And The Magician*, she had wondered if she didn't have more in common with Deborah than she realised, so she'd started to examine the self-help books, occasionally taking one home. But so far as she could see, they had nothing for her, nothing to address the sheer absence at the centre of her own existence. There was no cure for invisible.

And today she felt more invisible than ever. Today Grace felt close to non-existent.

Getting ready to come out, yet another thought had assailed her. Simon had never told her exactly when the affair had started, had been deliberately vague. And she, out of a kind of pride, had never asked. But suddenly she knew, was convinced that she knew. It was last summer, during the team-building exercise when the entire department had shifted to a luxury West Country Hotel. There had been raft building and fire walking and a sweat lodge. Simon had described it all and rolled his eyes as if it was beneath him. But now, she could see how it was, how it really was. Warm sunshine and sparks. Lucy walking with burning feet and a wet T-shirt. Simon watching her, sweaty with non-accountancy induced exertion, his memory a blank because when had he last looked at Grace, really looked at her...?

Grace, who had been at home changing her shoes when the thought hit her, had closed her eyes, jammed them shut; but now she had seen, she couldn't look away. She remembered Simon when he came home – how he had blushed when she greeted him, and seemed to keep blushing all through the weekend. Red, flaming up his neck and down into his shoulders. She had put it down to sunburn, to being in the open air, lashing oil drums together with the rest of the team. Gradually the flush had died away, and she had forgotten all about it.

But today, getting ready to come out, she had remembered; and yet another detail had slipped into place, freezing her to the spot before she had forced herself to carry on. She thought she had pulled herself together, but she was wrong. Because now, here in the shop, Grace looked down, and froze all over again at the sight of herself. On one foot was a normal outdoor shoe and on the other – a bedroom slipper. It was one of a pair Anna had bought her for Christmas, fluffy and white with the fronts rearing up in the shape of two snowmen that waggled and swayed as she walked around the house.

One snowman waggled at her now. Here, in the shop, right next to the self-help books.

Grace closed her eyes, and wished herself home. Then, with a deeper surge of wishing, wished herself in a dark hole, far below the surface. Not just because of a single slipper that waggled at her – although it was reason enough – but because of everything it said about her. A woman who could no longer even dress herself. Not invisible today. Today she would turn heads in the streets, like a girl – but only because of the snowman waggling at the end of her foot.

She turned and headed for the exit, defeated, head bowed to the inevitable and the long walk home. But at the door, urged by a prod of masochism, she found herself turning again, just to see who was there behind her in the store, chuckling at the woman who had come shopping in her slippers. She couldn't help herself.

And there, unbelievably, *he* was, sitting at a table with the wall of books behind him, and the pile of books in front of him. The face off the cover. The man whose eyes had quizzed her, and whose words had comforted her. Her staff. Her rock. Her safe place. The man who knew about the girl inside.

He was there. And he hadn't seen her. Not her or the snowman on her foot. His eyes (*those* eyes) were fixed at a point above her

39

head, with a gaze so distant, and yet so intent, she could see that, whereas she could only wish, he had actually *put* himself in another place, not here. A small sigh-like breath escaped her, as for a wild imagining moment she considered the sort of place that would be. A wonderful place. Far, far away.

The moment fled. In its place, agony. She wanted, she needed, to turn and walk back into the shop. Come and stand at that table, perhaps to touch him with a hand to bring him timidly to where she was, to where they both were, Richard Ortega and Grace. Together.

But on her foot, the snowman waggled his large woolly head. And not only that, Grace had left the house as she normally left the house nowadays, without looking at herself. She had dragged a comb through her hair, brushed her teeth. She was *clean*. But that was all. Her make-up was scattered over the dressing table. Her clothes, her good clothes, the ones that might have made her stand out, just a little, enough to show there was still a spark, a something, were locked inside her wardrobe as if under house arrest. Grace was wearing what she usually wore, jeans and a jumper (a grandmother's present to Anna) so nasty that Anna had discarded it the moment she unwrapped it, dropping it as if it burnt her fingers.

And Grace couldn't do it. She couldn't

present herself like this, without even the virtue of being invisible. The snowman nodded in agreement and with a sound of desolation in her throat, she carried on walking, out of the shop.

Immediately the street engulfed her, startling in its ordinariness. A bus passed, blasting dust into her face; a gaggle of girls of Anna's age, not seeming to see she was there, pushed past her, forcing her to stand in the gutter. In all directions young women with tired faces propelled toddlers in buggies, not realising that their babies were simply teenagers in waiting; that they, the women, were spending their years the way Grace had spent the years, recklessly, always thinking there were more years to come.

And here was something else she couldn't do: walk away into the clutch of all this ordinariness; turn her back on Richard Ortega, thinker of the extraordinary, so that he would never know Grace existed, that she was still here (if slightly damaged) because of his words, written like a bedtime story for a grown-up too unhappy to go to sleep.

She couldn't do it. She couldn't leave without making a mark, no matter how shallow or easy to erase. Grace turned yet again, eyes raised high above the snowman that waggled a warning from the floor, and walked with intent back into the shop.

This time, Richard saw her coming. He

had been gazing at a point above the door, thinking about lunch, about an acceptable Chenin Blanc and a decent wedge of cheese. All hours away still. Then a flicker of movement in the door, hitherto ignored, had brought his gaze downwards to meet with the face of the woman walking towards him.

His eye began the usual inventory of female flesh – fortyish, slimmish, dark ... but then he forgot the list, distracted by a single slipper, faintly grubby with wear and with what looked like a single dirty snowman swaying above it. And having noted the slipper, his eye rose again, almost unwilling, to meet *her* eyes. Already they were locked on his – huge eyes it seemed to him, blazing with some kind of emotion.

'Um...' he made the noise discreetly, looking for support behind him.

But the little fucker had vanished. Richard could hear him in the back of the shop, talking into the phone, laughing at something – or somebody. Richard probably.

'Um.' Louder this time. If only he could remember the little fucker's name. 'I think we might have...'

But she was right in front of him now, stopping just short of the table, making the snowman swagger back and forth with the whiplash of a sudden halt.

'Mr Ortega...'

Grace floundered. A hundred phrases,

42

some of them appropriate, flashed through her head, but none of them would fit her tongue. Already, with a sinking heart, she knew what she was going to say, and it was not in the least appropriate. Yet helpless, she knew she would say it anyway because it was the truth, and in this one brief moment with Richard Ortega, only the truth would do.

'Mr Ortega.' Out it came. 'You saved me.'

Instantly, inside herself, she shrank, hearing words that were too much, too desperate. Too odd...

Too late. There was a silence. Richard Ortega smiled tightly. And suddenly she had time to look at him, really look at him, the owner of the face. Long enough, on any other day at any other moment, for her to see. Namely that he was older than he'd appeared on the cover of his book; that his eyes, though still hooded, were less warm. And the mouth, although keeping the mobility suggested by the photograph, now betrayed a tendency to move in different directions than expected, creating a face less humorous, less giving. In fact, everything about Richard Ortega was less. Time enough to notice all this, leading to what should have been the inevitable result – the faint fall of disappointment that comes when absolutely nothing lives up to expectation.

But now, at this very moment, it was all time wasted on her. Grace was in no state to notice anything. Down below, a single grubby snowman had robbed her of the power to judge any appearance but her own, whilst the air still throbbed with the shaming intensity of her declaration. She could only stare at him, desperate, every nerve straining, trying to fathom what he thought of her.

At least he was smiling, if tensely, the lips stretched politely. The smile encouraged her, briefly. It gave her the idea that she could explain, make him see she wasn't odd after all, that those first words had blurted out of her for a reason.

'You see, Mr Ortega...' and out it came. The whole awful story, the shirts and the smells and the negligees. That feeling of disappearing and sinking beneath the weight of self; the wonderful effect of words offered like straws to a drowning woman...

It was like the first time she'd spoken – only far worse. Words, flooding out of her as if a dam had cracked. Locked behind the rush of speech, Grace gave a silent wail of shame. Already she could see his face freezing, then glazing. Everything about this man was in retreat, and who could blame him? Anyone would have retreated confronted with this, a woman pouring out her life, drowning him with words.

Oh God, she thought as the dam continued to flood despite herself. *He'll think I'm mad. One of those women who never go away. A stalker. Someone who latches on and never lets go.*

And with that she finally heard herself stop. Horror had cemented the crack. She stood panting, swaying slightly. Ready to go now, to turn and never come back. It's what he wanted. She could see it right there – the longing for her to disappear, written in his eyes, even though the smile had stayed where it was, fixed by politeness.

Not a real smile of course. Richard could feel it, wrapped tight across his face, like a mud mask that has hardened, pulling on the skin. The muscles were beginning to ache, but he knew better than to stop smiling. The woman was mad: an obsessive. The sort that thinks you're there to save them from themselves. Probably harmless, but who could tell? If a woman is crazy enough to walk the streets of a small town in a single snowman slipper, she could have anything up her sleeve. Someone like that could do damage, serious damage.

In fact, it rang all sorts of bells. Hadn't something happened to Seamus O'Connor only last month? Some crazed priest in New York, leaping out from behind the stacks in Barnes and Noble with a phial of what he claimed was holy water. He'd tried chucking it in O'Connor's face, but missed. It was only when the pages of the book O'Connor had been signing started to hiss that

45

everyone realised. That so called holy water had been acid.

Richard had found a real satisfaction in reading that story. This was what happened when you use an entire life as a prop for art. There's always the chance that life will spring right back out and bite you. Or throw acid in your face.

This woman didn't look like she had much left to throw at him, though. Something seemed to have switched off inside her, and now she was only standing there, breasts heaving. Quite nice breasts, actually, although a touch on the small side. The mad look had disappeared. If anything she just looked tragic, swaying there in her snowman slipper, ready to burst into tears.

Richard relaxed. A man knows he's safe when all a woman's got left in her is tears. Richard felt he could allow himself a small sigh of relief, let go the smile.

It was then another thought hit him. To do with O'Connor again. It was big news, that acid incident, and it certainly hadn't done his sales any harm. More to the point, Richard had noticed, no one seemed much surprised. Because that was the thing, wasn't it? A man like O'Connor, so called creator, thrived off what was real. Next thing you knew, he'd be writing about it. Wrapping up an actual event in a few extra words and calling it fiction. And like the dove returning to the Ark, the story would rebound with the touch of God on its wings. Another slice of misery. Another fucking bestseller.

Imagine what O'Connor would have done with this, then – a woman, not so bad looking, standing there with madness in her eyes, emptying herself in front of him, declaring he'd saved her life? The sort of woman who never went away, who could easily be there all the time, following him around. Not just a normal fan. And definitely not a lover, O'Connor was gay. Something else. A stalker. His very own stalker. Full time. She was a housewife, after all. Only a housewife would have the time.

Imagine what he'd do – Shameless O'Connor – the story he would write, if she had turned out to be a stalker, he'd have got a whole bloody book out of it.

A. Whole. Bloody. Book.

There was a stirring in front of him. The woman was about to leave, something heavy about her movements now, like someone on the edge of exhaustion. Richard felt a twinge of annoyance, regret even. A stalker shouldn't do this – walk away, weighed down by defeat, with the clear intention of never coming back.

And in that moment, in that very second, it came to him. He *wanted* her to stay. He wanted what the others had, what O' Connor had. He wanted his own slice of misery. Show the world that Ortega could suffer too.

Then write about it.

'Wait.'

Grace, on the edge of leaving, turned, snagged by that one word. And to her amazement, Richard Ortega was smiling at her, properly smiling, eyes warm and playful under those narrow hoods of skin. Eyes that seemed to reach inside her, penetrating the layers of disappointed flesh, in search of the person who was really there.

The Grace inside.

Finally she had found him – the man on the cover of the book. The man who knew about women, and the girl curled up inside. And he was smiling at her, at Grace, as if she existed. As if he could see her.

Made her shiver, the shock of it. Even so, outside the shop, the ordinary world called, ready – anxious even – to make her invisible again, inviting her back into its fold. Comforting in its way. Safe. So safe, she was tempted to carry on turning on her heel, and out of the door, as if Invisible was what she wanted.

But Richard smiled more warmly still. And so she stayed.

Chapter Three

Grace was carried home on a cloud of happiness, weightless, spirits rising so high they floated above her like an umbrella of sheer joy. In the street people must have glanced at the bedroom slipper, but it would have been her face that alerted them. Something was different about her. Everything was different.

She let herself in the front door of her house, and only then remembered that she had left by the back door, like a servant. Edging her way out of the side entrance as if working towards her own vanishing. Not now. She burst into her hall, surprising the workman she had forgotten was there. He was on his way back upstairs to the loft with mugs of tea for himself and his mate.

'All right there, Mrs Waites?'

'Grace,' said Grace. 'Call me Grace.'

'Right you are ... Grace.' He stayed on the stair, and smiled at her, as if noticing her for the first time. He nodded down at the bedroom slipper. 'I suppose you know...'

'Yes,' said Grace and giggled. 'I didn't even notice, not until I was – I don't know – *miles* from home.'

His smile grew broader, positively admiring. 'Well, I reckon you carried it off, Mrs ... Grace. Like they say, it's not what you wear, it's the way you wear it.'

Grace laughed. He was flirting with her now, a big twenty-five-year-old lad who was only puzzled that he hadn't seen the reason for it before.

'How's it going?' she asked him. 'Think you'll be finished today?'

'Yeah. Nearly done. Just tidying round we are really.' He sounded almost regretful. 'Kids too noisy up there, were they? It'll be all right now. After today you can have a herd of baby elephants in that loft and you won't hear hide nor hair of them. That's good solid soundproofing, that is. Someone could be living up there and you wouldn't even know it.'

'Good,' said Grace. 'Very good. I ...*we* ...never realised the floor was so thin.'

Thin enough to hear a husband talking to his mistress in the middle of the night, making his presence felt.

She waited until he had gone, then went upstairs to her bedroom. For a moment she stood, listening. And he was right. Apart from the faint sound of hammering, she could hear nothing. When Simon had come back downstairs for good, this had been all she wanted from him. Not a holiday. Not flowers. Only a loft that was soundproof. Just

50

in case...

In case of what? She had never given herself a reason, not out loud and in so many words. But she knew. It was in case it happened again. In case she needed an absence that was a proper absence, so that next time she would have the space to think.

And having listened to the silence, Grace went to do what she had come upstairs for. She needed to know what Richard Ortega had seen. The workman's smile had already given her a clue. She went and stood in front of a mirror.

And for a moment she was disappointed. There really wasn't so much difference between the Grace who had slipped out of her own back door and the Grace who had burst in through the front. Eyes, nose, hair still the same. Jumper still as nasty. And then there was the bedroom slipper...

But something *was* different, even if it took more than a moment to work out what. Then it came to her, gazing at her, square in the eyes. She could *see* herself, not just as a collection of features bearing no relation to each other, but as something approaching a whole. The vanishing look was gone, with the result that even a twenty-five-year-old man had noticed her and spoken to her and seen that she was there.

This is what he had done for her, Richard Ortega, and still she found it hard to believe. He had looked at her, had seen past the clothes and the snowman, the unmade up face. He had even seen through those first terrible minutes when she had been quite mad, past the flushed cheeks and the blazing eyes, and the flood of words poured into his lap. He had seen through all this to her, the real Grace. And he had smiled, properly smiled.

And not only smiled. After that first gentle command that she wait, he had begun to ask her about herself, insisting that she answer. It was as if he was a man incapable of having a conversation at arm's length, always needing to be closer, to draw the essence of a person to the surface. Empty, utterly exhausted, she had responded almost against her will until, before she knew what she was doing, he had drawn from her a quiet retelling of her life. And this time, it had all made sense.

And kind! He had nodded and sighed as she told him about Simon – no use leaving out the details of what had happened there; she had already told him all that. His eyes had been warm with understanding – but not pity. Betraying instead a kind of anger on her behalf, as if she was worth more than this. As if he cared.

He had gone beyond kind. At the end, he had reached out and touched her hand with his hand, and for another one of those amazed moments, bereft of words, she had stared at it, feeling his fingers closed over hers.

That was when he had said, almost in a tone of wonder, 'My dear Grace. And you say my book, my words, helped you. You tell me this? What kind of courage must it take, baring your soul in such a way? You humble me – at the same time as you make me proud. Can you imagine what it means to a man, to hear that his work has helped another man – or woman? It cannot end here, you see that don't you? There is a bond between us now. A friendship. Ah Grace, Grace. We need to meet again. Again and again.'

He had said this. To her. Now Grace could only stare at herself in the glass, wide-eyed. Already she was wondering if she had imagined it – all of it. Even the words he had used had a tinge of the unreal. Like something he was reading off a page, perhaps one of his own pages. *Did people actually speak like that?*

But then she remembered how he had smiled, and the shock of becoming visible as a result. And it didn't matter what words he used. Richard Ortega needed to see more of her. He had taken her telephone number. He knew where she lived. He had done everything a man would do when he needed to see a woman again.

No wonder suddenly she could see herself, and other people could see her too.
Maybe, just possibly, she was not invisible
after all.

Back at the shop the little fucker had looked
impressed despite himself.

'Richard, what can I say? I mean, I'm
really sorry you got landed with her. I was
so caught up on the phone, important call
and all that, I just didn't realise. Naturally
I'd have stopped her if I'd known. I mean
she *looked* all right when she came in.
Actually, she didn't look like anything. I
never even noticed her, not properly.

'But, man, I've got to say – hand on heart
– you handled it really well. Calming her
down the way you did, listening to her like
that. Most people would have run a mile, I
know I would. But keeping her talking,
making like you were genuinely interested in
what she had to say – well, to be honest, I
thought it was touching. Hand on heart,
Richard. Respect.'

Richard inclined his head. 'Writing's a
powerful thing. Sometimes with power has
to come responsibility.'

The little fucker nodded. 'Yes, oh yes. I
completely see that.' He paused and slowly
picked up one of the books off the pile on
the table. 'You know, I've never actually
read any of your work. But now I honestly

think I should. May I...?'

Richard stamped on the urge to slap the thieving little fucker's hand off with a snarling *buy your own*. Instead he smiled.

'Be my guest. Enjoy.'

Ten minutes later the little fucker was back with a mug of freshly brewed coffee, fragrant and steaming; no doubt from some special private supply. This is what Marcia Coyote and Alicia Milagro would have been given to drink when they were here. Not fucking tea.

He was frowning as he laid it down on the table.

'You know, Richard, I've been thinking. That woman. I mean, you were kind, really kind. But was it wise? Did you hear about Seamus O'Connor last month, and some mad monk throwing acid in his face? Apparently he'd been following him all over America. And Seamus, he never took him seriously, wouldn't get him banned or anything. Even now his agent has had to persuade him to press charges. I mean, the guy could have done damage, real damage.'

Richard swallowed coffee with a thoughtful, yet magnanimous, air. Then he shrugged. 'What can I say? It's a serious craft, writing. You put yourself on the line, you make a difference. You can't just hide away from the people you affect. Seamus and I, we both of us know that. Sometimes we just have to live with the result.'

The little fucker nodded wisely.

'Yeah, Richard. Absolutely. Respect.'

Chapter Four

How long did it last, that injection of self?

For a week, Grace smiled at her reflection, at Simon, at her children – and said nothing. She had discovered that she didn't want to tell anyone about *him*, Richard Ortega, the man who had stared deep into her eyes searching for the Grace inside. She had the feeling that words – hers and others' – would have ruined it. Tamsin would have asked questions, dry and searching as if they were in court, cutting the whole thing down to size. Laughing at words like *humble* and *proud*. Deborah would have become mystical and misty-eyed, regretful that Grace hadn't used the meeting for something deeper, more searching. And Simon – well Simon wouldn't have seen the point of hearing it in the first place.

All of them would have taken something away from her.

She even tried not to talk about it with herself. Or think about it. Thinking would have put a spin on it; she might have wondered why he had switched so suddenly from recoil to welcome. And thinking would have made it less immediate; she would have become used to it, the idea of Richard Ortega closing his hand over hers, searching her face. Grace preferred to be busy with something completely different and have the memory of the encounter hit her, catching her by surprise, making her blush with the delight of it. Still incredulous.

But a week went by and she became aware that she was waiting. Then another week, and time began to have its effect. The memory was still clear in her head, but it came gnawed at the edges now, nibbled away by doubts. One day she let herself imagine how it would have looked to a third person, seeing a middle-aged woman flustered and flattered by the kindness of a man. And she began to lose it, the wonder of it.

Half defiantly, half in despair she described the encounter to Tamsin and Deborah, and watched for the reaction of her friends. Already knowing what to expect.

'Well, what else should he have done?' snapped Tamsin.

'Sounds like you were the only one there. He should have been bloody grateful for the attention.'

'Oh Grace. Were you really wearing bed-room slippers?' Deborah's voice was soft, terribly disappointed, as if Grace had committed an act of *lese-majesty* so great it was impossible to recover.

That night, she looked at her reflection and she could see she was fading again, beginning to vanish back to the way she had been. Instinctively she looked to Simon, for proof that somebody could see her. On the other side of the room, busy taking off his socks, Simon had become intent on something not quite right with his big toenail. He was picking at it, devoting his entire attention to the task, flicking fragments on the bedroom floor, like a man thinking no one could see him.

'Don't do that,' she said. 'Please.'

He looked up in surprise, as if only now noticing that he wasn't alone. 'Sorry.' He was apologetic. But ten minutes later, he had forgotten, and he was doing it again, picking his big toenail.

It was as if she wasn't even there. Invisible. Again.

Three weeks went by and she understood. If Richard Ortega had needed anything from her, if there was any link between them, she would have known it by now. She had benefited briefly from the comfort of a stranger and everything else had been in her head.

Anna picked up the phone when it rang, displaying her usual indifference as she discovered it wasn't for her. Then the indifference vanished.

'Oh yeah,' she said after a moment. 'Oh, like, *yeah*,' She paused and listened. 'Yeah, yeah, yeah, like it's really going to happen.' She was beginning to giggle now. 'That's what they all say, like we've *really* got to believe you.' She listened again and then let her eyes go wide. 'That's bad, that is,' she said, half respectfully. 'OK, I'll get her. Just give me a sec.'

She covered the speaker with one hand and called to Grace, who was stirring a risotto. 'Mum, there's some guy on the phone, says you've won a holiday.'

'Oh, Anna.' Grace said helplessly. 'You know that's what they all...'

'Yeah but Mum, this guy's funny, I mean odd. He says if you don't get your fucking ass to the phone – I'm quoting – he'll come down and land the plane to Lanzarote in your garden. I think he must be pissed,' she added *sotto voce*.

Grace stared at her, then took the phone off her daughter. 'Who is this?' she said severely.

'Mrs Waites?' a voice said, sounding oddly falsetto.

'Yes.'

'Mrs *Grace* Waites?'

'Yes.'

'Then what are you waiting for, Grace?'

59

The voice had switched out of its strange register into something deep and infinitely more familiar. It spoke again, its timbre caressing. Tender. 'Tell me, Grace, my dear Grace. What is it really that you're waiting for?'

And instantly she knew.

'Why?' Her voice was limp with surprise. 'Why like this? Why a holiday?'

Richard Ortega laughed gently. 'Because maybe that's what I am offering. A kind of holiday. Time out from reality, from the life they are wrapping you up in. Not in Lanzarote, of course. You deserve better. If I were to take you anywhere, Grace, it would have to be, let's see ... Umbria. It's wilder than Tuscany. The wine is fresher, almost raw, the olives are sharper. And the wind comes scented with thyme, not traffic fumes from the *circulatione* of Florence. That, *that*, is what you deserve. Do they know this, the people who surround you? Those people who made you cry?'

Aware of her daughter's eyes, Grace murmured, 'I'm not sure that I...'

'Grace, my Grace. We are only human. How can anyone be sure of anything? Except I am sure of this: I need to see you again. I have thought about you every day, standing out of the crowd in that book store, unmistakable in your slipper. The sweet, *sweet* uncertainty in your eyes. That's what I need from you, Grace, your uncertainty. The fact that you are not sure. Do you understand what I am saying? You're being very quiet. Are you there?'

'Yes,' she said faintly.

'I am being too flippant. I am afraid you are not taking me seriously. Forgive me, it is shyness making me awkward. Didn't I say how you make me humble at the same time as I am proud? But I am drawn to you, Grace. Your intensity, your openness – they enchant me, surrounded as we are by automatons and liars. There is no passion in the world. But the emotions that you wore so nakedly that day, they inspire me. I need people who inspire me. And *you* ... you need to know of your own power to inspire. Do you understand me? Do you understand what I am saying?'

'I think that perhaps you...'

'Grace.' Suddenly he sounded hurried, as if something was happening behind him. 'There's not much time. I need you to come and be with me. Just as a friend, no more than that, I swear. A muse. Could you, *would* you, come when I ask you?'

Grace swallowed. 'I ... probably. I just don't know that I...'

'Ah, I know what you're thinking. That you're married and shouldn't be alone with another man. Literature is a strange match-maker. You know my work, but you don't know *me*. Look, have no fear of me. *Never* fear me, Grace. Come up to The Boho Club on Wednesday. There'll be people everywhere, you'll be tripping over them. You won't have to be alone. Nine of the clock – is that awfully late for someone like you?'

'Nine of the ... at the...' Grace echoed. 'Maybe I should write it down. I just need to find a...'

'Grace.' Now his voice was truly urgent. 'I have to go. You'll be there. You must be there. Promise me.'

The phone went dead before she could promise anything, before she could even find the pen she was scrabbling for. But it didn't matter. Time, date, place – all were stamped in her mind. How could she forget? She stopped looking for a pen and let herself be still, taking it in, little by little. Wondering if she would go, not trusting herself to know.

'Mum?'

Grace was still holding the phone, her eyes wide and unseeing. Time, date, place.

'Mum!' Anna's voice, louder this time. Not used to not being heard. 'What's the matter? Why are you just standing there like that? You look...' Anna searched about for a word that suited her mood. 'Stupid.'

Grace blinked. 'What?' she said faintly. 'Sorry, darling?'

And maybe Anna was right. Maybe she

was stupid. If not stupid, then dazed. Who had she ever met who talked like this, speaking of needs and bonds and enchantments? Certainly not Simon. Would she even have wanted him to? Slowly she replaced the phone. For some reason her head had begun to ache.

Then she remembered how he had told her she made him shy. Shyness of her, making him awkward. The thought made her want to laugh. As if it could be true – Richard Ortega, shy of her! Then suddenly she was remembering someone else, a younger Simon in a dim and distant past, confessing to exactly the same thing. So shy of her, so aware of her, he could hardly speak.

And with that she lost the urge to laugh.

The words seemed to slip out of her as if she was barely responsible for them. 'You know, I *have* won a holiday. They want me to go up to London on Wednesday. I thought I might, simply to hear what they have to say.'

And there, she had lied – just like that, without even intending to. Grace heard the opposite of truth as it made its way out and wondered at herself. There hadn't even been any need to lie. He had been asking for nothing but friendship. And she, *she* was married with an entire history behind her. Nothing was going to happen.

She hadn't needed to lie, but lie she had.

63

Richard Ortega put down the phone. Yawned.

Three weeks. He reckoned he had timed it about right. Any shorter and she might not have been so easy. Any longer, and she'd have forgotten about him. Probably got herself immersed in the books of Marcia Coyote or whoever and decided that they had saved her too.

But then there was the question of whether he had struck the right tone when he spoke to her. Was there a chance he was being too elevated, too high flown for a little bourgeoise, more used to the chitter of women in her kitchen?

Richard frowned, then relaxed. He had merely spoken as he wrote. Women loved it. Or used to until the *London Review of Books* told them to prefer the monosyllabic rantings of Seamus O'Connor and the rest. No, this was how a man should speak to a woman. It was almost a duty. *Noblesse oblige.*

He yawned again. He could see how the next few weeks would take it out of him, shaping, forming. Creating Grace.

Strange, Grace thought, how a lie changes things.

Before you tell a lie, no one seems to notice or remember anything you say. You open your mouth only to hear the words empty themselves into the ether. But you let fall a single untruth and suddenly everyone seems intent on what you have to tell them.

First there had been Anna, rounding on her in the kitchen. 'But ... Mum.'

'But ... what?'

'It's just a scam, you know. Free holidays, so called. They just want to sell you something.'

Grace bent her face into the risotto. 'I'm sure they do.' She picked up the spoon and waited for her daughter to lose interest, as she always did.

Instead Anna came and stood in front of her. 'I don't think you should go,' she said abruptly.

'Why ever not?' Grace glanced at her. A few weeks earlier she had told Anna that her father had been sleeping with another woman and her daughter's face had stayed like a peach, uncreased. Now, today, she was frowning, soft cheeks screwed up.

'He sounded ... odd. I mean, he made me laugh, but he didn't sound right, that man. He wasn't normal. Honestly, I don't think you should go. It might not be, I don't know – safe.'

'Oh.' Grace was taken aback. 'Darling. I'm sure that...' And she laughed, less because she was embarrassed by the lie than because she was suddenly in love with her daughter for the unexpected concern.

But she shouldn't have laughed. The

frown vanished. 'Oh, *don't* listen to me then.' Anna tossed long hair off her face. 'I'm only your daughter – what would I know? God!'

Then, later, at bedtime, there was Simon. Suddenly interested.

'What's this about a time-share?'

'Time-share?' Anna was wriggling into her nightdress. Now she stopped, letting her head stay hidden under swathes of imitation silk. She had given up wearing pyjamas although she preferred them.

'Anna told me. She says you've "won" a holiday. Now they want you to go to some kind of presentation.'

Under the nightdress, guilt closed Grace's eyes and prised open her mouth. She was going to have to tell him: there was no holiday, no presentation. Only a man waiting for her, who was not her husband. Already wondering how to explain why she had lied.

But before she could answer, he said, 'Look, you're not expecting me to go with you, are you? These so-called holidays, they're just ways to print money. People like you – naïve, gullible, to put it mildly – I'm sorry, Grace, but they can see you coming a mile off.'

And hearing that, Grace closed her mouth, let the nightdress slip all the way over her head. She stood in front of her husband with her eyes wide open.

'I expect you're right. And I expect they *will* see me coming. But at least they will see me.'

Something in her tone made Simon look at her again, sharply this time. Then his face changed. 'Hey,' he said softly. 'You look ... I don't know ... different.'

But Grace already knew it. She could see her reflection over his shoulder in the bedroom mirror. The difference was there, brought about by a phone call, by a few ill-chosen words and a sudden firm decision.

Chapter Five

Wednesday evening and Grace felt as if she was swimming with a tide of people in a foreign sea.

A warm night, somehow not British. Street after street where beautiful young men held hands with other beautiful young men; where girls drifted by in clothes that she would never have had the courage to wear, even at Anna's age.

She was in Soho, and according to her *A to Z* she had nearly arrived at The Boho Club. Unnerved by so much careless beauty, she had searched for her reflection in every window that she passed, and each time, to her own surprise, she was reassured. She didn't look like the young men and women. But neither did she look like the other women that she saw, closer to her in age. These stood in organised groups outside the theatres, immaculate in smart jackets and skirts, every hair sprayed in place, handbags at the ready. Grace had escaped that.

Because this evening, Grace glowed, and she could feel it. In the reflecting windows her hair spiralled round her face as if it had caught her excitement. Her blood tingled. She felt light and quick, ready to react to anything – an elbow touching her as she passed, or the look in a stranger's eye. Darting between cars and bikes, without having to stop, as if there were quicksilver in her heels. Animals probably moved like this, aware of being visible, of being on their toes. The only way to stay alive.

She arrived at a door with a small discreet sign: The Boho Club. Steps leading up from street level. It was nearly nine. She drew a breath and went quickly up the stairs, to a landing where a young woman sat behind a desk, busy on the phone, and up another flight of...

'Excuse me.'

The young woman at the desk had pulled the phone away from her ear.

'Are you a member?'

'I'm sorry?' said Grace, breathless and

already five steps up. She needed to find a cloakroom, somewhere she could check herself one last time.

'I said, are you a member?'

'Oh.' Grace paused. 'No, I don't suppose I am. I mean no, I'm not. But I am here to meet someone, so I suppose *he* must be.' She smiled down at the girl. 'I'll just run on up and find him, shall I?'

'There's a private party going on up there. I'll need to check they're expecting you. What's your name?'

'Grace,' said Grace. 'Grace Waites.'

The girl ran her eye over a list in front of her. There was a silence.

'I'm meeting Mr ... Richard. Richard Ortega.'

And still there was a silence. Finally the girl looked up from her list. 'There's no Grace Waites here.'

'Oh but...'

'I've checked twice. And your name isn't here. Do you have another name?'

'I'm sorry?'

'A work name, one you use when you're ... you know ... working?'

'Well no...'

'Then I'm afraid there's nothing here.'

Grace glanced at her watch. It was gone nine. A wave of impatience, almost panic, swept over her. 'Look, I'm late. I'd better run on up and find him. Just tell me where to go. Is it some kind of bar? I'll bring him down and he...'

'I'm sorry,' the girl interrupted. She had both hands resting on the desk now, eyes level with Grace. There would be no more checking of lists.

'But I need to...'

'I'm going to have to ask you to leave.'

'But he told me...'

'If Mr Ortega told you anything, then you can sort it out with him. Meantime, you'll have to go.'

'Please, won't you...?'

The girl shook her head. Impregnable. Smug.

Grace felt her jaw tighten. She had come so far. She had told a lie to her daughter and another lie to her husband. She had lost sleep. She had walked from her home to the station on legs that seemed ready to give way beneath her. She had had to learn to swim with the tide of beauty in the streets of Soho. She could not turn around without a struggle. Not when there was so obviously a mistake.

She came down the stairs. 'Look...' she began in a voice both quiet and reasonable; but the girl, scenting victory, merely bent over the list, feasting on names that did not include Grace's name.

'Look,' said Grace more loudly. But still the girl ignored her. Grace watched her a moment, then leant across the desk. *'Look.'*

And the girl looked. Maybe it was that one word, louder than intended. Sharper.

More quietly Grace said, 'There's been a mistake. I'm here to meet Richard Ortega. He's expecting me. If you don't let me in, he'll think I never came. You have to let me find him.' She saw the girl's lip curl, and with it something snapped. 'For God's sake just let me in,' she shouted, and banged the desk.

Hard.

There was a silence. The girl looked rattled, and suddenly very young, hardly older than Anna. *Anna.* Imagine someone shouting like this at Anna, frightening her, banging their fist under her young face. Imagine... Grace's anger drained from her.

She took a step back, colliding with someone standing behind her, and immediately the vacuum left by the anger was filled with something else. Embarrassment, no – *shame*. She knew exactly who was there, watching, listening.

She turned. And it was. It was him, Richard Ortega. Not alone either. Two women were there with him, eyes sliding away in distaste from a woman who shouted and banged desks to frighten young girls.

Something threatened to die inside her.

'Richard.' She tried to smile – and failed. 'I was trying to find you, but she wouldn't let me. She wouldn't listen. She just ... wouldn't.'

Hearing her voice beginning to rise again she stopped.

There was another, longer silence. Richard was standing very still. Impossible to read the expression in his face. Finally, he spoke.

'Ah.'

Just that. One of the women gave herself a little shake, ready to disengage from the scene. She said to him, 'We'll see you upstairs.'

He nodded, eyes still unreadable, watching Grace.

The other woman hesitated. 'Actually, Richard, maybe it would be better if you came with us. Let them sort it out.' She threw a glance at the desk girl – and now, a man, bulging and suited, who had appeared beside her.

But then Richard seemed to pull himself together. 'No.' His voice was brisk. 'Better leave it to me. There's obviously been some kind of misunderstanding. You go.'

It was a command meant for all of them, yet no one seemed inclined to obey him; not the girl behind the desk, not the women or the man in the muscle-bound suit.

'I mean it. I'll sort this out.'

His hand closed round Grace's arm, which immediately grew numb where he

72

touched her. Yet elsewhere her skin felt exposed, raw where the women's eyes had slid over her and away, as her eyes would have done if she had come across another woman shouting, refusing to leave.

She let the hand guide her downstairs. But she couldn't speak. She couldn't even look at him. Back on the pavement she braced herself to be abandoned there, alone, without even an explanation. Instead his hand stayed on her arm, firm but gentle. He led her along the street and into a pub.

Without consulting her, he ordered her a whisky. A triple. Sat her down.

'Take it,' he said. 'Drink it up.' He was speaking softly, as though to someone who was in shock. She picked up the glass and took a sip.

'In one.' He was smiling at her now. She tilted back her head and swallowed, expecting to choke. Instead, the whisky slipped down easily.

'See?' he said. 'You needed it.' He watched her a moment. 'So, tell me. What happened?'

Grace stared at him in wonder. Why ask, when he had seen it all for himself? Finally she found her voice. 'They – *she* – wouldn't let me in. She was so rude, and I ... well, I lost my temper, which was when you arrived with your ... with your friends.' She closed her eyes, seeing again the women and their cool distaste.

Richard chuckled. His eyes were tender, indulgent. 'Grace, my Grace. Always so intense. Are you ever different?'

She looked at her empty glass. 'Yes,' she said dully. 'All the time. I'm not intense. Not like this.'

He shook his head. 'I don't believe you. You are all intensity. All passion. It's what I...'

He stopped. Changed tack.

'Anyway, you haven't answered me. *What happened?*'

Grace blinked. 'But I've just told you. The girl wouldn't...'

'No, no, Grace. Silly Grace. That's not what I meant. That was nothing. What I want to know is where were you?'

'Where was I?'

'Yesterday. Nine o'clock. You promised to come.'

She frowned. 'Yesterday? You mean Tuesday?'

'I suppose you decided against me. I asked too much of you. Is that it? Is that why you didn't come? Were you frightened of me, Grace?'

'But I *did* come. I'm here now.'

He shook his head. 'Yesterday, Grace. That's what we agreed. Tuesday.' He spoke sadly as if all was lost.

'Oh,' she whispered. Finally she understood. 'I must have made a mistake.' Her eyes prickled. Time, date, place – she had been so sure, and she had been wrong. 'But I'm here now,' she said, stating the obvious.

Yet he continued to shake his head. 'I don't believe in mistakes, Grace. We are the creatures of our inner creatures. They tell us what to do, and only after do we choose to call it error. Your creature told you not to come. It told you not to trust me. And you obeyed.'

'No!'

'Yes! You know about the creatures, Grace. I wrote about them in *The Hierophant*. Our demons, the true reason we do anything. Tell me about the demons, Grace. You know my work.'

He was staring at her expectantly, confident that she did know. And suddenly Grace had no possible answer. How could she confess that she had never read *The Hierophant*? Unlike *The Maid And The Magician*, she had never got past the first few pages, which had seemed strangely wooden, expressing nothing she recognised. She had put the book aside, slightly guilty, as if her own reading skills had let her down, shown her to be illiterate. Now she had to let her eyes slip away.

In a small voice she said: 'I'm sorry, so very sorry. But if ... if you ask to spend time with me again, I would come. I'm sure I

75

would, no matter what the...' she swallowed '...the *demons*, the *creatures* say.'

She watched his hand cover hers, heard his voice reach her as if from a distance. 'But do you want to, Grace? *Do you?*'

She nodded vaguely, yet suddenly not absolutely sure she did want to. *Demons* and *creatures* – the words had seemed to stumble on her lips, as if somehow they had been chosen for her, words she would never use. Part of her was not even here with him now, not properly. She was still standing, shut out of the club, shrinking under the eyes of the women, so elegant and disdainful...

'Damn!'

Abruptly he took his hand away and jumped to his feet. 'I've got to go. My friends are expecting me.' He frowned at her. 'My dear Grace, my *darling* Grace – I would so love to take you with me, but I can't. It's a private party, and those women I was with...'

He must have seen her shudder. He sat down again. 'I need to explain something. One of those women is my editor, and one of them is my agent. I am sleeping with both of them and neither knows about the other. Naturally neither of them knows about you. They wouldn't understand. It's literature, Grace – do you remember I said it was a strange matchmaker? Well, it makes for strange bedfellows too.

'And here's the irony. They are both magnificent, literary women, giants in their field. Yet neither of them could ever understand this ... friendship of ours, Grace. Our wonderful, platonic, *inspiring* friendship. Because that is what we have, you see that, don't you? The seeds are there, the path is set. Already we seem to know each other.' He paused. 'Grace – are you listening to me?'

She gave a start. Despite herself, despite the seriousness in his eyes, she couldn't take him in, not the way she should. Too much of her was stranded, frozen for ever on the stair in front of the women, leaving only half of her to be here, numb to her surroundings. Numb even to him, Richard. The noise of the pub was like cotton wool in her ears.

What was she doing here? Was this what she had come for? To be numb, half blind, half deaf?

All the same she nodded and lied. 'Yes, I'm listening.'

Satisfied, he continued. 'You have spoken only truths to me – deep, painful truths. As for me, you have my work. My wares are on the table. You understand what is happening between us, don't you? Something that is beginning?' He let his voice fall. *'Grace, do you believe in the friendship of souls?'*

She looked up dully, almost ready to say *No.*

It was *then* the whisky hit her. It arrived with a blast that opened her eyes and finally pulled her back into herself. The disdainful women vanished and instead she found herself staring at him. His eyes were fixed on hers, intense and searching. Looking for something.

Looking for what? Another kick from the whisky, and she told herself she knew. She held her breath as the hubbub of the pub died around her, and waited for him to find it. And then he did. He found *her* – the Grace inside. Found her and rolled her up, and handed her back to Grace, who had been so sure she had lost her, just as he had done in the bookshop.

This was what she had come for. Now she felt the delight spread across her face. Relief. Gratitude.

And it didn't matter that a moment later he was standing up again, ready to go, still murmuring his regret. In fact she preferred it, already knowing what she wanted; to be left alone with her Self. Rediscovered, like something rescued from the bottom of a pool where she had sunk without trace. Back again.

Richard left, repeating apologies that barely registered, and Grace stayed, savouring the moment. Then slowly she stood up and made her own departure. She drifted with the tides of Soho, caught her train and went home. And none of it seemed real, not any more. Not the girl behind the desk or the women with their polite distaste.

Not even Richard, *especially* not Richard, who seemed like a creature of her own making, a dream of words, telling her what she had needed to hear.

It was herself that was real. Herself that she hugged on the train and the walk back from the station. Sixteen-, twenty-year-old Grace, back again. Alive again.

In the Booze Bar of The Boho, Richard's two companions waited for him. One of them was slightly older than Grace, the other slightly younger. Both looked oddly alike, beautifully yet loosely groomed, comfortable in their skin, and with each other.

Patricia, the agent, took a sip of cold white wine. 'Richard...' she said weakly.

'Richard...' echoed Regina, the editor. They sat for a moment, let the silence speak for them both, until Regina said:

'Has he – you know – tried it on with you recently?'

Patricia grimaced. 'Not for a while. A month maybe. You?'

Regina shuddered. 'Last week, after the Golden Chalice Awards. Drunk of course, but when isn't he? Good lord, Patsy, why does he do it?' She sounded weary, as if she would have been tolerant of this once. Amused. But not any more.

Patricia – Patsy to her friends – lifted her

shoulders, helpless. 'Habit? Because he thinks it's expected of him? His idea of saying hello.'

'Mmmm.' Regina put down her glass. 'I'm not so sure. Not any more. This last time there was a kind of steely determination to it. I fended him off, kept it jolly as one always does – and you know, I honestly thought he was going to hit me. Or burst into tears.' She paused. 'You know he blames us, of course? You and me.'

'Oh Reggie, darling, he blames *us* for everything. Falling sales, bad reviews, *no* reviews, the weather, the price of sugar in the shops.'

'I'm doing my level best for him, Patsy, you know that. But it's not working. He keeps churning out the same old stuff and people are bored. Our sales reps say they can't move him, but he won't see it. *And* he's making enemies. You know he nearly punched Max Farthing that same night at the Golden Chalice for not including him on the long list? Max was very good about it, but...'

She looked at her friend, preparing to break bad news. 'We're going to drop him after this one: you probably have already guessed. I'm so sorry.'

Patsy sighed, 'Oh God, Reggie. Tell me you don't mean it. You know Richard, he'll never...'

'Patsy, I *do* know. Look, I'll talk to people.

Maybe I can find someone who'll take him on. One of the independents...'

Patsy was still searching for a way out. 'The truth is, Reggie, you never know. He might pull something off, write something different. People do. Don't make any decisions yet. Maybe he'll surprise you...'

She had drifted to a halt. Neither of them was believing a word she was saying. Resigned, she changed the subject. 'So what about that woman?'

Reggie grimaced. 'The one downstairs? She looked utterly mad. It was Richard I noticed, though. He seemed quite shaken.'

'*Didn't he?* Almost panic stricken. You know, he's mentioned something like this happening before. Some woman who latched on to him in a bookshop, swearing he'd saved her life. He was quite kind about her – for Richard. But it rattled him, I could tell.' She turned to face her friend. 'I wonder if it's the same woman.'

Regina nodded at the door. 'Well, you can ask him. Here he comes.'

They watched as Richard made his way towards them.

'You know, Reggie...?' Patsy whispered. She sounded puzzled.

Immediately Regina answered her: 'Yes Patsy, I do know...'

But she couldn't have said what she knew. Over the years they had watched him move

81

across a thousand rooms just like this room, while they for their part sat a little straighter, readying for the ordeal that was Richard. Knowing exactly what to expect.

Except that this time, the expected didn't happen. Richard came and sat down. And didn't say a word.

Not a word.

Moments passed. Cautiously, Regina let down her guard. 'Are you all right, Richard? You look...'

She stopped and glanced at Patsy for support.

'You look bloody awful, Richard, that's how you look,' Patsy said firmly, and waited for the rebound.

He smiled weakly. But then silence fell once more. Richard was lost in thought.

'Well,' said Patsy at last. 'Aren't you going to tell us? What was all that about? What did she want?'

Richard's mouth twitched. 'Me,' he said finally. 'I'm afraid it's me she wants.'

He glanced at the wine on the table. They watched him, unconsciously urging him to behave as he would always behave, to grab the bottle and fill his glass, to the very top, the first of many glasses.

But he didn't. Tonight the wine had no interest for him, with the result that the two women stared at him as if he was a stranger.

Regina said, 'Forgive me, but is that the

same woman who jumped you in the bookstore?'

Richard looked up. 'You know about that?' He seemed startled.

'Patsy told me. *Is* she the one?'

Slowly, almost unwillingly, he nodded.

'And she's followed you here?'

Again, he nodded, then passed a hand quickly over his eyes.

The two women stared at each other. 'Well, I must say, Richard...' Patsy began briskly. But then she stopped. Regina was frowning at her.

Regina turned to Richard. Gently, she put the question: 'Have there been other times that she's come after you? Besides this time?'

He didn't answer.

'Richard,' Regina pressed him. 'Is she ... I hardly like to ask this ... but is she following you?'

And when he didn't answer they knew.

Chapter Six

After leaving Regina and Patricia, Richard went home. Fished a bottle of gin from the fridge.

God knows, he needed it. An evening with The Women would drive any man to drink.

Lesbians, of course, both of them. The literary world was full of them. Not that he was prejudiced. Perish the thought. He'd even taken it upon himself to attempt a cure, now and then, over the years. Kindly, patiently done his best to show them there was a better alternative, but he'd never got so much as a vibration out of them. Both had spun some kind of yarn about husbands and lovers at home. All lies, of course. Yet he'd never held it against them, the fact it simply wasn't in their nature to respond.

That said, it takes it out of a man, forced to conduct a relationship without any kind of sexual click to keep things smooth. And now it was becoming all too clear: he, Richard Ortega, had shown himself for a fool. A lesbian for an agent and another for an editor – who in their right minds would have trusted them to do their best for The Enemy? A mere man?

He shook his head grimly. He had been an idiot, a holy fool.

He poured out a tumbler of gin. No room for water. Lately he'd needed the mitigating effects of alcohol just to take the edge off the anger, to stop himself – loins girded with justice and righteousness – from charging them with crimes of neglect and commerce. And idleness.

Needed every bit of drink he could get.

The trouble was now, Richard, the *new*

84

Richard – the Richard who was facing a threat only Seamus O'Connor could understand – couldn't allow himself to drink. A man who was being stalked, who was being watched, preyed upon, would be a man who had to take care. Be aware.

Be vigilant.

So no more drink. Not in front of them.

Because in the end, this is what had impressed those two more than anything: the fact that he hadn't broached their bottle of Boho blanc. That's what really got the women staring, eyes popping, like he'd gone and grown a fucking tail.

He swallowed and smiled. Then smiled more broadly still. All in all, everything had gone quite nicely. Everyone had behaved correctly and on cue, with the result that suddenly he felt quite fond of all of them – Grace, Regina and Patricia, even the smug little bint at the desk who was guaranteed to make the Pope scream. Richard smiled and swallowed and smiled again. He remembered this feeling, this same impulse to smile at the end of the day. Isn't this how he used to feel after a good day at the typeface, sinking the first well-earned gin of the evening? Knowing that, thanks to his efforts, every character on the page had done what they were told and the story had stayed on course. Able to relax finally, the way a mother would relax, after she had spanked her babes soundly and sent them to bed.

Progress. The sort Seamus O'Connor would recognise.

Richard Ortega closed his eyes and let his mind play with the first line of a book. A prologue might be in order, some kind of introduction. *Sometimes a writer, if he is a true writer, is obliged to write true...*

He fell asleep mid-sentence and began to dream instead – the usual dream that inevitably would wake him without ever his remembering why, grinding his teeth and biting his tongue. He dreamt he was playing tennis with Martin Amis and, as usual, Martin Amis was driving the balls at him, one after the other, smashing them at points behind him on the court, like a precision bomber operated by remote control. Richard ran and sweated and cursed and reached with his racquet but it was wooden and heavy, with strings gnarled and warped, and every ball flew past him to its appointed detonation.

And almost the worst of it was, having beaten the shit out of him, Amis strolled off the court, without a look in his direction. Without even shaking his hand, just like he did at the end of every dream. And Richard woke briefly, snarling. Forgot he had fallen asleep smiling.

It was nearly midnight when Grace let

herself in.

She stood in the hall of her quiet house and considered if this was the way she liked it, coming home to a place where people had given up any hope of getting anything out of her and gone to hibernate instead.

Then came a movement on the stairs and it was her daughter Anna, descending like a beautiful ghost in pyjamas. Her hair was muzzy and her eyes dusky with sleep.

'Oh good, it's you.'

'Of course it's me,' said Grace and took off her coat. 'Who did you think it was...?'

Anna's clear brow puckered as if it irritated her, the brightness in her mother's voice. 'I told you I didn't want you to go. He was, well, odd, that man. He might have wanted to kill you, then rape you, then... I don't know what. Anyway,' yawning she turned and made to go back upstairs, 'it's good you're back. Rob was going to get one of his friends to follow you. Make sure you were all right.'

'Did he?' Grace was alarmed. 'Did he actually do that?'

'He tried but they were all too busy down the pub.'

Grace breathed a sigh of relief, yet something inside her had grown warm suddenly. She surprised herself by reaching out to her daughter and pulling her close, stopping her from going upstairs. Just for a

second Anna resisted – for form's sake –
then relaxed and they stood, breathing in
the warmth of each other, as they had done
since the day she was born.

Good to be home.

Upstairs, Simon was snoring lightly. But
when Grace climbed into bed, his hand
reached across the cover in the dark, checking that the warmth and weight beside him
was real, not a dream; that she was real.
Having checked, he rolled over and fell back
into unconsciousness, sighing, contented,
but not awake enough to know why. And
Grace drifted off to sleep, unaware that she
was smiling.

Outside The Boho Club, Patsy said goodnight to Reggie, who said, 'By the way,
how's Merlin?' She watched her friend.

A stillness came over Patsy. For the first
time this evening she looked tired. 'Oh, you
know. Same as ever. No pain. Mostly he just
sits, pretending to read, like a little boy
who's been told to occupy himself with a
good book.'

'Patsy...' Reggie touched her friend's
cheek. She gave a sigh. 'I remember the first
time I met him, oh, how many years ago?
How handsome he was. How clever.'

Both women smiled, both remembering a
short, dark, beautiful man from the Rhon-
dda with a passion for talk and the words

that were his reason for living. There were no words now.

Patsy said, 'Well, he's still handsome. And inside, who knows, he might even still be clever. In his own way.'

'And no pain?' Reggie's voice was soft.

'No pain.'

The two women stood a moment, as if reluctant to leave the shelter of the other.

'Richard...' said Reggie and for the second time that night, let the name hang between them. They had done this for years, editor and agent, sharing the burden, using the name like a secret signal only the other would understand. A wry, private joke.

'Ah yes, Richard,' replied Patsy slowly.

She was frowning as she hugged Reggie goodnight. *Richard.* Something else to worry about.

Chapter Seven

Daylight and Richard Ortega woke with a shudder. Limbs twitching as if electrodes had been feeding on him all the time he slept. A gin hangover buzzed in his ears and made the wind whistle in his chest.

He felt like a boy who had spent the night sobbing.

Why? He lay, teeth and fists clenched, and tried to remember who or what was to blame. Not the dreams, he rarely remembered his dreams. Or refused to remember them. Yet still they haunted him – wreathed catalogues of failure, miasmas on the edge of his waking life. But having not allowed them into his thoughts, still the resonances of them remained, so that the sight or sound of unrelated names or words would make him pant and sweat without his ever knowing why. Tennis. Martin. Balls. Bombs.

Books that bomb. The need for someone to blame pinned him to the bed. Paralysed him.

Then, as he lay, as if from nowhere came something new. A balm, a streak of comfort, like a hand smoothed across his brow. It arrived as a thought, a memory – something that actually happened. Real, not a dream.

It was the memory of a face. Grace's face. The way it had been when humbled by the bint of The Boho. Cheeks brimming with colour as the blushes kept emptying and replenishing. Small, high breasts, which might actually not be too small. Most of all, he remembered her eyes, after that one triple draught of whisky. The way they had changed so quickly: from uncertainty to trust, and finally to wonder.

When had a woman – when had *anyone*, man, dog or child – looked at him like this?

As he lay, other features of Grace returned in force – the curly brown hair, the small hands. The slim waist. All reminding him of something from a distant past, a picture from a book perhaps, highly painted in old-fashioned colours. A dairymaid chasing the cow that jumped over the moon. Lavender's blue dilly dilly... *Curly Locks, Curly Locks, will'st thou be mine?*

Richard lay in bed and gave himself up to a smile, huge, sentimental and lopsided. Unaware that suddenly he looked foolish and contrary as a wolf stunned by old age and too much moonlight.

Then he gave himself a shake. His head cleared, making way for the pain of the gin to return. Stupid, what was he thinking of? That wasn't what Grace was for. He had that all mapped out. Everyone was put on this earth for a purpose and Grace's purpose was catered for.

So what was she doing, stepping out of character, floating through his thoughts like a dairymaid hovering just out of reach, pink cheeked and cow-eyed? Suddenly Richard had the answer to his question: the reason for going to sleep perfectly happy and waking up with his teeth grinding. Not happy. Definitely not happy.

It was her fault. Grace. All set to complicate things with her diddly diddly smile and rosy posy cheeks. Stepping out of the role she was created for. Grace was responsible.

Richard bared his teeth, and stretched. Now that he had someone to blame, he could move again, think again. Leap out of his bed like a young man, like a youthful literary Turk on the edge of success. Ready for sweet black coffee and a head full of plans.

But slowly. Not too fast.

A leisurely breakfast of gin and eggs. A particularly enjoyable crap, while he considered the merits of chinos over cavalry twill for the day. He settled for the chinos. Years ago he'd noticed that male writers wore little else – if you ignored Iain Mc-Bankin, who wore only kilts. But having made his choice, he sighed for the uniformity of intellectual life, for the constraints it forced on men like himself. Still sighing as he reached for the newspaper. A writer has a duty to stay in touch with the world, keeping a pulse on the twitchings of other souls.

He ran his eye down the columns of print, skipping over famine in East Africa, sliding over a mass bombing in the Middle East; an elderly woman kicked nearly to death for the contents of her shopping trolley. Nothing causing him to pause. At least not until he came to a small paragraph in the left-hand corner of page five.

'Irish writer Seamus O'Connor was yesterday awarded the Prix de Serge Gainsbourg for literature in Paris, with screen legend Catherine

Deneuve presiding. O'Connor, who recently escaped a murderous attack by a stalker, thanked a worldwide readership that had embraced his work, based largely on his own experiences...'

Richard crumpled up the paper and tossed it aside, mourning a culture of information so utterly obsessed with the small and the mediocre. It threatened the good humour he had wrested from the clutch of bad dreams and night miasmas – so much so that he had to sit a moment and take himself in hand. After all, he had work to do.

He picked up the phone and waited for the soft voice.

'Grace,' he said gently. And satisfied, heard her catch her breath.

'A most beautiful day, my Grace. A day for walking under clear London skies. A day for bookshops and old haunts. A day for spending with a friend.'

He waited for a reply to tumble down the phone. Instant. Eager. Instead there was a silence. Hardly what he expected. He frowned to himself and checked his watch, was astounded to see it was only twelve hours since they had parted. *Only twelve hours?* He could have sworn it was longer.

But then came the reply. 'Yes. All right.'

And he sighed with relief.

He named an hour and a place later in the day. This time he had decided to be there waiting for her – alone. Not even a Patsy or a Regina present. It could be her treat, her one and only chance to spend time with him without the need to show the world. Time out from the rest. He could afford to be gracious to Grace. Just this once.

Lavender's blue dilly dilly. Why shouldn't it be? The eyes had it after all.

Grace put the phone down, not sure whether to be pleased or dismayed.

Although she had slept the night through, she was exhausted, as if she hadn't even closed her eyes. As if the events of the evening had played themselves over and over on a never-ending loop, even in her sleep. Over breakfast, Anna had cast her a sharp unforgiving glance and said, 'God you look knackered.' But then, looking closer still, she had added, 'You look good on it though. Sort of glowy.'

Which had made Simon look up from his newspaper. A moment passed while she felt his gaze, taking her in. Seeing her.

'Anna's right.'

And his eyes had followed her after that, around the kitchen as she stopped at all the usual places – the kettle, the toaster, the fridge, forgetting about his paper.

It was all she needed.

Yet here was Richard Ortega, back already, barely twelve hours since she had last seen him, when she could have lived off the effect of him for weeks to come. Ready, it seemed, to give her more of what had made all this possible. Now she felt her movements quick and light under her dressing gown, just the way they had been last night in the streets of Soho.

And decided that far from being dismayed, she was pleased. Pleased that he had rung so soon. Happy to see him again.

But it didn't last. They met in Hyde Park, not far from the fountain with the piping boy. And she saw him for the first time, by the broad light of day.

'Ah now,' he said indicating the statue. 'Look at that. I used to come here with my nanny. Every day. People even used to say I looked like him.'

She glanced at the stone figure, looking for a young Richard. But somehow her imagination failed her. She had been wondering – guiltily – what could have caused the stains spattered around the flies of his trousers. After the elaborate kiss on either cheek, it was the first thing she had noticed. Now she was trying not to look at them.

'Your mother worked?' she asked instead.

'Mother work? No, of course not. Good grief, what an idea!'

He fell silent so she would have peace to picture the scene: the artist as a small boy, hand in hand with a firm, uniformed young woman, lips and collars neatly pressed. It was necessary for Grace to see and understand the social divide that nonetheless he was willing to bridge for her sake. This was her day, after all. Her treat.

But all she said was 'Oh dear'. Her voice was soft as she added, 'She simply handed you over to a nanny. Poor Richard.'

Poor Richard? They caught him up, those words, startled him. He had painted one picture and she was looking at him as if she was seeing another, completely different. One that was closer to the truth. Namely a succession of cleaning women smelling of fags and carbolic paid to get him out of the house while his mother had...had done precisely nothing. *Poor Richard.*

He blinked at the picture, the true picture, too astonished even for rage, even when rage was what was called for.

Then he looked again at Grace, and knew he was wrong. She couldn't see a thing. Not a thing. It was *Poor Richard* because she just happened to be part of the generation educated by lesbians and left-wingers. Breastfeeders who disapproved of nannies and corporal punishment and tears before bedtime.

The threat of rage died away, and all he needed to do was smile. 'Grace,' he murmured. 'My sweet Grace. What a soft heart you have.'

Grace shook her head. 'I always thought it was sad, all those mothers forced to hand their children over, just because it was the done thing, because it was expected.'

'Ah,' he said. 'Well, there you have it. The tragedy of Class.'

She sighed again, and his heart swelled at the depths of emotion he was inspiring in her. Sweet Grace, sympathetic Grace. Suddenly he was happy just to be here, being kind to people to whom nothing was due. To be rewarded by ... this.

But he wasn't to know; they had been almost automatic, those words of hers. The truth was she was still too fascinated by the trousers, by the awful suggestion of the stains. Wondering how he could have failed to notice, almost feeling ill as she looked at them... And worse than this, was the beginning of a thought. What did it say about her if the only man who could see her, really see her, was a man with stained flies, and – for the first time she noticed – a musty, faintly acrid scent, detectable even in the fresh air?

Then a dazzle of sunshine, glancing off the fountain, seemed to catch her, throw a different light on everything. *What was wrong with her?* This was Richard Ortega. Writer, artist. Thinker of extraordinary thoughts. And surely that changed everything. Things that seemed important to ordinary people would mean nothing to a man like him.

Certainly not the things that bothered her. All they showed was that he was alone, uncared for. As alone as the man in the book had been – the man who could see women, really see women.

She could blush for herself, distracted by something so small. She must forget stains, forget everything except the fierce satisfaction it gave her, standing here by a fountain in the sunshine, the object of this man's gaze. Knowing that she was visible, inside and out. It was all she could do not to laugh out loud. If she had not been so shy, she would have flung her arms around him, just in gratitude.

The man who could see women could see her. And now even the crows of the city, flying and cawing a hundred feet in the air, would see her.

It was all she needed. She looked at her watch and smiled to herself. Already ready to go home, back to where she most needed to be seen. Wishing she could go now, at this moment, when everything was perfect, taking her visibility with her.

Chapter Eight

A week later and Grace woke before the alarm.

Simon was sleeping with his face turned towards her, head cradled in the pillow, his lips pressed firmly together. He was not one to sleep with his mouth slack and gaping. It was the reason he snored, of course. But it was better this way, she decided. A good-looking man who stayed good looking even when he slept.

Always the first to wake, she had watched him like this, all the years they had been together. Long ago, before the children, before time had passed, she used to feel she was watching *over* him. As if she was the one with the power. But then the years had gone by and something had changed. Somewhere the roles had switched and so had they, she and Simon. He had become the one with the power, the one to be watching over her.

How had that happened? How had the balance between them changed, and so completely? It startled her, only now recognising that it had happened at all.

Or if not how, when? *When* had it happened? After the children? Perhaps. But not straight away. In those first years, Simon had been the one who was always scared. Terrified by every baby fever, sleepless for fear of something worse. When the babies had screamed or flopped, she had been the one to keep calm. Powerful enough to keep them all safe.

Then it had been time for school. She remembered taking Rob in on his first day, his fist wrapped around her forefinger with a grip like a man's suspended off a cliff. She remembered catching sight of the headmaster in the playground and the activity that surrounded him. Clustered round him had been, not children, but adults. Women to be exact, gathered and fluttering like hens, all vying for his ear, while he stood in the middle of it all, making them wait for his attention. It had made her think not so much of a teacher but a Pasha, enclosed by his harem. Or a great walrus surrounded by seals. It had made her laugh. She had never seen anyone so important.

But two years later, on Anna's first day at school, she – Grace – had been right there, a member of the harem alongside the rest. Vying as hard as everyone else for a word or a look that would end in a benefit for Rob or Anna. So much power do we hand over to those who have power over our children.

So it must already have been happening then, irrevocable – the slow transfer of the power she'd been born with. Allowing it to leach away until she had simply become used to it being gone, used to being invisible. That must have been when...

Simon's eyes snapped open, he was looking straight at her. Wide awake, he had moved instantly, in that very moment from sleep to waking. Nothing in between.

He reached for her, and they began to make love. Not with polite murmurs and careful caresses of recent times, but sleepily and slowly, without ceremony. As if it was the only thing to do, the obvious thing; which of course was the way it had always been, before the children, before there was a question of doing anything else. Before she became invisible.

They finished at the very second the alarm went off, making Simon laugh as if the radio signalling seven had been the fanfare. Then more soberly he lay, looking at her for a long moment, before getting out of bed.

She watched him move across the room, naked, his penis still half erect – until with a small lurch, she realised this was how the other one, Lucy, would have watched him. Approving the long line of his thigh, the balls she had just been cupping, like a comice pear, in her hand. But it was then, with another kind of lurch, Grace realised that she had been awake for twenty minutes, maybe longer, and this was the very first time *she* had thought of her. Twenty whole minutes, and not one thought of someone else.

Nor had Simon thought of Lucy. Grace knew this as well as she knew the sun was in the sky. He had woken to see and smell and taste only her, Grace.

This was what came of being visible again. Powerful again.

Downstairs Rob was smearing peanut butter on slices of bread, slapping them together and then throwing them into a tin box she had previously only seen used for set squares and protractors.

'What are you doing?'

'Making my lunch. Save you the trouble.' He opened the box again and threw in another sandwich, this one made of jam. He started on another sandwich, with nothing in it but tomato ketchup. Grace watched him close the lid on half a loaf of bread and remembered why she had continued to make his lunch for him, even now.

Anna meanwhile was eating toast. Fastidious, spreading slivers of butter with the very edge of her knife. Open in front of her was a book, which she looked at casually every now and then, between tiny bites and careful scrapings. It didn't seem to be holding her attention much.

As usual Grace opened her mouth to chide her to eat more, remembering chubby

102

polished knees, now pared down to two dainty knobs of ivory under pelmet skirts. Then closed it again. Simon had caught her eye with a slight shake of the head. Apparently more expert in Anna than she was.

Afterwards, she picked up the book. Anna had broken its spine and seemed to have spread more butter over the pages than on her toast. It was Richard's book. Grace turned it over with a pang of annoyance. Richard's face stared from the back cover, now smeared with a light acne of toast crumbs. Hurriedly, she brushed them away, instinctively knowing that he wouldn't like it, wouldn't like it at all.

Later though, she must remember to ask Anna what she thought about it.

Books. This book had put her in mind of other books. With the house now empty Grace opened a cupboard and took out a pile. A year ago she had started a distance learning course, half-heartedly going over ground already covered at school. With no clear idea of what she would do with it, she had wanted to resurrect her French. Then came the discovery of Simon's affair, and she had dropped even the pretence that it interested her. She had fallen behind with the work like a teenager with problems at home. Today, though, she wanted to look at it, as if a space had been cleared in her mind.

All the same, her fingers shook slightly

when she opened her exercise book. This was what she had been doing, the hour, the minute, the comet struck and the world had turned upside down. Three months ago she had been writing an essay on *Madame Bovary*. The problem was, the Grace who had so earnestly written the opening lines had had no idea that the deadline for completion would come and go while she would never get beyond the first paragraph. The essay had shuddered to a halt, right in the middle of a sentence. This had been the moment Simon had walked into the room, drunk, his face contorted as if he was ready to cry. His voice had sounded odd when he asked her if she was busy, and she had put down the pen.

Yet Grace remembered now, three months later, exactly what she had intended to say about poor, silly, doomed Emma Bovary with her frantic itch for attention. A cautionary tale. Grace stared at the page, at the place where the essay stopped. Then she picked up her pen.

She finished before lunchtime, dotting the final *i* and crossing the final *t*. Then she sat, panting slightly as if she had been running. She had followed Emma to her sickly exit, made all the necessary contrasts between her search for romance and the squalor of her death. And she had drawn the usual and inevitable conclusion that, while Emma had brought doom on herself, society had conspired against her. If the essay had ever been marked, Grace knew she would have been ticked for all the right responses. But it never would be marked; the deadline had passed. Yet she was perfectly satisfied. She had been able to pick up where she left off, go back to the place where disaster had struck. Like getting back on a horse.

She was not Emma. She was not invisible. She gathered up the pile of books again and stacked them back in the cupboard, knowing she would never go back.

Something else happened that day. Simon came home from work, carrying a giant bunch of flowers. Beautiful, expensive blooms that filled his arms like the bulk of a large child. He had to struggle just to get them through the door.

And seeing them, she felt her face fall. There had been too many flowers, too many gestures gleaned from the indispensable manual of men who have discovered they don't want to leave home. But this time, Simon saw her face. Without a word he dropped them, so they fell with a hard, abandoned flump against the floor. He grabbed her into his arms, snatching her close and holding her so hard her hands were locked against his ribs. She didn't resist. Grace let him pull her face into his neck and breathed deep.

Later, in the bedroom, she sat at her dressing table and looked at herself in the glass. Behind her, Simon's eyes met hers, observing her, watching her every movement. And she was satisfied.

Later still, on the edge of sleep, she thought she saw Richard Ortega and Emma Bovary moving together against a flat landscape that looked suspiciously like a page. Small far-off characters that could loom suddenly large or become infinitely small, the way that literary characters do. There when you need them, vanished when you don't.

Then she had turned over and breathed in the warm accountant smell of her husband, falling asleep to the sound of his faint, familiar snores.

She stayed away from the phone for the next few days, allowing Rob or Anna to answer. Why it was, she couldn't say. Perhaps it was that one lie she had told Anna. Sometimes she felt she couldn't look her in the eye. It played on her mind like an incident in childhood, when a small sin seems huge, and you wait for the sky to fall in pieces on your head.

Why should lying to a daughter seem so huge? Making her blush when she thought about it?

It didn't matter that she had lied the same lie to Simon. He had lied and lied, and then stopped lying at a time to suit himself. So now, although she slept with her face pressed into his back and woke to find his arms wrapped around her in the morning, she told herself she had no illusions. He could lie again.

Or maybe not.

Sometimes she was almost ready to doubt it. And the reason was Simon himself. After all those years of invisible, suddenly he was watching her. She would look up from what she was doing to find his eyes fixed on her, as they must have been fixed all the time she had been reading or stirring a saucepan, or talking to the children. Once she opened her eyes in the small hours, with the dawn only a suggestion below the curtains, to find him bent over her, watching her even as she slept.

And when she caught him looking, he blushed. Awkward as the young man she had unsingled all those years ago. Except that now he was almost fearful, like someone who finally understood what he could have lost. He had added nothing to what he said to her the night he came back to her, but again something had changed. Grace counted his blushes and could feel it happening.

Power shifting.

But at last the phone did ring, when there was nobody but Grace to answer it.

Richard had made sure of it. Choosing his

moment when no one else was likely to be at home – unless they were sick or skiving or unemployed. To tell the truth, he had been surprised the first time, when the daughter had answered. At that age he had been away at school. Somehow he had expected Grace's own children to be packed away in the same fashion. Isn't that what people did?

This time, he phoned in the middle of the morning, sat and doodled his autograph over his latest copy of *Literary Lives* until he had completely covered the face of Seamus O'Connor on the cover, and from the other end came an answer.

'Yes?' He could hear the fluster, just in that one word.

'Grace! My *saving* Grace.'

'Oh,' she said faintly.

At his end of the line, Richard took nothing for granted. He let his face fall into the familiar lines, as if there were a photographer in the room.

'Grace,' he said again. 'Tell me.'

'Tell you what?' she said.

'Tell me where you are. How you are sleeping, what you are wearing. Tell me the book you are reading, the thoughts you are thinking. Tell me how the world fares for you. Tell me why you didn't answer the phone.' There was a silence. He could hear small light breaths. Gently he said, 'Speak to me, my dear. I am sitting here with the sun on my face and a wise old cat on my lap. The page is blank and inviting. I would be in heaven, but first I need the sound of your voice.'

'Well,' said Grace cautiously. 'I'm fine. How are you?'

He chuckled. 'Oh Grace, sweet Grace, you are priceless! I am very well, my dear. And how are *you*? Are your children obeying you, is the milk fresh, are the sheets ironed? *Is your husband faithful?*'

And now, at last, he heard her catch her breath.

'...He is a lucky man, Grace. So lucky, he has luck to spare. I need to borrow some of his luck. Grace, I need to borrow you. The sun shines, the cat is fat. But the well is dry. I need inspiration. Come and replenish me. Come to me, Grace. Please.'

'Of course but...'

'Grace, don't desert me. Come at a time to suit you. Come when you are hungry so I can feed you. Thirsty so I can quench you. Olives and fresh bread, wine and good cheese. Come to my house, Grace. Let me show you how I live.'

He listened to the silence. Let his voice drop.

'Is it too much to ask, Grace? Small time out of your day? For friendship's sake?'

Grace cleared her throat. 'No.' She sounded calm suddenly, as if at last she had reached something firm. 'Of course it isn't. I'll come.'

'Grace, you unman me. Tomorrow, no, the day after. All shall be made ready for you.'

He told her his address, pausing only to listen for evidence that she was impressed when he mentioned Holland Park, but it never came. All he could hear was her breathing as she wrote it down. Too stupid. A rosy posy milkmaid woman who couldn't recognise a good address when she heard it.

He put down the phone and went back to defacing Seamus O'Connor. There was no cat, and no sun. And no blank page. At night Richard Ortega went to sleep with first lines floating through his brain, but he hadn't come near to writing anything. That was for the future. Meantime he was busy, working towards the task, gathering his material. First there had to be a life. He had to see it happen. Make it happen. He was being a writer on whom nothing was lost – even when it meant having to pay court to an ordinary little bourgeoise who didn't know the value of an address.

To be honest, there was something of the marvellous in the work he had set himself. Something ... something almost *Parisian* about this wholesale adoption of a life so different from one's own, tuning in to a mind so different from one's own. And all for art, for the sake of creation.

Suddenly, he could see what he was doing, what he was becoming – a Zola perhaps. Or better – a Flaubert, observing the bourgeoisie in honourable close up, not sparing himself. Plucking the stories of their small lives in order to create something bigger than anything they could dream for themselves.

He was doing Grace a favour.

He stopped doodling, and straightened up, transcended by the thought. Then the sheer squalor of his house hit him and he remembered that the day after tomorrow Grace would be here.

Better phone up Molly Maid.

Then phone up Patsy.

Chapter Nine

As usual, Grace woke before the alarm, and as usual turned to look at her sleeping husband...

...And he wasn't asleep. Simon was lying propped up on one arm, watching her.

'You're awake,' she said unnecessarily.

'I was watching you. Watching you sleep.'

Now, inexplicably, she was the one to blush. 'Was I snoring?'

He shrugged. 'A bit. But I was thinking how ... how young you looked. Not a whole lot older than Rob. No more than a girl, really. I suppose,' he added, not quite so satisfyingly, 'it's because people's muscles get all relaxed when they're sleeping. It irons out the wrinkles. *Wait...!*'

She had moved to get out of bed.

'It's a good thing, though, isn't it, Grace? Not being Rob's age. Or twenty, or twenty-five? Not being so young any more.'

'What could possibly be good about it?' Suddenly she was irritable.

'Well, it means you're alive, that you've lived this long, got this far. *We've* got this far. Grace. Don't you see...?'

But then the alarm went off. She got right out of bed, quicker than she needed to, knowing he wanted to say more, wanted her to stay.

It wasn't the end of it.

Later she overheard Simon giving Rob and Anna money to go out after school, enough to take them to a film, then for a pizza. She listened from the stairs as Simon winkled guarantees that they wouldn't be home till late, and guessed what he was after – time with her, alone, without children or interruptions.

Something was coming to fruition. She had known it for days. She had known it from the way he looked at her, touched her. From the way he clung to her in his sleep.

112

Everything moving towards this.

He had something to say. Words unspoken until now. Finally knowing what he needed to tell her. He loved her. He had stayed because he loved her. Only her. Words he should have told her weeks ago.

But he was ready to say them now: words that would make the last necessary adjustments to an engine that had stalled. He would speak, she would listen, and that finally would be the end of the breakdown. Everything would be back in its place. She and Simon would carry on. The children would carry on: growing, leaving home, or taking up residence in the loft, the in-between place. It would be as if none of this had happened. Lucy gone, discarded – the unwanted spanner discovered in the works – while, like one of those sensible, designed-for-family vehicles, they would motor on. And on. Nothing between them and a flat, unthreatening horizon.

This was what she had wanted, wasn't it?

Yet suddenly she was wishing he weren't quite so ready. That it could all be put off, just for a day, two days. Because once Simon had spoken, she knew she wouldn't go to London, to – where was it again? – Holland Park. She would listen to what Simon had to say tonight, then tomorrow, out of loyalty and duty and maybe even love, she would phone Richard and tell him she would be staying home, unable to explain that there was no place for him either.

Meanwhile, her children were pocketing the money, their faces knowing. Tutored by soaps, versed in happy endings, they knew exactly what Simon was up to. Almost cynical, she thought. Was this how they would be as adults? Expecting life to be as obedient as the switch on the TV remote. They didn't know or care that things only worked because people made them work, adjusting, compromising, sometimes doing the complete opposite of what they wanted.

And more often than not, jettisoning things that got in the way. Not just things – people. Lucy. Richard. Although unlike Lucy, Richard had done nothing but help her. Unlike Lucy, he had been generous, possibly the most generous man she had ever known. He had given her back her Self and wanted nothing in return but her time...

Now she couldn't give him even that, not after Simon had spoken. And she wondered why she wasn't happy.

She prepared for his homecoming the way she would for a lover. Bathing and dressing and smoothing. Touching scent to her lobes and wrists.

She heard the front door open. Simon stepped into the kitchen and smiled at her, holding up a bottle in either hand.

'I've got wine...' she began.

He interrupted her. 'Look at the labels.'

She looked.

'The date,' he urged her. 'Grace. Look at the date of the vintage.'

And still she could see nothing unusual.

'It's the year we came together,' he said. 'Don't you see? Our year. A good year.'

'Oh yes,' she said. 'Our year. I see... Ah yes.'

She told herself to be soft. Soft from head to toe.

They never ate the meal she had prepared. They took the wine to the sitting room, lay down on the rug in front of the fire.

'Twenty years old,' she mused. 'They must have been expensive.'

He shrugged. His eyes were anxious and watching, even now.

'Drink, Grace. It's our wine. Our vintage.'

'You just want me to be tipsy.' She smiled at the effort he was making.

'...Sun shining on the vines. Filling the grapes with sweetness.' And still he watched her. 'You know why wines improve, don't you Grace? Why some wines do and some don't. There has to be the right mix. Sunshine and rain. Proper care. Tenderness. Those are the wines that get better and better over the years.'

'Like some marriages, you mean.' As she

spoke, she felt she was helping him labour a metaphor that was already there. Almost too obvious.

He nodded. Then blushed. There was a silence. She was aware that she should say something to help him. Words, these words, were hard for him. The trouble was, she couldn't think of anything she wanted to say. A small voice inside her was even whispering that the problem was all his. He had to make the effort. His fault they were here, looking for parables in wine labels.

She didn't want to be like this. Surely sixteen-, twenty-year-old Grace would have been more forgiving, more willing to be kind. Forty-year-old Grace listened as Simon toiled to find the right words, and realised she didn't feel either forgiving or kind.

They finished the first bottle and started on the second. But there was no sign of either relaxing under the alcohol. Simon was watching the level of the wine descending, like a man with his eye on an hourglass, conscious that something had to be achieved before the sand ran out.

So she wasn't surprised when, just before the bottle emptied, he turned.

'Grace ... there's something I have to say.'
She smiled. But he was finding it hard.
'I don't know how to tell you...'
'Tell me anyway.'
But still he floundered. This was how it

used to be with Rob when he was a child, always sure that the truth led inexorably to disaster. Confessions had to be patient affairs. And having remembered Rob, her mind continued to drift, towards the children, wondering where they were. Thinking Simon could have chosen another night to bribe them to stay out, when there wasn't school the next morning.

'I've turned it over and over, Grace, how to tell you. And I still don't know.'

She nodded. She was hoping Anna and Rob were together. She preferred it when it was the two of them, looking out for each other.

'I know I haven't any right to ask anything of you, no right at all.'

Absent-minded, she shook her head, agreeing with him.

'It's just that last week ... last week, Grace, I went to see a doctor.'

He stopped. And Grace blinked. So sure she'd known what was coming she wondered if she had heard him right.

'A *doctor*?'

He nodded. 'A specialist. It had to be. They had to be sure.'

Now, finally, she was beginning to see what she should have seen all this time; there in his face. Not anxiety but misery – carved deep into the contours. She felt the certainty ebbing away.

'Why?' Her voice was fainter. 'Why did you have to see a doctor?'

He was telling her why. Trying and failing. Opening his mouth, but the words wouldn't come.

'Simon?'

He looked at her. 'I've got... Oh Grace, I can't say it. I can't make myself say it.'

His eyes pleaded with her and she wondered how she could have been so blind. Complacent, smug. Thinking adultery was the worst crime, the worst thing that could happen to them, not realising there was worse, far worse. An absence more final than anything Lucy could have brought about.

Her hands flew out to cup his face. To hold him, letting the strength and warmth flow through her fingers into his skin. 'Say it.' Her voice was soft. 'Just tell me what the doctor told you. I'll be here, no matter what. Whatever it is, we'll fight it. Together.'

'No matter what?' He whispered the words. 'You promise me that?'

For answer she kissed him. He closed his eyes. Then said:

'It's gonorrhoea.'

Her hands grew stiff. The very air seemed to freeze.

'Grace. I've got gonorrhoea. It means you have it too. I'm so sorry.'

And all she could do was stare.

'*She* gave it to me. Passed it on and never

said a word.'

Still her hands had not moved from his face, frozen there like flesh to metal. She didn't have the strength to pull them back; she had just this minute poured that same strength into him. All of it.

'But it's going to be all right, isn't it Grace? Because we'll work through this, won't we? The two of us, we're like the wine. We just get better as we get older. No matter what. Because I love you, Grace. You know I love you.'

It was these last words that seemed to release her, allowed her fingers to fall away from his face. Slowly she got to her feet. As she did so, she heard the stem of a wineglass snap delicately beneath her heel. The tiny sound of something fragile, breaking.

He heard it too. She knew he did.

On her way out of the room she saw the book – Richard's book. His face greeted her as if he had been waiting. Eyes meeting hers, knowing all, understanding all. She reached for it with what small strength she had left, held it to herself. Her rock. Her safe place.

She had crawled into bed, was huddled under the duvet when Simon came into the room. She heard the noises of him moving about, collecting things, getting ready to go elsewhere. To the loft, where else? Eventually she heard him move towards the door, and pause there. Then she heard him again, not leaving but climbing into bed beside her.

He lay for a moment, then said out loud, into the dark, 'I'm not going, Grace. I'm not going back upstairs. I'm staying here, with you, until you tell me to go. I'm staying with you.'

She opened her mouth to tell him she didn't want him. But nothing had changed since she had poured every bit of strength into him. She didn't even have the energy to answer him. And so he stayed.

She thought she would never sleep, but she did, almost immediately, aware that she was falling into something like a vast expanse of black, deep and dangerously peaceful. She didn't hear the snorts and giggles of her children coming into the house, finishing off the wine left abandoned on the floor. Sleep, the best place to be. All this time she had thought he had been watching her because he could see her. Now she knew. He had been watching because he was frightened.

Only frightened.

Chapter Ten

When she arrived at Richard Ortega's door, she almost expected him not to be there. Or that he would open it and stare at her like a stranger. It was how much faith she had now.

But Richard had opened the door and looked at her. 'Grace,' he said simply, 'My dearest Grace.' And drawn her inside so warmly that his house had bent around her like an embrace.

For the first half-hour she could do nothing but cry. He had sat and watched her, saying nothing. But all the time he held her hand, moving only to mop her face with a silk handkerchief that had smelt musty; and every so often, pouring tots of clear liquid into a glass and making her drink. Not having swallowed gin neat before she didn't even recognise it, but knew that, gradually, it was making her feel better.

She didn't tell him the reason why she cried. Not even a man who looks at a woman, really looks at her, could have seen past what she was now. Unclean. This morning she had attended a clinic where people had treated her with absolute kindness, yet whose voices were lost on her, merging instead with the educational posters on the walls and the pudgy unformed features of young girls who blew bubbles with their gum and waited for their names. She had lain with her feet in cradles above her head and stared at the ceiling, at a spider's web studded with a myriad of tiny dead flies while a young male doctor had probed inside and talked about the weather.

Now she was here, weeping while Richard kept a silence that seemed magical in its tact and tenderness. And for so long! Never protesting that she should stop. As if he knew that every tear was necessary.

Meanwhile Richard Ortega had sat and let his mind wander. Not bored exactly. He sat as he had sat two days before, until finally she had answered the phone, waiting until he had her full attention. In truth, it was almost a relief to see her in tears, nose wet and swollen, lips puffy. It mitigated those annoying images of milkmaid Grace that still had a tendency to float unbidden, as if she had a mind and destiny of her own.

Finally though, he stole a covert glance at his watch, remembered that he was working to a timetable.

He stirred, gently withdrew his hand. But only so as to brush the latest of the tears from beneath her eyes. A delicate signal that it was time for her to stop.

On cue, she looked at him, and tried to smile. Took a long shuddering breath. And stopped crying.

'Sweet Grace,' he murmured, whilst he wiped his hand discreetly on his trousers. Tears, like snot, repelled him for the same reason that he found them useful: for their ability to make anyone seem less than they had been. His own bodily fluids upset him not at all.

'Richard,' she whispered. 'You are so kind.' She smiled, this time for real. 'You haven't even asked me why I'm crying.'

His eyes played over hers, amused, affectionate. 'The kindness is yours. You are here, weeping in my house, making me a witness. It's a sacred trust you show in me. Only the honour is mine.'

Then he stood up. 'But after tears, sunshine. It's necessary. Soil needs heat as well as rain. As the French say: one weeps, then one blows one's nose.'

With a flourish he handed her the silk handkerchief. She took it, hesitated – then buried her nose and blew. Richard looked away. He shook his head benignly when, timidly, she offered it back. 'Keep it, Grace. I give it to you. And when next you need to cry use it and think of me.'

She nodded slowly. And put it away carefully in her bag.

'Now,' said Richard. 'We eat. What did I

promise you? Good bread. Good wine. Food ancient and modern. Food as a remedy and prayer. Almost religious you might say.'

He led her through partition doors to a table, sat her down. Poured her a glass of cheap Bulgarian red and placed it in her hand. 'A moment,' he murmured and returned to where they had been sitting.

She had left her bag in the chair where she had been crying. Through the partition doors he could see her, her back to him. Despite the gin, she was sitting much straighter now, shoulders spread more widely. He could see she was recovering, the tears having served some kind of purpose. Not his own purpose, it occurred to him. Richard frowned. He was beginning to notice that Grace had an annoying habit of apparently hearing, seeing, only what was useful to her. Like not noticing the value of an address. Or willing to sit for hours exercised by some private concern of her own, incontinently leaking tears.

Not quite formed. Not yet. Not the way she should be. Bobbing out of true like a character refusing to lie flat on the page.

Well, he'd get her over that. As Grace sat, sipping wine on top of the gin, Richard rummaged through her bag. Not with any specific intent, but rather with the forward thinking of a planner, an author never knowing what he might need to drive a story on. A plot can only come together where there are enough threads to be knit. And they have to be created.

So it was creative thinking that made him rummage, looking for anything he could use, scribbling down the number of her mobile phone. Creatively removing the house key from her bag, whilst thoughtfully leaving behind the keys to the car.

Then he returned to Grace and poured his own glass of wine. Raised it to her as a salute. 'To passion, Grace. To that which makes men and some women different from each other. To tears and laughter, and ... *love.*'

He held her eyes as he spoke the last word, his voice deepening. He thought she would blush or catch her breath when she heard it. He thought it would move her in the direction that was already there, mapped out for her.

To his annoyance, however, all that happened was that her eyes filled with tears once more. And she looked away, breaking the gaze that should have held her. He had a sudden urge to slap; he had talked of love, and the woman was off on a frolic of her own.

He watched her try to eat, and fail. Again it occurred to him: Grace was barely aware of him, not the way she should be. Mind elsewhere, like a child with its own preoccupations. He was moved to prod her slightly, draw her attention back to where it should be. To him.

'Don't feel you have to speak, my dear.' Small chance of that, it seemed. 'There are moments when a man must let a woman be. Let her work through the passions that shake her. No questions. He needs only to be there when she turns to him. *Her rock. Her safe place.*'

And there, somehow he had hooked her. For with these final words, she turned to him with something close to wonder. He had her attention now. All of it.

He poured the last of the Bulgarian into her glass. And like a priest held it to her lips.

But to his annoyance, she shook her head. She stood up – a little unsteady. 'Richard, you don't know, you can't know, what you've done for me. I was mad, completely mad when I came here. My whole world was...' She checked herself. 'I can't explain. I shouldn't even try. I have no right. But I needed to cry – only not in front of them, not in front of the family...' She gulped down another sob. 'You did that for me. You let me cry, sitting there so beautifully, like ... like someone from out of your books. Thank you.'

He prepared to murmur a suitable reply, but already she was turning, heading for the door. *Filling him with dismay.* It was too early. Leave now and she would ruin everything, make the entire encounter a waste of time. But then his eye caught the hands of the ormolu clock on his mantelpiece and he relaxed. He hadn't realised it was so late. Sitting here all this time, holding her hand, watching her cry, feeding her gin, and never noticing the hour. Almost as if he had been enjoying himself.

In fact, according to his own timetable it nearly was time for her to leave. Nearly but not quite.

'I just need to...'

'...Visit the little girl's room. Of course, of course.' With relief, he pointed her towards a door. A few minutes more and they would have arrived at the appropriate time. Whilst she was gone, he cleared the table and all traces of lunch.

When she emerged from the bathroom she made straight for the hall. She had been crying again. Richard forebore to notice this. He was clock watching now, aware that every second counted.

Then, praise be, the doorbell rang, making her jump. He frowned as if at an intrusion, then bent to squint through the peep-hole in the door. And jumped back.

'Damn,' he said between clenched teeth. 'It's Patsy. *Damnation.*'

Yet Grace only stared at him, mystified. He could see that already she had forgotten what she was supposed to know. What did this woman do with information? Suppressing another urge to slap, he said, 'Patsy – I mentioned her to you. You saw her. She's my agent, the one I'm sleeping with. Jealous is hardly the word. She's going to play merry hell when she sees you.'

But Grace was already turning pale. She was remembering the two elegant women who had witnessed the shame of The Boho Club, the look of distaste as both had turned away. Richard, however, was staring at Grace. Shock and sudden pallor had conspired with the red around her eyes to make her look ... well, mad. Quite mad.

Time for Patsy to see her. Just like this.

He motioned towards the door, feigning helplessness. Grace sighed and tried to be ready. He pulled open the door and Grace walked, fast and straight as she could, brushing up against Patsy on her way out, looking neither right nor left.

Patsy watched her go, then gasped, turning wide-eyed to Richard.

'Did I ... was that...?'

Richard returned the stare, his face blank, and nodded. Then he slumped against the side of his door.

Inside Patsy took control. Had to. He was clearly in shock.

She looked around the room for a remedy, registering a house unnaturally tidy, but not thinking to wonder why.

'What are you looking for?' Richard's voice was dull.

'A drink for you,' she said firmly. 'Something with a shot of alcohol.'

'Patsy, I hardly think I...'

'Nonsense. You look like death. That woman has traumatised you. Oh Richard, what the hell was she doing here?' She pulled open a cupboard door and found a bottle of gin, not quite empty, thank goodness. She tossed some into a glass and wrapped his hand around it. 'There, get that inside you.'

She sat back and watched him, noted the shaking in the hand, the fine line of sweat along his brow. Richard Ortega as she had never seen him. It stirred in her a feeling normally directed towards friends, relatives, pets. Even clients, occasionally. But never towards him. A feeling of concern – anxious, affectionate, almost maternal – reaching out to him now despite herself.

'Richard,' her voice was gentle, 'why on earth did you let her in?'

He shrugged weakly. 'She was so sad, Patsy. So hopeful. And I suppose I was shocked. I mean, imagine opening one's door to find ... to find...'

'One's very own stalker standing on the step.' Dryly Patsy finished the sentence for him. 'Face it, Richard – that's what she is. Why didn't you tell her just to fuck off, then phone the police. *The police!'* She cried and jumped to her feet. 'That's who we need.'

Richard shook his head.

'No, Patsy. Not the police. You saw her. She's just a woman. A poor lonely woman who thinks – wrongly – that I'm some kind of god. I won't set the police on her. I can deal with it. At least, I'm learning to deal with it.'

Patsy's eyes narrowed. *'Learning?* She's the one who's learning. She's learnt where you go, what you do. She's learnt where you live. She's even learnt how to work her way through your front door.'

'She's sad,' he said again.

'Mad, more like. Did you see the way she pushed me aside, the look in her eyes? Vicious! Oh Richard, wake up. Don't be so nice. Think of Seamus O'Connor, letting that lunatic follow him around. Think what happened to him.'

She stared at him, frowning. Then her face softened. Once again, it was striking her; this was a Richard she had never known. Kinder than she had ever suspected, braver. Above all, sober. On the table, his glass of gin was almost untouched.

'We need to talk to Reggie. She has to know about this latest thing.'

He raised his eyes, questioning. 'Regina? Why?'

Patsy hesitated, then said, 'because she's a friend, Richard. When all's said and done, that's what she is. And God knows, you need friends at the moment.' She let the words hang between them, then said briskly: 'So – what did you call me, for? What was so important that you needed me here at three o'clock sharp?'

An hour later, Richard walked her to her car.

'Damn,' she said. A piece of paper was wedged behind the windscreen wiper. 'Bloody traffic wardens.' She glared round at Richard for sympathy. She had been doling out enough of it herself.

But Richard, who had been strolling beside her, was gone. He was striding ahead so as to be there first, removing the offending article. He was scanning it as she arrived.

'Well, hand it over,' she said, resigned.

To her surprise, he only pushed it deep into his trouser pocket.

'Richard...!'

Slowly she said, 'It's not a parking ticket, is it?'

He hesitated, then shook his head.

'She's left me a message, hasn't she? She thinks that you and I ... that we...'

Richard shrugged.

'Let me see.'

He flinched, but the paper stayed in his pocket.

'Richard...?' Then she understood. 'It's horrible, isn't it, what she's written? So horrible you can't even bear to let me look at it.'

'I'm sorry, Patsy. So sorry.' There was a tremor in his voice.

She stared at him. Suddenly she was thinking of Merlin at home, of all the people who depended on her. She was thinking about the calls she had to make, editors to be pursued, people to be supported or else gently let down. And it all made her so tired. So tired, that suddenly she didn't want to see what a mad woman had written to her. She didn't want to read threats and insults. She didn't even want to touch the paper they were written on.

'I'll deal with it, Patsy. I won't let her get away with this.' Not tremulous now, Richard's voice was low and determined. Utterly trustworthy.

She gave a sigh of relief. And gratitude. She touched his arm, then unlocked her car and drove away. And forgot that Richard never had explained what he had wanted her for, at three o'clock sharp.

Richard finished off the gin in the glass, then emptied the rest of the bottle and finished that too. After that he reached for his cheque book and made out the fine for the parking ticket, filling in all the required spaces, making sure nothing came back to

132

her, to Patsy.

A piece of luck, that was, finding the ticket planted just then. The sort of luck that makes one feel that fate is right there, applauding and supporting. A religious man would go so far as to see it as proof that God was on his side.

That said, there was the argument that genius will always create its own luck.

Richard Ortega was not a sporting man. Indeed some of his blackest memories of St Olave's of the Faint Hearted were of the drubbings that met his every best attempt at prowess on the field. But seeing that parking ticket and then dealing with it the way he had ... well, it was like being an expert batsman having a ball hurtle towards him, only to send it spinning into the wide blue yonder, past the boundaries of the imagination, into a place of pure art.

Well played indeed.

Outside her front door, Grace searched in vain for her house key. She felt ill and dazed, and put it down to the antibiotics that she was taking for 'her' venereal complaint.

There was no one home to let her in, so she sat down on her doorstep and cried until, in the middle of crying, she fell asleep, propped up and snoring against the front door. Which was where Anna found her when she came home.

'Mum?'

Grace opened her eyes. Anna was staring down at her in disbelief. Grace stared back, confused. She had been dreaming that the children were young and that she had simply closed her eyes against the sun while they played in the sandpit or ran between the sheets hanging on the line.

Now here was a young woman staring at her, and for a stark second Grace couldn't think who she was.

'*Mum?*' Anna said again. 'What are you *doing?*'

'Beautiful,' murmured Grace, drunk with gin and wonder.

'What?'

'You. You're so beautiful,' said Grace. 'It's just struck me, as if I was seeing you for the first time. You're your father and me, rolled into one, yet completely different from both of us. Somehow it makes everything better. Oh, so much better.'

Her eyelids fluttered, ready to go back to sleep.

Awkwardly, Anna put out a hand. 'Come on, let's go inside. I'll make us both some tea.'

Grace followed her inside. She didn't feel like crying any more. Or not so much.

Chapter Eleven

Only now everyone had taken to watching her.

Anna's eyes followed her anxiously across the kitchen. Simon's across the bedroom. Even Rob was falling into fits of absent-mindedness, his gaze resting on her while he ate, mouth open as he forgot to chew. That was the trouble with being found asleep and snoring against her own front door.

'Anna says...' Simon said, timidly raising the subject.

'Anna says what?' Grace had snapped in return, and immediately he had retreated, bitten, now shy. Yet he never retreated far enough. He had stayed in their bed, as if some kind of waiver had happened, making it too late to change.

But now Grace, who a month before had felt that she could lie down and die without anyone noticing or commenting, found that her entire family was watching her, wondering if it could happen again.

One could be too visible.

Once, serving spaghetti to a silent yet watchful table, she couldn't bear it any more. 'I wasn't drunk,' she rapped. 'It was medication. That's all.'

And all they had done was smile at her, sadly. She needed to talk. Eventually she phoned Tamsin in the middle of the morning, knowing she would be busy.

'I'll phone you back,' Tamsin said. 'Soon as I'm finished here.'

Grace spent the rest of the day waiting for the call. But when it came, Tamsin's voice sounded tinny and temporary.

'I'm at the airport, Grace.'

'Holiday?'

'Don't be daft. I'm off to the Cayman Islands. Remember that case I told you about? That big pensions fraud?'

'Of course,' Grace lied, finally understanding that for three months her friends had been talking and she had heard not a word. 'When are you back?'

'God knows. Weeks probably. Everyone's going to be lying through their teeth. It will take a month just to hear them admit to their own names. Anyway, got to go. Look after yourself.'

'And you.' Already she could feel herself falling behind, something left on the ground as Tamsin took off. Suddenly she wondered why Tamsin had stayed friends with her all through the years, when all she had had to talk about was children and husbands and the occasional death of a pet.

On impulse, she dialled Tamsin's number

again. 'Yes?' Tamsin's voice was clipped.

'Tamsin, I've got VD. Simon gave it to me. He got it from her.'

She heard an intake of breath, then Tamsin's voice. 'Oh my God, now you tell me. What a bastard. What a bitch. Wait till I get home, Grace. Just you wait, you hear me...?'

She was cut off. But it was enough. In danger of forgetting, Grace had remembered exactly why they had stayed friends.

Patsy and Regina were waiting.

They had ordered the best table in London's best fish restaurant, Richard's favourite. Not that he particularly liked fish, but it was expensive and it had never failed to soothe his soul, watching Regina hand over a plastic card that would cover the lobster and all the wine that would have washed it down.

Also, ten years ago the head chef had made an unprecedented outing from his kitchen to have him sign a napkin for his wife. It was the sort of thing that Richard remembered.

They hadn't brought him here for years. Now they were waiting for him to arrive.

'Seamus O'Connor has just written a long piece in *The New Yorker* about his acid attack,' Regina said. 'It's incredibly good. The man's a genius. And generous.'

Patsy replied, 'He can afford to be. He

survived *his* stalker. He's lucky it's not other people writing his obituary instead.'

Regina looked at her friend. 'You really are worried about Richard, aren't you?'

Patsy sighed. 'If you had only seen the woman. Dead white, with these mad, red eyes staring right past me. And Richard ... oh Reggie, Richard was shaking. I can't begin to imagine what had gone on in that room before I arrived. And thank God I did arrive. I mean, what if I hadn't? Then there was the note she left on my car...'

'He still hasn't shown it to you?'

'He refuses. It's as if he's trying to take the burden of it all himself. And he still won't go to the police. Apparently she's married, and he's – stupidly, gallantly – trying to keep it all quiet, for her sake.'

Reggie shook her head in wonder. 'Who would have thought, Richard of all people, showing this side to him...?'

Patsy looked uncomfortable. 'I don't know, Reggie. You could say it's all there, in the books. It's what he writes about isn't it – men with a sympathy for women, what they're going through? Men who at least try to understand.'

'Well yes, but that was just the books. That was art. Or rather...' Regina corrected herself '...artifice.'

Patsy looked more uncomfortable still. 'I know, I know, but...' She prepared herself for a confession. 'Reggie, I have to tell you. When Merlin was first diagnosed, and he took it so badly, when everything looked so black and awful, you remember...' she swallowed. 'There were times when nobody could say anything to me. And Merlin, he just closed himself off. He knew what was coming and he couldn't, he just couldn't, stand it. It was as if he blamed me for not being able to stop it happening, for not keeping him safe. Those were terrible days, Reggie, and no one, not even you ... I mean you were wonderful, the best a friend could be ... but still no one could *say* anything. It took something else to do it, to get me through that time.' She smiled sadly. 'Now I'm almost ashamed to tell you. What helped me was that bloody book of Richard's, *The Hierophant.* All the time I was reading it, I knew it was just pseudo philosophical *stuff.* Stuff to make your toes curl. But it stated things that were true for me at the time. It said – you remember – that sometimes a woman needs a man to be bigger than herself, bigger than the awful things that are happening. To be able to see past his own tragedy and recognise how it affects the ones who love him.' Her voice fell. 'I needed Merlin to be like that, to carry us both – just till I got the strength back enough to carry him. And he *wasn't* strong enough. Early onset Alzheimer's – how could he be? So I had to get the strength elsewhere. And Reggie, I got it from that bloody book.

'You say it's artifice. But sometimes artifice can get you where you need to be further and faster than art. And Richard was good at that stuff. *Is* good at it. I don't suppose it's his fault if people want more and better. He gave them the taste for it. And maybe, just maybe, Reggie, it wasn't just artifice, pure and simple. Maybe at some level, he meant every word.'

She looked at Regina. There was a silence while Reggie thought. Finally she said, 'I agree. I do – I agree. Up to the point that he might ever actually have meant what he wrote. Darling, this is *Richard*. We know him.'

'Or thought we did,' said Patsy quietly and she nodded towards the door. Richard was making his way across the restaurant floor, seemingly unaware of the two women watching him, more carefully than they ever had.

He sat down and smiled at them. He looked tired.

'Did you come by yourself?' Patsy said softly.

He winced at the unspoken reference, then nodded. 'A taxi, then another taxi. Like in *The Third Man.*' He blinked as if in wonder at his own resourcefulness.

Regina pointed to the bottle already on the table. He shook his head. 'To be honest,

140

it's coffee I need. A lot of it. Can't pretend I got much sleep last night.'

He winced again as he spoke, this time for real, briefly haunted by a fleeting image of balls hissing past his left ear. Richard Ortega in fact had slept too well, borne away by gin and satisfaction into the land of tennis singles.

At least the satisfaction remained. This morning he had phoned Grace, listened to the sound of surprised joy, as she had gasped:

'You...'

Things were back on track. He could hear it just in that one word, followed by the torrent of what came after. Something about falling asleep and being misunderstood. And being watched. She would have talked all morning if he had let her. Finally he had let her know he was about to have lunch with Patsy and the other one, the women who had seen her at The Boho Club, and she had juddered to a halt just as intended. Nothing like shame to silence a woman.

'Patsy thought you could do with cheering up. That's why we're here.'

He switched from thoughts of Grace to concentrate on Regina, yet it was difficult. Thoughts of Grace, silent and blushing, were beginning to take a familiar resonance. Inexplicable – in the same way that thoughts of tennis balls making him feel ill were inexplicable. All he knew was that thinking of Grace could lend an aura, a fleeting glow to the moment.

So he forgot to concentrate on Reggie and began to think again about Grace. Grace weeping in his room. Grace blushing. A pleasure, a joy even – when she behaved. He kept his eyes on Regina, and let his thoughts wander where they willed.

Oh good, thought Patsy to herself. He's actually smiling. Poor old Richard. Maybe all he ever needed was a bit of tenderness.

When the time came to order, he surprised them both by asking for only a small plate of sardines. Still, even this modest dish seemed to revive him. The waitress had a ready smile and this also served to inject a trace of the old Richard into his veins. Patsy and Regina watched him, waiting for the moment when he would crack, when he would come out with the usual proposition, the one that was so obscene it would force the waitress to retreat hot-faced, demanding that somebody else serve the man on table twelve. It had happened so many times before.

But this time it didn't happen. The waitress stayed sunny-faced, and Richard's mouth stayed closed.

He's being careful, thought Patsy. He's thinking what can happen when a woman takes him at his word. Now everything's changed. And suddenly, contrarily, she missed the old Richard, the one you couldn't take anywhere.

Yet now that they were drinking thimble-fuls of hot, fish-scented espresso, Richard was slowly returning to form. He was talk-ing, re-telling the story of how decades ago, he had worked alongside Salman Rushdie on an advertising campaign, back in the olden days when both had been copywriters not artists.

'Mere pushers, the two of us. Servants of the masters of production, my darlings. You could say that Salman still is, in his modest way...'

'Oh Richard!' cried Regina. 'How could you possibly? After everything he's...' She stopped. 'Is that yours?'

'Is what mine?'

'Phone. Is that your mobile I can hear?'

He listened, then felt in his pocket, absent-minded. It was clear that his head was still full of invective, words still forming on his lips, so close to the old Richard as to be almost indistinguishable. And yet Patsy had a sudden intuition, an urge to warn. She opened her mouth to do just that.

But it was too late. He pulled out his phone. 'Yes?' he said cheerfully, 'What fresh hell is this?'

He listened, then his face changed. 'Oh...?' He listened until his hand, with its phone, fell on to the table, nerveless.

Regina looked at Patsy, who looked at Richard. Who was looking at ... nothing.

'Richard?' Patsy said in a low voice. *'Richard?'*

When still he didn't answer, Regina put a hand on his. He jumped at the touch, as if he'd been burnt.

'It can't be,' whispered Patsy. 'Is it her? Phoning you here, on your mobile?'

'Yes, but I don't know how.' Richard shook his head in wonder. 'I never gave her my number. Barely anyone has this number.'

Regina gave a small, mirthless laugh. 'You didn't have to give it to her, darling. You let her into your house, remember? What happened after? Did you leave her alone at all?'

He shrugged helplessly. 'Only to fetch her a glass of water. She was behaving so ... strangely. I thought turning my back on her would give her a chance to, well, collect herself.'

'Ha,' Regina nodded. 'That's how she did it then. While you were acting like the perfect gentleman – for which I would ask you to read *idiot* – she punched into your phone and got your number. Which means that she's got your number in all senses.'

'All senses?' Richard echoed the phrase limply.

'She knows you for what you are,' Regina said briskly. 'A fool with a soft heart, who lets weirdos into his house, then turns his back so they can do what they like. Now she's got you at the end of a line, like a fish on a hook. You're going to have to jettison the mobile,' she finished, matter of factly.

Patsy however was staring at the phone. 'Richard,' she said softly. 'What did she say?'

Richard blinked, then looked away. 'Oh, you know, the usual rubbish people pour into their phones.'

Patsy's eyes bore into him.

He hesitated. Then the words seemed to tumble out of him. 'She was asking a question. She wanted to know if I had the lobster. She's heard it's very good here.'

There was a silence, then Regina said, 'You *told* her this was where you were coming?'

He shook his head. There was another silence, longer this time. Suddenly Patsy jumped to her feet, almost knocking over her chair. 'Where is she?' she cried fiercely. 'Where is the bitch? If she knows where you are, then she's got to be here somewhere.'

She glared around the restaurant, catching people's eyes with a basilisk stare that made them forget they had ever had an appetite.

'Patsy.' Regina put out her hand. 'It's no good. She's probably outside in the street. Obviously Richard didn't throw her off when he thought he did.' She waited until Patsy had sat down, then she turned to Richard.

145

'This has gone too far. You have to tell someone, get help. If she's coming to your house, stealing your number, if she's following you – and then letting you know she's following you – if all this is happening, it can only mean one thing.'

'What?' Richard's eyes were unfocused. He seemed to be having difficulty concentrating.

'It means she's going downhill, caught in some kind of spiral. She probably can't help herself. Because that's how it's going to be now. Everything is going to get worse, until it gets to such a point that...'

She stopped, as if suddenly unwilling to go on. She looked to Patsy. Who took a deep breath, and took up the argument.

'What Reggie's saying is, you won't be safe any more. This woman is going to turn your life upside down, more and more each day. She's doing it, right now. Wherever you are, that's where she will be. Whatever you're doing, she'll be behind you. Watching. Waiting. It's your life she wants, under her control. And if she can't have it, she'll just take it. She'll take your life, Richard. It's what they do, people like her. People like Seamus O'Connor's stalker. She'll end up killing you.'

There was another silence, longer than any before. And when the waitress with the ready smile stepped up with the bill (which she placed in error next to Richard's plate), all three jumped, violently, as if she had crept out from behind a bush and surprised them all.

At home, Grace put down her phone. She could tell from Richard's voice that they were still there, together in the restaurant. She was not put out by the curt way he had spoken to her. He had told her this morning how it would be.

'They reel me in, these women, like some great ocean beast. I'm their meal ticket, you know, the reason they're alive. The more I give, the more they want. And it's not just my art they want. It's me. Myself. I. Body and soul. Sometimes I swear they'd rather see me dead than belonging to anyone else.

'Phone me, Grace. Phone me at the very moment when they think they have me. Let me hear your voice, if only for an instant. Your lovely voice, so soft, so utterly giving – it will be a lifeline in my ear. Freedom for my soul. It will be my salvation, my sweet consolation.'

At her end of the phone, Grace had protested. 'But won't they know it's me? Just from the way you talk?'

'My dearest girl! Do you honestly think I would let them find out? No, they'll guess nothing. I'll speak to you as if you're the last person I want to hear. In fact, I'll cut you dead, my darling. Make them think it's some deranged fan who's tracked me down. But you can smile as I do it, knowing the truth. That from the very depths of my heart I am thanking you.'

And so, exactly as instructed, Grace had phoned at three o'clock, sharp. And just as he had promised, he had cut her dead. But as she went to fill the washing machine with more shirts, she had begun to smile, despite herself, and then to laugh, picturing the two women, so greedy, so grasping. So sure of him. Never knowing that together she and Richard had tricked them.

In the taxi home, Regina leant against the window, thinking of a time Patsy knew nothing about, when she had first met Richard. How long ago? Fifteen years, longer? A manuscript, titled *The Hierophant*, had landed on her pile with a note from an out-reader that just read 'CRAP'.

Yet still it had been placed on her desk, waiting for attention, as if the same out-reader had seen something that required a second look. And Regina, so much younger then, about to be married, had picked up the typescript and begun to read. It hadn't taken very long. Like all of Richard Ortega's works still to come, it had been short and horribly sweet. A sugar-coated pill to slip down easily. Regina had read philosophy

and literature at university. She had emerged with a starred first. Her special subject
had been Cynicism in the Novel. Now she
read *The Hierophant*, and spotted each
cannibalised nugget of other people's
thoughts as it appeared, ticking them off
one by one – Sartre, Plato, Nietzsche. All
the usual boxes.

She finished the book, then scanned the
photograph that the author had sent along
with the manuscript. And reached for the
phone.

It was early June, the beginning of the
short summer that Regina would spend in
love with Richard Ortega, and never say a
word about it to Patsy. The first time she
had met him to discuss the novel, he had
been waiting in a café with a Gitane in one
hand and a copy of *Meditations of Marcus
Aurelius* in the other. The second time it had
been *The Second Sex* he'd been holding. On
either occasion he had lain aside his reading
matter with an air of reluctance, as if even
now he would have preferred to stay in the
company of authors. He had just split up
with his wife, refused to talk about her.

The third time Regina had gone home and
ended her engagement, something she had
never really explained to anyone, not even to
her fiancé. Not even to herself. She just
knew she would rather live alone than be
misunderstood. And no one would under-

stand her, because the truth of life was that no one could understand anyone – not unless they lived in the pages of a Richard Ortega novel.

She never slept with him. She never even kissed him. The first move he had made towards her was so clumsy, so obscene that her summer of being in love stopped, dead, in the middle of July, leaving her with one exception to attach to her general rule. It *was* possible to understand another person, all too well – so long as that person was Richard Ortega.

But she never did get married, and she never did regret that.

Now, in the taxi, she remembered that summer, the shock of falling in and then out of love. Then she began to think about Richard's refusal, even after today, to report the woman to the police. Here was another shock to add to the first shock of all those years ago: Richard could be kind. Had she misjudged him, then? Measuring the man not by his work but his outward behaviour. What if, despite all these years, she had been wrong? If so, it would only mean she had always been right. It never was possible for anyone truly to understand anyone. Not even Richard Ortega.

Later, sitting at her desk, an idea came to her, so obvious, she wondered that she hadn't thought of it before. She seized her phone.

'Richard, I've got an idea, something for you to think about.'

'Oh?'

'What you're going through, it's very common. I've been reading about it. Apparently 90,000 people are stalked every year. Or is it 900,000? Something like that. Anyway, usually it's just normal people – women, shop girls. Lower income, not well educated, that sort of thing. They know something terrible is happening to them, but they can't describe it to anyone, the horror of it. The sheer *strangeness* of it – having someone shadow your every movement, never going away. They don't have the words. And even if they did, they could never begin to analyse the situation, make any kind of *philosophical* sense of it.' She stopped. 'Richard, can you guess what I'm going to say?'

'No, Regina. I'm afraid I can't. I'm a little preoccupied at the moment, as you might understand...'

'Then I'll tell you...' she interrupted him in her eagerness. 'Richard, I think you should write about this, everything that happens to you. Everything. The frustrations, the fears. The feeling of being drawn slowly into someone else's world. The terror of losing oneself, becoming their creature. Can you imagine the sort of book it would make, if *you* were to write it?'

There was a pause. Then Richard said,

'Reggie, I think you may have misunderstood. What's happening to me is so...' she heard him struggle for a moment '...unpleasant. Why would anyone want to read about something so bloody miserable?'

'I've just told you. Because it's true. And because it's you. People know you from your work. They know you as a philosopher – of sorts. They know you would write about it in a way that no one else could. Not even ... not even *Seamus O'Connor*.'

There was another silence. Then Richard said, 'Reggie, I don't think you know what you're saying. This woman – you want me to expose her, lay her poor, mad mind open to all who would read about her, to sell a book? Flay her poor twisted soul and leave it swinging in the breeze? Oh, Reggie, *Reggie*. All these years and still you don't know me.'

'You're right!' cried Regina with some emotion. 'I don't believe I have known you, Richard. But I think I'm beginning to now. Look,' she forced the calm back into her voice, 'what's happening to you is happening to others, right now, as we speak. And all of them thinking they are alone. A stalker takes over their lives and yet no one else can really understand how it feels. But then someone – *you* – writes a book and suddenly everyone who picks it up will understand. Don't you see, Richard, what a service you'll be doing? Imagine – the writer of *The*

Hierophant examining the darkness of a mad soul as it tries to take possession of another soul. And every word of it real. Imagine it, Richard.'

There was another long silence.

Finally Reggie sighed. 'You're not going to do it, are you? You simply refuse to expose this woman and what she is.'

Still she met with silence. Yet Reggie's hand only tightened on her phone, not done with him, not yet.

'Then tell me one thing, Richard. Do you keep a diary?'

'A diary? But of course.'

Hearing his reply, Reggie let out a sigh of sweet relief.

Richard put the phone gently back on its cradle. For a moment his face retained the expression it had used all throughout the call. Patient, weary, forbearing. Then it came – the grin to wipe the same expression clean off his face. He stood up and thought a moment. Then he began to dance, slowly, on the spot, lumbering in circles like a dervish who's been shot through the knees, still determined to whirl for pure joy.

Chapter Twelve

Grace glanced out of the kitchen window. It was the first hot weekend of the year and in the garden Anna lay on a towel. Her long pale limbs were flexed, hair scraped back to allow a maximum amount of sun to burn into her skin. She hadn't moved for nearly three hours unless to turn over, keeping the exposure even, allowing the rays to reach and damage every part of her.

Grace frowned. Couldn't help herself. All those years on all those beaches, coaxing and slathering sun cream into every fat little crease on fat little bodies. Chasing through rock pools to make sure the coverage was complete, nagging, scolding, bribing. And all so it could come to this, to Anna pegged out in the sun, having rubbed oil, yes olive oil, into her grown limbs to magnify the rays, activating who knows what cells under the fragile membrane of the skin.

And Rob too, slouching round the garden with a wheelbarrow full of wine bottles he was about to trundle down to the park for recycling – he wasn't wearing a shirt. His shoulders were already pink from lying face down on the grass. Yet at least he was moving, somehow creating the impression in Grace's mind that he was dodging the rays, lessening the effect.

But Anna... Grace pressed her lips together, then walked out onto the lawn, trying to look as if she just happened to be there, and no intention or purpose behind it. Walking past the slim prone body, before casually looping back.

'Sure you're not burning up?'

There was no answer, only the flip of paper as Anna turned a page of the book she was reading.

'There's lemonade in the fridge, why don't you go inside and grab some before Rob drinks it all?'

Still no answer.

'Anna, it's awfully hot. Don't you think...?'

'What?' Anna looked up and around, her eyes genuinely surprised, as if she truly had only just now noticed her. 'Sorry? Did you say something?'

'Well, actually...' Grace began, but then Anna gave a shriek.

'Oh my God, Mum, I'm burning up. Look at me.' In panic she touched her face. 'Oh shit, my nose! It feels like it's about to split. Quick, tell me. Is my nose all red?'

Grace looked, 'Maybe, just a little...'

'Oh bum,' Anna moaned. 'Why didn't you tell me?' She glanced at her watch and moaned even louder. 'I've been out here three hours, three solid hours. Why didn't you stop me?' She glared at Grace.

'But darling, I thought you wanted...'

'Noooo,' wailed Anna. 'I'm going out tonight. Why would I want to go out with a face like a tomato? Now look what's happened.'

She got up and began to examine the backs of her legs, muttering to herself.

Grace said, 'If you didn't want to burn, why didn't you keep an eye on the time?'

'I meant to, didn't I? I was only going to read for as long as it took. We started this book at school. All we had to do was read a chapter for Monday. And I dunno, I just carried on. I didn't realise. Look, I've practically finished it.'

'It must be a good book then,' observed Grace.

'It's OK,' Anna said stiffly. But then something stronger than ritual pride overtook her – a desire, a need to communicate something, even if it was only to her, to Grace. 'Mum, it's brilliant. I can't get over it, it's a school book – it should be dire, but I think it's the best thing I ever read.'

Grace put out her hand. Almost reluctantly, Anna gave her the book.

'Alicia Milagro.' Grace read the name aloud. 'I've heard of her. But isn't she quite black? I mean very black?'

'So?' Anna snatched at the book as if

Grace had insulted it. 'Are you saying I shouldn't read her?'

'No. I just thought, when a writer is as black as that, you might not want to...'

'I can't believe this.' Anna was scandalised. 'Are you trying to tell me I shouldn't read someone just because of the colour of their skin, just because they're black?'

'Oh!' Grace gasped. 'No! Goodness, oh lord, no. I meant what she writes about is black. Sad. Terrible things happening and all of them true. Tamsin's talked about her...'

'Oh, you mean *dark?* Well, why didn't you say that?' Anna was stern. 'Instead of calling her black, like black is something to object to. If you mean what she writes about is dark, then say *dark*. People hear black and they think of something bad. It's ingrained propaganda. It says so here.'

'Is it?' said Grace. She thought a moment. 'Well yes, maybe it is. Sorry.'

'Don't say sorry to *me*,' shrugged Anna. She was moving towards the house.

Grace moved beside her. 'So...what made you keep reading?'

Anna stopped. And there it was again, the sudden shine in her daughter's eyes, the need to communicate. 'Because it's real, every word of it. And terrible. She grew up in New Orleans, and had to fight, really fight, to get educated. Then she was raped and became a lesbian, and had to go to prison...'

'For being a lesbian?'

'For shooting the man who was dealing drugs to her brother. She only winged him. At least the bullet shot off one of his testicles – is that what they mean by winged? But the dealer was a white police officer who swore it was only meant to be a sting operation. Alicia Milagro had to prove he was lying and there was a whole gang of officers dealing drugs to black kids, which she did. But before that, they got her family evicted, and then her father was killed in a robbery. Well, he was doing the robbery – did I tell you she had a terrible father? And ... and it's really *funny*.'

'*Funny?*' echoed Grace.

'Yes! That's the thing about her. She talks about all this, but she never feels sorry for herself, and if something funny happens in the middle of it, even though it's black – I mean *darkly* – funny, she puts it in. She's not sentimental. She just wants you to know that if you face up to things, if you're determined and you're sure what's right, you can make life better. Not just for yourself, but everybody. See what I mean? Brilliant.'

And with that, she left to run upstairs. Grace could hear her in her bedroom, greeting her sunburnt nose in the mirror with tragic cries. But later, she found her in the sitting room when she was supposed to be getting ready to go out, still absorbed in the book, deaf and blind to everything around her.

Eventually Anna did make it out. So did Rob, leaving Grace and Simon alone together. They ate in silence then pretended to watch television until it was time to go to bed.

'Coming?' said Simon. His eyes spoke to her, saying things accountants rarely even think about. It seemed to her that Simon had become eloquent without ever once using his voice.

'I'll wait up for the kids.'

It's what she always did now: find an excuse to come to bed long after him. And, having made the excuse, she waited, knowing what always arrived after. Depression, closing in and curling around her. Familiar to her now, like something that had come to live with them, like a cat that followed her around. It followed Simon too, she knew that.

At her shoulder now, it was. Ready to jump into her lap...

If she was less shy, if she weren't married, so very very married, she would pick up the phone, unbidden, to Richard, just to keep it at bay. She had kept his handkerchief and washed it, and forgotten that it had ever smelt musty, not quite pleasant.

Tonight, though, she had a thought. A brightening, a possibility of comfort, remembering how a book had helped her before. There was another book in the house now, a remarkable book by all accounts. A book that had kept her daughter pinned beneath the sun's rays and made her forget to put on make-up.

She found the book on Anna's desk. Grace took it and held it a moment, as if to weigh it in her hands, trying to guess its worth to her. Then, remembering that other book, she turned to study the photograph on the back cover. An African-American woman, big even in the confines of a photograph, looked directly back at her, eyes challenging. She wore an African headdress and her skin had a sheen that suggested health and strength and life. Grace stared at her and felt a fall of disappointment. As if so much strength could only make a distance, point up the difference between them.

She turned to the first page and read.

'I was born among the weak but I became strong. I was a child in the dirt who never forgot to gaze at the stars. People put me in the places they rejected for themselves but I have never stayed. I am the woman my mother fought to be, and her mother before her. I am and always will be – Alicia.'

Grace sighed – then closed the book. Already she knew this was a book that would make her feel weak, breakable. Less than the woman writing it. Grace Waites could not see herself as a fighter or the daughter of fighters. She couldn't remember her mother battling for anything, unless it was to grow the biggest, brightest dahlias in her street. As for herself – Grace – when had she fought for anything except not to disappear? She tried to imagine a different Grace, one she could fight to become. But all she could come up with was herself as she used to be, the girl inside, used to the attention, used to being loved. And what had happened to her?

Then she remembered. Richard Ortega approved of her, exactly as she was, breakable as she was. He had told her, so often. He had the gift of sight. A man who could see right through to the girl he knew was there. Unbidden, it came over her, a tide of sheer gratitude for the one man who could still see her.

She put the book back on Anna's desk, and went back downstairs, still using her children as an excuse not to go to bed.

Chapter Thirteen

Eleven o'clock in the morning and laid out on his sofa with its tufts of leaking horse hair, Richard opened his copy of *Literary Lives*.

He almost couldn't bring himself to do it. Hogging every inch of the cover was an oversized image of Shameless O'Connor; head fashionably shaved, gurning at the camera, his face a study in faux modesty. Chubby. An intellectual ping pong ball. Inside was the article to go with it, stretching page after page. Revolted, Richard put the magazine down.

Then he thought again and, manfully, set himself to read.

O'Connor had just returned from the South of France, where he'd been hanging out with an American film star who famously had been pursued by her stalker for two years. (Here Richard's eyes narrowed as he tried to remember what else she was known for, and came up with – nothing.) Finally, despite the fact that no physical harm had been done to her, the starlet's pursuer had been arrested, tried and put away. Federal law in America frowned at people turning up at premiers with more than an intention to cheer.

Different in this country, the magazine noted. In Great Britain, harassment had to amount to more than merely hijacking a life. There had to be harm done, usually physical. Which meant that every year up to 90,000 people in the UK were able to be harassed without penalty or proper protection.

'90,000?' Richard became alert. He had heard that figure recently. But where?

Regina of course. His eyes flicked to the end of the article and, sure enough, there was her name. She had written this. He let out a sigh of satisfaction and continued to read, happy now.

And here was the paragraph he was looking for. After an over lengthy concentration on O'Connor's literary genius, his generosity, his bigness of soul – Richard yawned – Regina got down to business. *'O'Connor admits that he is lucky. If Father Murphy had been blessed with better aim, he might not be around to tell the tale. Add the fact that American law gave him the opportunity to be rid of his stalker before harm was done, and you could say the gods smiled on him.'* Richard winced. It was clear why some wrote while others could only dream. *'Over here, amongst our own, we are not so lucky. It is a sad truth that one of our most singular writers is suffering a daily assault on his safety and freedom. The genuine attraction his books have always exerted for needy souls has in, one instance deepened into something more sinister. A fan's admiration has become what fandom always threatens to be: fanaticism, and this man is now at the mercy of a woman who dogs his every step. Yet he can do nothing. British law does not allow it.*

It is a function of literary life in this country that writers are not protected like film stars, or cosseted like statesmen. Like all artists in this art-forsaken land, their value is ignored. Safety has to lie in their own hands.

The man I speak about is astonishing in his generosity to his tormentor, astounding in his courage in the face of daily threat. His life depends upon the whim of a woman who is spiralling into madness, and yet he fights to remain sane. All one can hope for is that he survives and one day sees fit to tell the tale of a life turned upside down.'

Richard smirked. Then frowned. Then seized up the magazine again. His name. Where was his name? He went back and read through it all again. And again.

Nothing. Regina – all this and she had never mentioned his name. Not once. *Singular writer* – that could be anyone. Worse, it could be any fucking no-hoper in residency at some fucking university that no one had ever heard of, someone you have to describe

164

as *singular* for want of a proper term of abuse.

He was so angry that he had to get up and walk around, fury driving him into walls and pieces of furniture. A table corner caught him in the groin and threatened to lay him low, snarling with pain. All that, and no mention of his fucking name. He grabbed a bottle of vodka and pulled the stopper out with his teeth. Cold liquid trickled down his throat, but did nothing. Nothing.

No mention. No name. *Singular* writer. For a moment he paused mid-stride, snagged by an image of Regina. An image of her, bound and gagged. Naked perhaps. Eyes pleading for forgiveness. Perhaps one hand released, simply to allow it to scrawl across a page of parchment set beside her. To write – in blood – *talented, genius. Ortega; man for our time.*

He shook his head, and his eyes cleared. There was no Regina. No parchment. Just his room tossed around him in its usual disorder of spiky antique furniture that already had done enough harm. He stroked his aching groin and could have wept.

The anger was there. But so was the need. He needed something to take the anger away. To soothe and make it better. Something to float gently across the suffering with the dainty eagerness of a milkmaid.

The eyes have it. And if he couldn't have

the eyes...

He seized the phone and let it ring. Let it ring and ring. And when still Grace didn't answer, he felt he could see her, with all the clarity of a pure-bred psychic. Grace with her back to the phone, refusing to pick up. Not doing what she was told. A character ignoring the plot. Fury whirled up inside him again, like a wind, a hurricane that has changed its direction to concentrate on a different target. With a roar, he threw the phone at her, aiming at that pretty, silly head.

It fell with a clatter at the far side of the room – and immediately began to trill. He stared, then with the heavy tread of undispelled rage went to pick it up.

There was a silence broken by the sound of a gulp.

'Richard?'

It was Grace's voice. And somehow the sound of it, so tremulous, so unexpected, so *longed for*, made the anger falter, so it was almost with a whimper that he said: 'But I was just phoning you.' Then his voice hardened. 'You didn't answer.' Rage welled inside him again.

'Were you?' There was a throb of wonder in *her* voice. 'Then I was right. You *were* thinking about me.' Not pausing for breath, she carried on. 'I'm not at home. I'm in a church. I shouldn't be using my phone at all, but there's no one around... Anyway I was passing and, I don't know, it just seemed to invite me in. It was the peace, Richard, the silence. You could practically hear it from outside. I just had to follow it. So I did. I came and sat, and suddenly I felt so peaceful. The way I haven't felt in months.'

Richard sat, unaware that he was cradling the phone, that his face had grown soft as putty. Happy just to listen.

'And then it came to me, the reason I felt so peaceful. It was because of you! Such a strong feeling that somewhere, somehow, you were thinking about me, right at that very moment. I was so sure of it. I told myself I was being silly, that it was all in my head, but finally I had to phone, just to find out.' The wonder came back into her voice. 'And look, I was right. Because there you were at the exact same time, trying to phone me!'

And still Richard only listened. One hand clasping the phone, the other cupping his testicle, a rapt look on his face. Indeed, the longer he listened, the more it seemed to him that the hand pressed against his aching groin, easing away the pain, was not his hand at all. But another hand altogether – softer, smaller. Infinitely more gentle.

He closed his eyes, overwhelmed by an emotion that had veered dangerously close to true. Then finally he spoke:

'Grace, my saving Grace! How right you are! I have been sitting here thinking of nothing but you. And there you were, in a sacred place, thinking of me.' He could feel the strength coming back to him. 'And why? Because our thoughts, our very souls have embraced in the ether, untrammelled by the bonds of earth. And in your charity you have told me. Thank you for this, my dear. Thank you.'

And he meant it. Every word. Never had a mind so seized been soothed so well. Pain fled, anger gone – Richard felt he was floating, a man buoyed up while all around a sea of troubles seethed. Couldn't touch him now. Couldn't even make him wet.

He put the phone down gently. He didn't need to hear more. Here was a Grace who could be summoned simply by the force of mind. Like an image conjured up in the brain. His brain. His brainchild.

Surprised at having been cut off so quickly, Grace tucked her mobile slowly back in her bag. She wondered if she should take offence then smiled at the thought. There had been no mistaking the warmth in his voice, the emotion in his words. It was that emotion that had overwhelmed him, robbing him of speech.

She wished she felt the same. Already the exhilaration of the call was leaving her. An hour ago she had come away from the

168

GUM clinic where they had told her she was clear. In other words, she could consider herself cleansed, wiped clean of other people's grime.

But nothing else had gone away. The depression was still there, at her shoulder, ready to pounce. Leading her into the church she had happened to be passing. A place to welcome cleanliness in all its forms.

And immediately she had begun to feel calm – calm in comparison with the plethora of plaster saints frowning and suffering in the semi-dark, every gout of blood lovingly recreated in paint. It was a reminder that at least she wasn't actually in pain. She had inhaled the scents of wax melting, hot wood, the threat of fire, and all this too had made her feel safe in comparison. Yet still something had been missing and she had decided it was Richard, as if somehow, the church had connected them.

And look! she had been right. They were connected. She could only marvel at how right she had been. But still it changed nothing, being connected. Everywhere else, the threads of her life lay spliced and frayed and she couldn't see how they could ever come together.

With a sigh, she stepped out of the porch just as a figure was hurrying inside. Dressed in long black clerical robes that flapped around his legs, he crashed into her and

169

hissed as if the fault had been hers. She murmured an apology and kept walking, away from the parish church of St Olave's of the Faint Hearted in the direction of home.

Richard lay down on his sofa again. Put the phone on the ground, noting vaguely that the small aerial had become bent. Already he was beginning to forget what had caused it. A feeling of peace had settled over him, a feeling that seemed natural to him, as if he had never known another. The ache in his groin had switched to a warm glow which wiped out all memory of pain.

He had forgotten the sloughs and the rages of the past hour. Nothing left to disturb him now.

Calmly he picked up the pages of *Literary Lives* again, skating past the not quite acceptable article about Seamus O'Connor, until his eyes, ever trained to pick out his own name, settled on something better. Much better.

Max Farthing had written an editorial. Lengthy as always, reflecting what Richard took to be self evident: editorials were the only works of fiction Farthing could ever hope to see in print. But today Richard read and nodded. Because for once Farthing was not far off the mark.

'Literary Lives *supports the comments made by this month's contributor, Regina Forbes, with reference to this country's legal response to stalking. It also notes her reservation in attaching a name to the 'singular writer' presently suffering the attentions of a crazed fan. While we respect her restraint, it seems right to speculate on his identity, if only to give credit where credit is due.*

Literary Lives *feels able – obliged, even – to do this in the light of information reaching us from various sources that the writer in question is Richard Ortega (known for* The Hierophant *etc). Incidents of escalating degrees of seriousness have been relayed to us – as has the man's quite extraordinary forbearance in the face of growing threat. It is in consequence of this ordeal that* Literary Lives *would like to proffer its sympathy and support to Ortega, something that, tragically, is a great deal more than the law of this land is willing to provide.*

Such impulse to sympathy may come as a surprise to many readers, knowing as they do of past events that have put Ortega in nothing if not a poor light. (See Literary Lives, *vol xxiii, pps 37 and 45, and vol xxvii passim.) Especially memorable is the incidence of near violence instigated by Ortega at the recent Golden Chalice Awards (cf* Literary Lives *vol xxx, pps 1 to 54 inclusive).*

It is however a benchmark of cultural life in this country that, in the absence of state recognition of art and artist, we writers stand by our own. Ortega must be reassured, therefore, that as an artist, Literary Lives *stands by him.*

And we endorse the hope of Regina Forbes that in the course of time, just as from the lion comes forth sweetness, so out of his ordeal will proceed a work of greater art and insight than Ortega has thus far been able to produce. We can wish for him no better outcome than this – life forged into art. Our prayers go with him.'

Richard Ortega sat very still for a moment. Yet another feeling was sweeping over him, this time so unexpected that he could barely put a name to it. Goodwill. Pure, unadulterated goodwill, reaching out to that unreconstructed bastard, Farthing. Who would have thought it? Who would have guessed that such a closed mind could suddenly see through to so much truth? To be honest, it gave a man faith – even a man as clear sighted in the face of the squalor of human failings as Richard Ortega. Faith in his fellow artists, faith in the future. Hand shaking with emotion, he groped for the vodka and poured a generous measure into the murky reaches of a nearby glass, and toasted him – Max Farthing.

Later, much later, having fallen asleep in his chair, he woke up. *Literary Lives* was spread out on his chest, like a small blanket someone had considerately placed there to guard his slumbers. There was a smell of cheap perfume in the air that he refused to recognise as the fumes of exhaled alcohol. Mind still neutral from sleep, but with a vague memory of recent pleasure, he seized the pages again to continue reading...

...Only to toss them aside with an exclamation of disgust. The last article in the magazine was a short piece reporting that Alicia Milagro was returning to the UK to promote the final volume of her autobiography, detailing the dates and venues of her tour.

Richard Ortega got up with difficulty from the sofa and stood, swaying. It had been a long day. He had been wrung out by successive blasts of emotion, each more powerful than the last, all adding up to this – exhaustion. Sheer bloody exhaustion.

Only in bed did the feeling of peace come back to him. And that was because Grace came back, floating across his field of vision, huge eyes more pleading and cow-like than ever. This time he didn't mind. She came because he told her to, just as earlier she had phoned when it was necessary that he hear her voice. He watched her hover, then float away like a solid, yet graceful cloud blown by the breezes of his own mind.

A mind that was in control. Ready to sleep now.

Chapter Fourteen

Grace climbed into bed. She had come long after Simon, as she always did now. But he was awake and waiting for her as he always did wait.

'I'm clear,' she said briefly. For a moment neither of them moved, then in the dark she had felt his hand steal over her own. She let her own hand stay still, neither responding nor rejecting. It was a small gesture that seemed large. It was all she could muster.

The next morning she noticed a line in her newspaper and handed it to Anna.

'What do I want this for?' Anna glared at her. Never good in the morning, it was as if she blamed Grace for a world that demanded she be torn from the sempiternal dusk of her bedroom.

'Read it,' said Grace. 'It's about Alicia Milagro. She's doing a book signing up in London. You could go with a friend. Talk to her even.'

As she spoke, she felt a pang, knowing that her daughter would have more in common with this woman than with her. If Alicia Milagro spoke, Anna would listen.

Meanwhile, Anna was looking thoughtful.

'*You* come with me,' she said after a moment.

'Me?' Grace could not have been more surprised if Anna had suggested they go clubbing.

Anna scowled at her surprise. 'Well, unless there's something else you'd rather be doing – like staying at home. Watching TV.'

'No, no.' Grace was quick in her reply. 'Of course I want to come with you.' She smiled at her daughter, a full-on beam, couldn't help it. 'I'd love to come with you.'

For a split second she thought she saw the answering spark in her daughter's eye. But all Anna said was, 'OK,' before sliding back her chair.

Simon looked up briefly from his own newspaper and nodded at his daughter. 'That skirt's a bit short isn't it, Annie? For school...?'

Anna didn't look at him. 'Like I care.' And she was gone.

Simon shrugged and went back to his newspaper. Something had happened and he had missed it, never even noticed it. But Grace had seen it and she was shocked; he had become irrelevant to Anna. So irrelevant she couldn't even be bothered to argue with him. It had had an effect after all, deeper than the TV glow of the soaps, more profound than the sheets of the teen magazines. It had had an effect on their daughter – the fact that her father had done what the stupidest

175

people did in the stupidest of scripts.

Something had changed for ever and yet, because Anna's face had stayed peachy smooth, he didn't know it. Suddenly, Grace felt sorry for him. She had just witnessed the death of another love affair, and still he didn't know what he had lost.

But later, when he bent his face to hers, tentative and timid, she turned away. A hand closed over her hand was as much as she could bear. Simon himself drew back, flushing as if he understood he had over-stepped a mark. And again she felt sorry for him. But it made no difference; she could no more have kissed him than a stranger. It would have been easier to kiss a stranger.

The hospital was wrong; she knew for certain now. She wasn't clear after all. Infection was still there, a different kind, that no course of antibiotics could hope to cure.

Tamsin phoned from the Cayman Islands. 'What's happening? Tell me everything.'

And Grace told her. How the disease was gone but the infection remained. 'I don't even want him to touch me, Tamsin.' As she spoke she felt the ache inside, memories of years of intimacy, of not knowing where her skin ended and his began. Gone now.

'It's natural, isn't it? You're just plain angry, that's all.'

'Am I? It feels more than that. It's more like...' she heard herself choke on the word

'...disgust. I thought yesterday when I was cured it would go away. I thought I would be ready to start again. But I'm not.' Voice dropping almost to a whisper as she said, 'What's the cure for disgust, Tamsin?'

There came a silence, stretching all the way from a hotel verandah in the Cayman Islands. With a pang Grace heard it and understood that here was a question Tamsin had no answer to.

And yet she was wrong, because after the stretch of seconds Tamsin's voice came back. 'Maybe the cure is to climb off your high horse, Grace.'

'What?'

'You heard me. You were doing all right the two of you. He'd had an affair, but you'd begun to understand that these things happen, that people screw up. Then you discovered that he'd got more than he'd bargained for and it all got nasty again. Am I right?'

'No! Well, not exactly...'

'OK, maybe not exactly then. But at least your skin didn't crawl when he touched you. In fact, each time he did touch you, it meant that he wasn't touching her. You'd got him back. It meant you'd won. And you were pleased about that...'

'But Tamsin...'

'Hear me out, darling – otherwise there's a chance that this time you'll be the one that screws up. He caught something, that's all. He exchanged bodily fluids, it was bound to happen. But it might just as easily have been a cold he got off her, or measles. Or ... I don't know ... tonsillitis. Instead it was this. Yet you wouldn't have minded it if it had just been measles or tonsillitis.'

'But that's because it's different. This is *VD*.'

'Only different in the way you look at it.'

'But for God's sake, Tamsin...' Grace was beginning to feel indignant.

'I'm just pointing out that it's all in the perception, how you see him and how you see yourself. If you *want* to see yourself as some pure creature besmirched by some crawling monster, then you will. And that's fine if that's really how you want to look at it. But how do you make a marriage work if you're going to keep on seeing him like that?'

With a touch of acid, Grace replied, 'I don't know. That's the problem.'

'Well, how about this? Maybe you need to be less pure, darling.'

'What do you mean?'

'I mean you've got to forget all this stuff about being the one on the pedestal, the one who's been so wronged. Do a bit of wronging of your own. God – get yourself a lover. Then you'll be in less of a position to judge. Because that's the trouble, Grace, you're judging.'

178

'Oh Tamsin,' Grace began to laugh. 'Me, with a lover. How could you even think of it?'

And Tamsin laughed too. But her laugh was dry, ironic. 'I don't know. But I did think about it, didn't I. And if you can think something, you can do something.'

'Get myself a lover!'

Grace repeated the words to herself in exasperation. As if she could. As if she could simply snap her fingers and hey presto! a lover would appear, someone she could summon and then dismiss at will, like a character in a book.

A lover to bring her down a notch, make her ever so slightly grimy. Ever so slightly dirty. And just a little bit less able to judge.

She shuddered, half in pleasure, though she didn't know why. Besides, she told herself, there was no one. She'd been married so long the only men she knew were married to her friends, and she could never do that – betray a friend. This was what she should have pointed out to Tamsin with her easy advice. There was no one.

And it never even struck her as strange how, as she played half seriously with the idea of a lover, she never once considered Richard Ortega. Not even for a moment.

But that night he came to her, Richard Ortega.

Stealing into her bedroom in the cover of dark. He walked to the bed and slowly drew back the sheet, watched her while she lay, pretending to sleep. She knew he was there and held her breath, eyes closed, her body waiting, curious. In twenty years the only man to watch her as she lay naked was Simon. Now here was a man, not Simon, taking in the small breasts and small waist, noting the tuft of hair between her legs that she kept so carefully trimmed because that was how Simon had first seen it. Eyes following the curve of her thighs and the dents in her knees with their scars from pavements and gravel where a younger Grace had had her first collisions with the world.

Eyes that observed a forty-year-old Grace, and then, from under narrowed hooded lids, looked deeper still, to the girl inside.

And naked under that gaze, Grace had blushed, sheets of blood stealing across the entire surface of her skin, everywhere his eyes had been.

It was the heat under the skin that woke her, as the warmth turned to a fine, all-over sweat. She lay, paralysed a moment, aware that if someone removed the covers from her now, her entire body would be shining, slippery as an eel. And all because a man, not Simon, had been watching her.

And not just any man. But Richard Ortega.

'Oh!'

The exclamation was out before she could stop herself, making Simon stir in the bed beside her. After that she lay very still, needing to be alone with the thoughts pouring into her head as if through a newly opened hole in her skull. Simon sighed and seemed to settle back to sleep. She gave a sigh of her own, of relief.

Why had she never thought of him like this? As a lover? How could she not have thought of him?

It must have been because of Simon, filling her thoughts. Simon, making himself the centre of everything, first by threatening not to be there, then by threatening to be there all the time. He had made her blind to every other thing, even the erotic possibility of another man. Even when that other man was Richard...

Yet all this time, perhaps she had been falling in love, and didn't know it; and with the very man who had shown her it was possible. Slowly but surely falling in love with the one man who could see her, right through to the Grace inside. And it had taken a dream to tell her, to show how it could be to lie, naked under his eyes...

But then another, colder voice, speaking from a part of her skull she didn't know was there, told her she was wrong. Simon was not the reason she had never considered

181

Richard as her lover. It told her she didn't love Richard, couldn't love Richard. And the only strange thing about it was: *why?* Why, wondered the voice, *why* had she not fallen in love with Richard Ortega, when she had fallen in love with everything about him? She had fallen in love with his book, with his picture. She had fallen in love with the kindness and the depth of his gaze. She had fallen in love with the look of him, the way that he smiled. Everything.

But she hadn't fallen in love with *him*. As if all those other things were nothing more than clothes. Things that could be put on or put off, cast aside – thrown away and burnt, even. As if they had nothing to do with the man.

In the dark, Grace lay and frowned. The sweat cooled, then dried. She lay and she thought and she frowned, and still she couldn't fathom it. *Why* didn't she love Richard Ortega?

She fell asleep, still frowning, unaware that in her sleep her body moved towards Simon's in the dark, closing up the space between them. Unaware that Simon could feel her beginning to breathe softly against his neck, as he felt her every night. The moment he waited for every night.

The moment when he too, finally, could fall asleep.

Chapter Fifteen

Richard Ortega was woken by what had become in the last five years an unfamiliar sound, that of mail sliding in a torrent through his letter box, to gather with a protracted flump on the floor.

He remembered that sound. It spoke to him of fan letters, queries from Californian students studying him for their Masters' (usually alongside subjects like astrology and the tarot). It whispered of cheques and royalty statements and requests to appear on literary panels. It made him think of invitations to functions and prize-givings, not to mention letters recounting forgotten encounters from the past... *Dear Richard – or should I say Dickie? I don't know if you remember me, but we were together in the Remove at good old St Olave's. Couldn't help noticing your name has begun to crop up everywhere...*

It was a sound he hadn't heard in half a decade and it was enough to raise him from his bed with the bound of a barely dead Lazarus.

A moment later he was standing in his hall. For a further moment he seemed reluctant to do anything more than that – to stand, his toes touching the edges of envelopes, handwritten in all hues of ink. Blue-black, mostly, his name scrolled out in fat rolling As and Rs from under the nibs of fat ink pens of good make – Montblanc, Sheaffer, Cartier. Thick white envelopes. Not bills. With a trembling hand, he opened them, one and then another.

'Dear Richard, so sorry to read about your misfortune...'

'Dear Richard, just to let you know I stand by every word of Max Farthing in this month's...'

And so on to his personal favourite: *'Dear Richard, **devastated** to hear about sheer bloody talent landing you in such a mess...'*

They were written by people who hadn't talked to him in years, who kept their backs firmly turned at parties and festivals; who never mentioned him except in articles with titles like 'Where Are They Now?' or 'Books I Never Have to Pretend I've Read'. Now Richard held their good wishes in his hands and was humbled. They weren't turning their backs on him, not any more. Miriam Rapko had even included a pressed flower in her missive. And most tellingly of all, given their so-called scorn for his previous body of work, each one had ended their letter with the same plea:

Write about it.

He nodded solemnly, his face serious, as if

all the correspondents were in fact there, gathered around him. He was still nodding when he picked up the last envelope, the only one in the pile to be made out of cheap paper and written with green ink.

'*Dear Dickie, don't know if you remember me, but we were in the Remove together at good old St Olave's. Couldn't help noticing your name in the pages of* Literary Lives. *My advice is:* get to know the lady in question. *Stalkers often turn out to be very nice people as I happen to know...*'

He threw that one away.

'Grace...' His voice purred down the phone.

'Richard...' She sounded pleased to hear him. Pleased but not thrilled. A shadow passed across his face, but only for a moment. He allowed himself to consider: she was a woman talking from within the bowels of her home, cramped by the trappings of her existence. Bovine as a little French housewife with no talent for adventure. Fearing that she would be overheard.

So Richard closed his eyes, opened them again. And forgave her.

'Grace of my heart. I need to see you.'

'Oh, I'd like to see you too, Richard.'

Again he had the urge to wince. Her voice sounded warm and natural. Eager, even. But not in awe of him. It sounded as if she genuinely wanted to see him – but genuinely would not be devastated if she didn't. The wince deepened to a scowl. The woman might have been speaking to a favourite uncle.

Then it came to him. She had an audience, people to impress. She was not free. She had to speak this way to throw them off the scent. He relaxed. To understand all is to forgive all.

She was waiting to hear what he had to say.

'Grace, Grace,' he sighed. 'I am not my own man. Every hour, every day filled, accounted for. And yet I have to see you, make space for you, like a man parting the bars of a prison to allow a tiny bird to enter. A small token for a soul in chains.'

Grace made a noise. Indistinct, it could have been anything. Richard decided to take it for encouragement. 'Grace, my darling, if I juggle, if I throw enough irons in the air, I could fit in a small pocket of time for us, just you and me. Wednesday, Grace. There's an opening at an art gallery where a friend of mine...'

'Oh Richard, I can't.'

'Can't? *Can't?*' He spoke the word a second time, more sharply. He had made plans for Wednesday at the gallery. There would be an audience, people including more than just the usual suspects. Miriam Rapko would have been there. A chance for her and others to see what he was going through.

He tried again, furiously gentle. Reminding himself of what he needed to be – a man pleading with his muse. 'But Grace, couldn't you *make* time – for me?'

'It's Robert's birthday. He's my sixteen–, I should say my, *seventeen*-year-old. We're going to a film and then for a pizza. It's quite wonderful actually, he wants to be with us. I'm really so pleased... I'm sorry, Richard. Not Wednesday.'

Not Wednesday. Richard tugged at the sides of his mouth to keep the smile in place. 'Tomorrow then. Lunch with me. I could just...' *make sure* somebody *saw her.*

'Lunch?' She gave a small sigh of apology. 'I couldn't, Richard. I've promised to pick a friend up from the airport at twelve. Sorry.'

'My dear Grace.' *Careful now.* 'Hasn't your friend ever heard of taxis?'

'She's flying all the way from the Cayman Islands. She's been working so hard, and it's much nicer than just getting in a cab. No, really, I'm sorry.'

'Thursday then?' Richard snapped the words. Not that he had a plan.

'Thursday? Oh maybe, but I thought that you...' Then she laughed happily. 'I can't see you on Thursday. I'm coming up to London with my daughter. We're going to a book signing.'

'A book signing?' Richard said sharply. 'Whose?'

'Alicia Milagro's. Anna – that's my daughter – she adores her. She says her books are sad, but full of light.'

An odd noise reached Grace, unidentifiable yet reminding her curiously of their old cat, a Tom, coughing up a hair ball. 'Richard?'

'Just a frog, my dear Grace. A small obstruction. Alicia Milagro, you say.'

'Yes.'

'Ah...' He released the word gently, like something on a leash, holding back more than he let out.

Immediately she was alert. 'I'm sorry?'

'Oh ... nothing. Ignore me. Not my place and all that.'

'Ignore you? Why?'

'She's your daughter. Far be it from me to...'

'Richard, ignore what?'

'Oh...' He took a breath, then let the words tumble out. 'It may mean nothing to you, of course. But you know that Alicia Milagro... I mean you know that she's black...'

'I know that much of her writing *is* dark.'

'Oh indeed, that's perfectly true too. But the real problem, the thing that would make me pause as a mother of a young girl is ... well the woman is ... how do I put this? The

188

woman is not like you, Grace. Her desires are not your desires. Alicia Milagro is ... not to put too fine a point on it ... a lesbian.'

'Yes?' said Grace slowly. She was waiting for his point. And continued to wait until it occurred to her that this was his point. For a moment she was at a loss. Then suddenly she burst out laughing.

'Grace?'

'I'm sorry, Richard. I was being stupid. I actually thought you were being serious. Can you believe it? As if you, of all people, would hold that against... Oh, how silly of me.'

Grace continued to laugh, but at the same time, she blushed to herself for thinking he could be serious.

There was a silence from the other end. Then Richard was laughing too. More heartily than Grace, a man laughing at his own joke. Ha. Ha. Ha.

He put the phone down. Then kicked it. Then picked it up and put it gently back on the table, so as to make another call.

'Patsy?'

'Richard!' Patsy's voice was warm. Then alarmed. 'Oh my God, has something happened?'

'Not exactly. At least nothing that I would want to... Look Patsy, what are you doing on Thursday?'

Patsy hesitated. 'I'm arranging a talk for

Alicia Milagro at Weatherby's. And please don't say anything, Richard, I know your feelings about her and...'

'*Au contraire,*' Richard was meek. 'I never said the woman didn't have talent, simply that her work had nothing to say to me. Now ... well, now things are different. Circumstances have changed. One takes one's comfort where one can. Patsy, my love – did you just say she was giving a talk?'

'Yes, but I can't see that it would be your sort of...'

'Not at all, my darling. It's absolutely my sort of thing. At least it is now. The woman is wonderful. Very ... dark. But full of light. And it's light I need in these dark, dark days.'

There was a pause, then Patsy said, doubtful, 'All right. I'll make sure to keep you a seat.' More doubtful still, she added, 'You know Max Farthing will be there, and Miriam Rapko.' In other words, the Enemy. People to make his hackles rise. But she wasn't to know, he loved them all now. Needed them all.

'Count me in, my dear,' he said earnestly. 'Count me in.'

He put down the phone and hugged himself. Then he began to rock. Hardly noticeable at first, then rocking faster and faster still, as it came home to him how beautifully, how beautifully it all worked out.

190

Chapter Sixteen

In the days before Thursday, Grace tried and tried again to read the book by Alicia Milagro.

There never seemed enough time. First there was Tamsin to be picked up at the airport. Grace arrived to find her already waiting at the kerb outside the terminal, quivering with lack of sleep and slightly pasty. Three weeks on a tropical island and yet she was paler than when she went away. She pointed to a man stepping into a taxi a few yards away.

'That's my boss. He came back in first class.'

He tossed a glance in their direction and waved. He was smiling and wide awake, with the deep, ingrained tan that comes from hours spent uninterrupted in the sun.

'So ... tell me everything,' Tamsin said, strapping herself in.

Grace took a moment to answer, negotiating her way between the streams of airport traffic. But when she turned to face her passenger, Tamsin was fast asleep, dribbling a little against her seat belt.

Then there was Rob's birthday, a Vin

Diesel film to be sat through, and pizza to be eaten. He had unwrapped a new Play-Station game with the same broad smile as when he was a twelve-year-old, unwrapping almost the same thing. During the film, Simon had held her hand again, and again she let him, and there they had sat, chaste and uncommunicative as a pair of backward teenagers, too awkward to do more.

But late that night, as Simon slept, she picked up the book. And once again, it seemed to have nothing for her except reproach. No easy answers, no possibility of rescue. No magicians. Alicia Milagro's world came right because she faced it and fought it. Once again, Grace felt weak when she read it, a woman of no substance.

She dreaded the comparison Anna would make between this insubstantial woman and Alicia Milagro.

Thursday, and on the train, she watched Anna apply yet another layer of foundation, another coat of mascara.

'You do remember she is a lesbian?' The words were out before she could stop herself. Sitting opposite, a man in a business suit and with a well-folded newspaper glanced at them surreptitiously.

Anna's hand stopped, mascara stick waving perilously close to her eye. 'Yeah. So what?'

Grace flushed at her own clumsiness, yet somehow she was committed. 'It's just, you're piling on all that make-up, wearing those clothes,' she nodded towards the scarcity of skirt. 'It's as if you're getting yourself up to see a man. As if you *want* her to notice you in a certain way.'

'But I do,' said Anna sounding surprised. 'Of course I want her to notice me. What's wrong with that? If you were going to a book signing by that stupid, what's his name? Ortego man, the one who wrote the book you keep leaving around – I looked at it and God it was so dire – if it was *his* book signing you'd want to be dressed up, you'd want him to notice you *in a certain way*. I just want to be sure she notices me.'

She carried on with the mascara, creating a fence of short, sharp wands all around her eyes. Shining eyes, Grace thought, ready for anything. She sat back in her seat after that and watched her, while deep down, sixteen-, eighteen-year-old Grace stirred and wished she'd had this girl as her friend, all those years ago. The man in the suit looked away and opened his newspaper, wistful.

'Anna.'

'Mmmm?'

'You know you said you had read Richard Ortega's book...?'

'I didn't say I'd read it. I said I *looked* at it. Simply because you always seemed so mad about it. But it was such complete crap I had to put it down.'

'Why do you say that?' The sternness of her daughter's answer surprised her.

'You only have to read it for five minutes to see what he's up to. He writes about people who couldn't possibly exist, and not just because they happen to be mermaids and freaks like that. I mean – even if there were such things as mermaids, they still wouldn't exist, not the way he writes about them. He's got them all saying, doing things, just to make it work. Just to get a story.'

'But Anna, he's a writer. He has to tell a story...'

'Yeah, but that's the point. There's not even a story. Not a proper one, because nobody's real. They're just puppets he's made up. You can just imagine him, making them all have to line up on the page and behave like he tells them to. They're all in his head, doing what he says. You should read Alicia Milagro to see the difference. Everybody's real. Like they're the ones telling the story, not her.'

She went back to work with her mascara stick. No more to be said.

The tubes were delayed and when they arrived, late and flustered, the bookshop was already full. They weren't even allowed through the main door. They had to creep in through the back to the last remaining seats. Someone noticed them however. A young man dressed in black approached with a tray of wine, and offered it to Anna while ignoring Grace. But Anna only glared. He was standing in her way, blocking her view of a figure already too far distant for her satisfaction.

But they could hear her. Alicia Milagro was reading from near the beginning of the book, words Grace recognised, and which had been empty of meaning for her before. Yet now, as she listened, she seemed to hear the familiar passage as music, sentences gathering like phrases in a melody. Milagro's voice was not so deep, yet it occupied the lower spaces of a register all its own, where the words resonated and echoed in the wake of words that came before. Like a song, Grace thought. Music first, words after. Beside her, Anna shuddered with similar recognition before leaning into Grace.

'This is what I heard when I read, Mum. I knew she'd sound like this. Somehow I just knew.'

At long last Grace understood why the book had failed to speak to her. She had simply refused to listen. But she listened now, sitting next to her daughter, as rapt as she was. Finally hearing every word.

Up at the front of the crowd, wedged between Patsy and Regina, Richard suppressed a yawn.

God, he hated these affairs, strapped into a seat, forced to listen to other people's words. Sometimes you could work it so you could drift off, nodding sagely while the mind attended to better things, like porn; but you couldn't do that when the Milagro beast talked. Her voice was like a horn, one of those vast, pot-bellied things you'd spot in the depths of an orchestra and could never put a name to. Once you'd noticed it, you'd hear it in the middle of everything. A voice you couldn't get away from.

Bloody voice. Bloody woman. And no sign of Grace.

He'd expected her to be there when they arrived. Little country bumpkin, the sort that's early for everything. Never the sort to roll in after curtain up, carelessly apologising for blotting out entire first scenes with her bottom. No, he had confidently expected Grace to be there. He'd had his face of frozen horror ready. So practised now, he could practically pale at will.

But no Grace so far as he could see. Only the big black woman with a voice that got everywhere and kept a man from drifting away into the privacy of his own place of small delights.

And whose fault was it? Grace's, that's whose. Not turning up when she had told him she would be here, turning down his invitation. Liar. Turning her back on the script again, as if she had a life and purpose of her own. Turning and turning in all directions except where she was meant to be.

Without his being aware of it, the skin tightened over his face, pulling his lips back from his teeth in something like a snarl. An hour passed, slowly as a day trapped underground. And still Milagro carried on. It was as if she was an engine, one you'd find under the bonnet of a bus, never seeming to lose power. What was wrong with people that they could put up with this? On either side of him Patsy and Regina sat, never taking their gaze off her. At one point Patsy even wiped a tear from the corner of an eye.

When had she ever done that for him? Wept for him?

Fucking lesbians, it was the only possible answer. All of them. Even Max Farthing, an honorary lesbian he'd have to be, sitting there with the rest. All fucking weeping and wailing for each other because of what fucking men had done to them. Fucking ... women.

Finally, finally, she stopped talking. She sat back in her chair and smiled into the silence. Blissful silence, thought Richard.

Then a ripple of sound ran through the crowd, as one by one people began to clap. The ripple grew, became a rising tide of applause that broke against her like a wave. Sitting there, a big, black, gleaming rock stopping the sea.

But at least it meant it was the end. Richard sat forward, coiled as a spring, waiting for the noise to stop, for the first moment of release. Ready for the first moment of freedom in the street, and the first blessed gin of the evening.

He was ready ... and then it started. Question time. With a silent groan, he threw himself back into his chair. It was never going to end now. Never. The writers had the floor. Here was Miriam Rapko already standing up, wearing a cardigan she'd probably woven for herself, set to kick off. And after Miriam there was Farthing, gearing up. He could even feel the future in Regina, sitting beside him, waiting her turn. The silent groan turned into a howl as deep, deep inside, the creature that rode Richard to the edge of every pit began to gnaw at its own flesh. Which was Richard's flesh.

And then he heard another sound. Different from the rest. The sound of a voice. A sweet, familiar voice. It rang from the back of the crowd, a little tremulous, but eager. A voice to make the air throb.

A sound to make Richard throb. Sweetness suddenly playing through his entire body, like a lost chord.

'Miss Milagro, I have a question.'

Alicia Milagro craned her neck, ignoring the writers who had been so sure the moment was theirs. Then she smiled. 'Well stand up honey, so I can see you.'

Right at the far corner of the room, Grace stood up. Beside him Richard heard Patsy gasp.

Yet now that she was on her feet, Grace was at a loss, bringing a soft, lopsided grin to Richard's face. He knew her so well. He knew the impulse that had made her leap to her feet – just as he knew the impulse to panic that would follow as the rest of her caught up and found itself exposed. Even from here he could see the red beginning to light up her cheeks like beacons.

But then she drew a breath and in a voice that was almost calm, said: 'Miss Milagro, when I first read your book, I thought it had nothing to say to me. But now I know different. It has everything to say. Yet I feel so sad. It feels so late in the day. I would need to be a girl to be able to use the messages it sends. What can you say to women of my age? Women eager to learn, but who are like dogs, too old for new tricks. Miss Milagro, what can you say to us, to women like me?'

And Grace plummeted back into her seat,

cheeks burning, aware of Anna's face, averted and scandalised. She had done it again – heard the words erupt from a place so deep she had been powerless to stop them, helpless as a peasant living on the side of a volcano.

And as so often seemed to happen after she had heard herself, there was silence.

But then Alicia Milagro spoke: 'What would I say to women like you? What would I say? Honey, I would say "rejoice". And why? Because you are the age you are and because you are a woman, *not* a girl. "Girls" are our fragile baby daughters when they are running around our feet with milky breath and a belief in Santa Claus. "Girls" are what the plantations masters called the negro women who slaved in their fields and served in their beds. "Girls" are what the bosses are used to calling their secretaries, knowing so long as there are girls in the typing pool there will never be women on the board. You hear what I'm saying? You're a woman, just like me, just like the young woman sitting next to you.'

She nodded at Anna who immediately flushed, harder, deeper than her mother.

'You don't need to be a girl to be something in this life. But you do need to be a woman. A fully grown woman with her eyes open and her heart the same. You say it's too late to learn? Well, listen to me – it's not

200

what you learn that changes you, but what you teach. I'll say that again. *It's what you teach*. Because the only real lessons are the ones we teach ourselves. If my books help, that's a fine thing for me. That does my soul and my bank balance no end of good. But *you're* the one, honey. You're the one with the knowledge deep inside. All you have to do is listen to yourself. Be the woman you were meant to be. It's never too late for that.'

For a long moment Grace and Alicia observed each other across the room. It seemed to Grace that they were taking each other in, accepting everything they found in the other. Then Alicia smiled and looked away as other questions burgeoned around her.

Leaving Grace to sit in the aftermath. Aware of some of the crowd still watching her, aware of Anna, red-faced and hissing over and over in her ear, 'How could you, oh how could you? This is the last time, the last time I go *anywhere* with you.'

Yet she was getting no answer from her mother. Grace was not ignoring her daughter exactly. Rather, the agonised whispering simply added to the fabric of the moment. Something she needed to take home and unpick to see how it all wove together. Only then would she think about answering. Besides, despite the fierceness of the whisper, it seemed to her that Anna had been only half serious. Almost proud.

Meanwhile, up at the front neither Patsy nor Regina had been listening to what Milagro had to say. They were sitting, staring at Grace.

'My God,' Patsy was repeating the exclamation under her breath. 'How dare she? How dare she?'

In no time at all, no one else was listening to Alicia Milagro either, not among the writers. The word was spreading, *sotto voce*, reaching Max Farthing and Miriam Rapko. The woman, Ortega's tormentor, was right here, in this room, drawing attention to the fact. Exploiting the spotlight on Milagro, turning it on herself.

'See what I was talking about?' seethed Patsy to Regina. 'Do you see the mad look she's wearing?'

Regina said nothing. She was holding Richard's hand very hard, eyes narrowed, trying with nothing more than a daggered stare to penetrate the mind of the woman sitting on the far side of the room. But when the woman stayed oblivious to her, lost in whatever nightmare vision fuelled the madness, Regina had had enough. She dropped Richard's hand and stood up, to pick her way through the crowd in search of the person she needed to speak to.

Meanwhile, Richard sat wearing the look

he had needed after all – frozen horror, shoulders stiff with the helpless rigor of the victim. Unlike everyone around him, he *was* listening to Milagro, every word she had to say. Worse, he was watching the eyes of Grace, *his* Grace, growing wide as if the woman was feeding her pearls straight from the lap of the Virgin Mary. Believing every fucking syllable.

Frozen horror, that is to say – real horror. Unable to speak or look away, unable to do anything except watch Milagro's influence grow, he listened and let his mind play with solutions. Cutting the brake cables on the Milagro mobile or poisoning the pilot before the flight back to the States. Something, anything to stop the seed being sown in Grace's mind. Yet all he could do was watch her sit in the aftermath, her dairy-maid features stained by thought.

Yet unknown to him, help was at hand, something to mitigate the worst of it. Richard was unaware that, as he seethed, a couple of heavy set men had begun to push their way through the crowd to where Grace, still spellbound, was similarly blind. It was the girl next to her who saw them, her black rimmed eyes – smoky, mascara-ringed – narrowing. She watched them as they closed in, leaning towards Grace as if to protect her, one hand reaching for her arm, trying without words to warn her.

Richard saw Grace look up from her reverie to find two men bending over her, saw her expression change. At the same time he heard Regina, back from wherever she had disappeared to, snarl, 'Go on, throw the bitch onto the street.'

'Regina!' he turned to her.

She gave him a look of triumph. 'She can follow you around, Richard, she can send you threats, she can do anything she likes – *but not on my watch*. Let's see what happens now the heavies have arrived.'

Richard watched as the two men, suited and shaped to look like large black coffins, hid Grace from view. 'Who are they?' he said in wonder. 'Hit men?'

Regina shook her head. 'Shop managers. Tim Weatherby employs them to beat the sales reps from the door. That's what we've been up against, Richard, with your books lately.' She gave him a significant look. 'If Tim Weatherby doesn't like an author's work...'

'Good God,' said Richard aloud, ignoring her. He was watching Anna. She had leapt out of her chair to face the men, sizing them up like a small fierce animal looking for a point of attack. 'I know who she is. That will be the daughter.'

'Who?'

'The girl next to her. The one who has just started kicking the ankles of the man on the right.'

'Hell's teeth,' said Reggie. 'Whatever is she doing?'

'Defending the indefensible, I'd say.' This was from Patsy who had also begun to watch.

But not for long. Suddenly Richard stirred. 'Oh, I can't have this. She shouldn't have to get caught up. She's just a child. She'll be traumatised.'

As he spoke, they saw the slim figure switch from the man on the right, to lay furiously into the man on the left. Both men seemed to have forgotten Grace, forced to deal with this small, potent force arrived, it seemed, from nowhere.

'She doesn't look as if she's being traumatised,' observed Patsy. 'She looks as if she's enjoying herself...'

'Nonsense. Listen to me, both of you, I'm going to have to step in, stop those men. I can't have a young girl exposed to this kind of thing. I couldn't live with myself.'

He was gone before he'd finished speaking. Patsy started to go after him, then stopped, her face softening as she watched him wade through the crowd. *Who would have thought it – Richard Ortega willing to risk everything to spare the feelings of a child?*

Regina, meanwhile, glanced over at Alicia Milagro. She, Milagro, was aware of a commotion at the back and was craning to see what was happening; but her bookshop minders were making a wall around her that made everything invisible. Tapping their watches, they were already beginning to hustle her from the room, making sure she stayed out of it. Everyone cautious now, thanks to Seamus O'Connor, fully expecting mad monks to step out from everywhere.

And no wonder, Regina thought, turning away from Milagro just in time to see a further development in the fray.

The crazed woman had joined in, had launched at the larger of the men as he struggled with the girl, was seizing both his ears in a twisting grip that made him squeal like a large, rutting pig. Savage, thought Regina with a shudder. Utterly mad and dangerous.

She hoped Richard was making notes.

In the middle of everything, Grace stared in bewilderment at the huge head she suddenly found in her grip. It was all too dreamlike, beyond comprehension. A moment ago she'd been sitting quietly with Anna, lost in her thoughts. Now she was here, trying to control a man twice her size; a man who was screaming, describing in chapter and verse exactly what he would do to her when she let go of his ears. Unnerved, she gave them another – hard – twist. The man dropped to his knees and the threats changed to pleas.

They had appeared from nowhere, these men, demanding that she leave. Or, to be more accurate, *that she shift her fucking arse onto the street and let decent people live in peace.* And when, paralysed by shock, she had only stared at them, they had sneered and let their hands fall like vices on her shoulders, seizing her in a grip so hard she had heard herself yelp.

That's when Anna had sprung. Hurling herself at the first of the men, kicking and kicking until he had had to move away, before turning on the other. And even then Grace had been too horrified to move. It was only when the first man had retaliated that Grace stopped being paralysed. Seeing him, suddenly massive and threatening, closing in on her daughter, *then* she had moved, leaping to grab him by the ears, pulling until she could feel the soft tissue begin to tear.

Now here she was, with a man on his knees and his ears in her hands – afraid to keep hold, but more afraid to let go, while all around them the crowd simply stood and watched, mouths hanging open. No one making a move to help. And here was almost the strangest thing of all. Why was no one helping them?

Except, thank God, someone *was* helping. A voice, smooth and familiar, unexpected, yet suddenly there. A voice to change everything. A saviour.

Not that she could hear what he was

saying. But she saw the hand come to rest on the shoulder of the other man, saw the man listen, and shake his head. She saw Richard speak again, saying words only the other could hear until finally the man nodded, reluctantly, before stepping forward to whisper something to the man whose head she held captive.

And of course he couldn't hear. She was holding both of his ears, twisting them so hard no sound could have got through.

'Let him go,' the other man said curtly to her.

Terrified she shook her head. She knew the danger, after all. Chapter and verse. But Richard Ortega was there, making sure the worst never happened.

'Grace,' he said softly. And his eyes held hers in a gentle grip. 'Let him go. He won't hurt you, I promise.'

She opened her mouth, but the words refused to come, gathered like frightened chickens in her throat.

Richard said, 'Grace, you have to trust me. Let the chap go and I promise you it will be all right.'

'He was going to hurt Anna,' she whispered.

'Let him go.' Again Richard's eyes spoke to her, reassuring, promising safety.

Then Anna touched her arm. 'Go on, Mum.'

And so, slowly, very slowly, Grace released her grip. And just as she'd known he would, immediately the man reared above her. Above them all. She caught her breath and spread out her arms to protect her daughter. But Richard made a sign with his hands and the man stepped away. His ears were scarlet but his face was dead pale. He didn't look at Grace.

'Now,' said Richard, 'I think you should come with me. Somewhere less...' he looked over his shoulder, at Patsy and Regina, at Max Farthing and Miriam Rapko, all of them staring at him, watching every move '...less visible.' He finished his sentence, and had to cover his mouth with his hand.

Fucking smile refused to stay off his face.

Chapter Seventeen

Out on the street, Grace forced herself to stay calm. Had to, for Anna's sake.

'They were there, right on top of us, but no one stopped them.' She couldn't keep the wonder out her voice. Or the hurt. 'All those people and no one lifting a finger to help us.' She broke off. 'What am I doing? I should be phoning the police. Those men, they need to be locked up.'

Richard coughed. 'I don't think it would help, to be honest. It's happened before and she always talks her way out of it.'

'Who?'

'Alice Milagro. No doubt she has her reasons, but sooner or later, someone is going to get hurt. I mean, I know why she feels bound to do it. What with Seamus O'Connor nearly coming to grief, everyone's a little edgy. All the same...'

'Richard,' Grace's voice was faint. 'I don't know what you're talking about. What has Alicia Milagro got to do with those ... those animals?'

'Oh,' said Richard. 'Oh my dear, didn't you know? They were hers. Her men, her praetorian guard, so to speak. She's put so many backs up, made so many people angry she can't travel without them. Poor thing, she's convinced someone's going to kill her one day. And as I said, after the fracas with O'Connor – I suppose she feels she can't take any chances. Those men's jobs depend on keeping her happy.'

'You're not saying they thought that I was...?'

'...I'm saying that sometimes it's a case of shoot first, ask questions later. Very American, don't you think? Dear Alice, I'm afraid we've learnt to live with it, with her.'

'But it can't have been her,' whispered Grace. 'It couldn't be ... she spoke to me.

We...' her voice broke as she remembered. They had looked into each other's eyes, Milagro and she. Woman to woman – like people, like friends.

Richard sighed. 'Ah, my dear Grace, always so willing to think the best! But who knows? You may be right. Messages get mixed, commands get ever more jumbled down the line. Maybe poor Alice said one thing and meant something completely different. Then again,' he allowed himself a gentle smile, 'maybe she didn't like a woman standing up in public to say that her books had nothing to say to her.'

'Oh,' Grace gasped. 'But that's not what I meant. That's not what I meant at all.'

Richard shrugged.

Then a voice cut in between them, icy cool. 'It's rubbish, all of it. *You're* talking rubbish.' It was Anna, addressing Richard. 'Alicia Milagro had nothing to do with what happened in there.'

Richard turned to her with a smile. 'This must be your daughter. How lovely. Anna, my dear, how do you do?'

Anna said nothing.

'Anna,' Grace murmured, wanting her to take the scowl off her face. 'Say hello to Richard – Mister – Ortega.'

But the scowl not only stayed where it was, it deepened, causing Grace's heart to sink. She knew that look, it always led to something worse. But then to her intense relief, Anna stopped scowling and smiled instead – so sweetly, so unexpectedly, it took her mother's breath away. Only to say:

'Hello, Mr Ortega. I must say you do talk a load of *fucking* crap. And her name's Alicia, not Alice.'

It took a moment, so completely had the smile and sweetness of tone fooled them. Grace gasped. Richard's eyelids drooped.

Anna carried on: 'Those men had nothing to do with Alicia Milagro. Didn't you see their badges? They had *Weatherby's* written all over them. One of them took our money off us when we came in. And as for Alicia Milagro not liking the question, I heard what my mother said, *and* what Alicia said back, and I know this: she liked the question.' She turned to Grace, and her voice softened. 'She liked *you*, Mum.'

And there it was, the thing Grace had suddenly most needed to hear. She didn't care who was to blame for the men, so long as it wasn't Alicia Milagro.

Richard's eyelids drooped still further as he surveyed them, mother and daughter smiling at each other. They had forgotten him. *Him!* They needed to be reminded who they were ignoring. He said, 'This ... this is indeed a privilege for me. Enchanting! She is absolutely your daughter, my darling Grace. I can see it so clearly. The eyes have it.'

But he was lying. Anna's eyes, now turning sharply to meet his, were nothing like Grace's eyes. They were hard, ring-fenced in black. Eyes that told him they could see right through him. Lying of course. Eyes that lied. Richard shuddered, reminded suddenly of the eyes of his first wife, which in turn had been so uncannily like the eyes of his mother ... never so hard as when he begged to be allowed home to stay, never to have to sleep in a school again...

...He was in danger of being distracted, and all by a pair of eyes. Not just distracted, but laid bare, stripped naked by a woman's eternal intent to flay. *Damn!* If it wasn't Grace doing it to him, now it was her bloody daughter, calling in reinforcements. Lining up his mother, his ex-wife... Suddenly he couldn't take it, not another second.

He snapped off the smile. Without a word, he turned on the spot and walked away.

'Oh,' said Grace softly in surprise. 'He's gone!'

'Like I care. What a creep.'

Grace turned. 'Anna, how can you say that? Swear at him like that? He rescued us from those terrible men and...'

'...And then tried to spin you a lie about Alicia Milagro, when it's obvious he can't stand her – hates her. Saying those things just to try and make us hate her too.'

213

'Anna!' Grace protested again. 'That has to be nonsense. He doesn't hate her. He wouldn't be here otherwise. Why sit and listen all evening to someone he doesn't like?'

Anna shot her a look that was both sharp and hesitant. 'Maybe he didn't come because of her. Maybe he came because of you. I mean he obviously knows you. And you know him. All those weeks with his book hanging around the house. *And you never said.* You never said you knew him. Did he know you were going to be here tonight?'

She stopped and suddenly her cheeks were pink.

'Why does he call you *darling?* And how did he know my name?'

Her eyes met Grace's. Already beginning to answer her own questions.

Grace's mouth had dropped open. She had forgotten that Anna knew nothing about Richard. Forgotten that he had been her secret, kept from the family, from Simon, from everyone. She had lied about him from the start, and Anna was the first person she had lied to.

Now here was Anna. Standing in front of her, doubts tumbling like numbers falling into place. About to think the worst, and there was nothing Grace could do to stop her. Nothing she could say.

So Grace did the only thing she could.

Pulling herself up to her full height, lifting her chin and stretching her neck. Tightening the sinews and shutting down the channels through which the blood was pouring into her face.

The voice, the voice too was important. When she spoke it was with the voice her own mother would have used.

'Anna, how dare you? How dare you think that I would ever, *ever,* have a relationship with a man in that sort of way? With that man or any man.' Coldly she added, 'I think you should apologise.'

She saw the change come over Anna. A moment ago, her daughter's eyes had been accusing, but clear. Now suddenly they were clouded. And all the fight, all the power that had driven the ankles out from under a man twice her size, seemed to ebb away. Anna bit her lip and began to walk, away from the bookshop, away from everything they had been through together there. Away from her.

They sat in silence on the train home, a weight of years between them, keeping them apart. Grace stared into the dark of the window, at the woman reflected back to her, and knew that for the first time in her life she looked middle-aged.

It was that night she knew: she didn't want to see Richard Ortega again. Ever.

Chapter Eighteen

Next day, his phone didn't stop ringing, its small bent aerial throbbing as yet another call bleeped its way to Richard's ear.

And frankly, he was overwhelmed. He put the receiver down for the tenth time, and clutched his chest in emotion. He imagined his heart, his tough old writer's heart, sinewy and stoical; a heart that had continued to beat through all the outrages and injustices, a heart forced to harden itself against acts of betrayal, large and small. He imagined this same heart swelling and growing soft at the turn around. A heart, despite everything, still able to be touched. The heart of an artist as a young man.

Richard had forgiven his fellow writers. Even the successful ones. Even the poison pen pushers, the toxic reviewers who had given way to reviewers who refused to review. He forgave them all because they were here now rallying to his side. Artists who stood by their own.

Over and over again he murmured quiet thanks into the phone, gratitude for such support. And over and over again, he listened to the replies.

'My God, Richard, what do you expect? Miriam says the woman bit a man's ear right off. Imagine if she'd actually got to you...'

'...fighting like a wild thing...'

'...screaming like a banshee...'

'And poor Alicia Milagro having to be bundled out. Absolutely terrified by the sound of it.'

He'd particularly liked that one.

The phone went again. This time it was Patsy. 'Richard?'

There was a note of urgency in her voice, making it the best call of all. Calmly he said, 'Patsy,' and waited. He knew something was coming.

'Richard, the phone's been ringing off the hook here. It's the papers. Everybody wants to talk to you. The *Observer* wants a full interview, the *Sunday Times* are running a profile. The *Mail* wants to tie you in with the stalking of that actress in America, and the *London Review* wants a Zeitgeisty in-depth essay from you about the writer teaching us all how to live with modern obsession.'

Richard's mouth opened, about to shout a joyous *yes*. Yes to all of it. Then he closed it, just in time. 'No,' he said.

'No?' Patsy was startled. 'But why?'

And oddly, the answer he gave her was the absolute truth. '*She'll* see it. I don't want her reading that sort of thing.'

He heard a gasp of disbelief.

'But don't you see, it might make her stop if she reads about herself. She'll see what people think about her.'

'It doesn't work like that, Patsy. She'll just be convinced they've got it wrong. Then she'll get angry. Then she'll start trying to attack me in other ways...'

'But Richard...'

'...Trust me, Patsy. I know rather more about this than you. She'll say I encouraged her, she'll say all sorts of things. She'll swear blind there's a relationship between us. That's what they do, these sorts of people. It's what they tell themselves after all. At the same time, she'll still be right there, but more careful. More dangerous.'

'But how do you know?'

Richard allowed his voice to become stern. 'My dear Patsy, don't you think I've been doing my homework? I know how these people operate. Just believe me when I say that if the newspapers run with this, nothing will be achieved, except that others will suffer. Innocent others – young, easily damaged.'

'Oh, you're thinking about her daughter again.'

'Yes, Patsy, I am.' And that was true too. It would be the daughter who would take him on, taking her mother's part. She'd swear there had been a relationship too. It was the reason he shouldn't have talked to Grace while, what was her name? Anna, was there. He regretted that.

Patsy sighed, tried a different tack. 'All right. But Richard, there's something else to consider. Your sales for instance. We both know that they haven't been ... well ... quite what we would want. Something like this, going public, have you thought what it might do for you? For your sales?'

'Patsy,' he said shocked. 'Do you really think that's all I think about? My sales?'

He listened to the awed silence in which she took this, then put the phone down. The silence was almost a relief. A man needs time to think after all. For a moment he even considered taking it off the hook. Then he remembered: there were still so many others he hadn't heard from, probably still trying to get through. To block their calls, to turn his back, smacked of ingratitude. Ungenerous, and quite beneath him.

All the same, it was almost a matter for regret, having to be on hand to answer the phone. Because something was happening inside him now – a stirring in the stomach. Something growing, delicately unfolding from the confines of a seed.

The seed of a story, the knowledge that if he sat down now, pen in hand and a sheet of thick white paper, the story would begin to flow. *Sometimes a writer, if he is a true writer, is obliged to write true...*

Yes, yes that was it. Richard was nearly, nearly ready to write. He could feel it welling up inside – the Act of Creation. He closed his eyes for sheer joy. He drew a breath, and felt for his pen – his favourite pen – trembling. A modest man, humbled by his own power, now fumbling for paper, his blank page...

...But here was the phone bleating again, and he couldn't bring himself not to answer.

'Yes?' He had perfected the voice of a man under siege.

Weary, yet resilient.

'Ah, Dickie.' This time he sat up. *'You won't remember me, but we were together in the Remove at good Old St Olave's...'*

Richard put the phone down hurriedly. Immediately it rang again. Richard winced and took it off the hook.

Sometimes a writer, if he is a true writer, is obliged...

Blank. Nothing there.

He'd lost it. He poured himself a gin. Drank it, then another, then another. The cheated look began to clear from his brow, as he started to brighten. He knew what was required: a good deed. He'd phone Grace, lighten her day. An act of kindness.

Call it a kindness because he didn't need her now. She had served her purpose. Done her duty. The morning's phone calls were proof of that. Stories of Ortega's stalker had taken on a life of their own, flourished like greenfly on the vine. He could release her, into the ether, like a character that's done and dusted. No need to occupy the reader any further.

No more need for Grace, yet still he picked up the phone. A true man, a man of soul, takes time to disappoint a woman. He lets her down slowly. Gently.

Besides, he liked the sound of her voice.

He heard her voice now.

'Ah, Grace...'

'Richard!' She sounded flustered.

'Indeed, Richard.' He mocked her fondly. The foolishness of her. 'It's your Richard, who should be hard at work already. Creating, carving his thoughts into the good earth. Richard for whom the page waits and who instead is here, talking to you...'

'Well, I'm sorry if you...'

'Yes, my dear, and so you should be. Distraction is death to a writer. You should be punished – gently of course. But punished all the same.'

He had a happy vision, suddenly, of a dairymaid Grace lying across his knee, petticoats adrift, her cheeks pink. And not just the cheeks on her face...

Grace's voice interrupted him. 'Richard, if you have so much to do, maybe you should just get on with it. You know, just buckle down and do it.'

The vision vanished. Astonished, Richard gaped. He winced, then frowned, then decided to laugh. 'My dear Grace, you make writing sound like a mere chore, something one can simply hammer out.'

Grace replied. 'Well, maybe you should see it like that too. Put your head down, get it done. Rest when you get there.'

'*Rest when you get there?*' he said and the laughter vanished from his voice. 'I don't believe I've heard that particular...'

Expecting she would falter.

She didn't falter. Her voice was, if anything, firmer. 'It's a family thing. What we'd say to the children when they were little, when they were dawdling and we needed to be somewhere.'

Richard let silence be his answer to that. A dignified refusal to speak. Only after seconds had passed did he understand that Grace wasn't saying anything either.

Then he remembered. He had left her so abruptly last night. Revolted by teenage yapping, he had simply turned and walked away. No wonder Grace wasn't sounding like herself. Precious little bourgeoise, brimming with middle-class ideas of how people behaved – she was offended. Now he really could laugh.

'Grace, I should speak plain. I am phoning to apologise. Deeply and profoundly. I left you so badly last night. But I had to, my

222

dear! I turned and there they all were – not just Patsy and Reggie, but Miriam Rapko for heaven's sake. I haven't mentioned Miriam have I? Forgive me, I should have. There's a history between us – a long one alas. If for a moment *Miriam* had suspected that you and I ... oh my dear, it doesn't bear thinking about. Anyway, my darling, I had to disappear. There wasn't even time to explain. Anything to stop them making a scene, and in front of your daughter, your lovely daughter...'

'It's all right, Richard.' Grace interrupted him. 'Don't say any more, not to me, and not about them, those women.' She paused. More slowly she said, 'You see, I've been thinking. You seem to have so many difficulties in that ... that area. You shouldn't be adding to them, not because of me. Not just to be kind.'

'My dear Grace, when have I ever been kind?'

'Oh Richard, all the time! You have been endlessly kind. But now I think I should let you be, and not impose on you any more. In fact... In fact, I really think it's better that I don't.'

'Don't? Don't what, my dear?'

She hesitated. He imagined her struggling to speak. Again his face softened without him being aware. Such a nervous Grace, so anxious to say the right thing.

But then she did speak and her voice was strong. Shockingly so. 'See you again. I don't think I should see you. You have your ... women friends. And I have my family.'

Family. Her daughter, that's who she meant. The husband didn't even come into it. Richard fought to keep the panic out of his voice.

'But my dear Grace, what is there to fret about? All we have is a friendship, a beautiful, enriching friendship. Why should it be a problem?'

Again the hesitation. 'You don't have children, Richard. It's impossible to explain. But Anna, my daughter, she's seen and heard so much recently because ... because of Simon. And because of me. She's not thinking very well of either of us at the moment. And you...'

'...And I?'

'Confuse her. She doesn't understand about friendship, you see. Not the sort between men and women. She thinks that everyone behaves the same way. She's seen that her father was friends with a woman and that they...' Grace sighed. 'Oh dear, I knew I wouldn't be able to explain.'

'On the contrary,' Richard said coldly. 'I would say you have explained it well enough. Yet you forget who I am, Grace. You forget that my life's work has been bound up in understanding others. Mothers, fathers, lovers, brothers. My books are evidence of that. And what I understand is that you are letting a child, a mere child, interfere with your freedom to live. To love, even.' He added slowly and with meaning: 'She is killing the girl inside you, Grace.'

There was a long silence. He couldn't even hear her breathing. Eventually she spoke:

'That's not the problem, Richard. There's no girl here. And Anna's not a child. As for freedom – well freedom doesn't come into it. Not when you have family. I'm sorry, so sorry.'

And then, to his utter disbelief, Grace, *his* Grace, put the phone down. On him, Richard Ortega.

Confusion first. Staring at the phone in his hand, like a glass that has emptied itself without touching his lips. Then rage. Rage beyond endurance. Rage like pain, like noise. Nowhere to hide from it. Nothing to penetrate it. This time when Richard hurled his phone away from him, it went with a roar that he would have sworn never came from him. It flew through the window into the street where it smashed into hundreds of plastic pieces scattered across the pavement. Just more litter.

The next few minutes came and went. Richard had no knowledge of them. With the dispatch of his phone something white, like mist or snow, had come down, blanking out the world. He wondered briefly if it was the whites of his own eyes he was seeing, then stopped wondering, stopped thinking all together.

Grace stood in her kitchen, trembling slightly. She hadn't wanted to say goodbye to Richard, but it was all she could do. In a few minutes Anna would be home from school and somehow she, Grace, had to start again, from scratch.

Start everything again. After Anna, Simon. Grace knew what she wanted now. A road back to where they used to be: before Lucy, before disease, before infections. Before an Anna who found her father irrelevant. Further back, even, than all of these, to a place where Grace had been happy to be an adult, a grown-up. Happy to be herself. Forty years old – she should be happy she had lived so long. *Rejoice,* that's what Alicia Milagro would say. Rejoice.

This was where she wanted to be. Yet she couldn't find the road to any of it when there was Richard. He complicated things. He was the lie she had told to Anna.

All the same her eyes were wet as she put the phone down. Now finally she could see what he was. Not a lover, not a friend even. What then? An uncle, perhaps. Yes, that was it. A magical, mysterious uncle who, for a brief sparkling time, had snatched up his favourite niece and carried her to places no one else could visit. The sort of uncle you'd read about in books as a child and look back upon for ever with a smile. An uncle who sees the world as a place designed only for himself, and daringly wants you to think the same way. The sort of uncle that stops you growing up.

Dear eccentric uncle. Her rock. Her safe place.

She didn't want him now.

Chapter Nineteen

When the mist cleared Richard found himself lying on his sofa. His head throbbed as if it had been bludgeoned. In a moment of hope, he wondered if that wasn't exactly what had happened – a thief stealing into his home with a cosh to lay him out before making off with his most precious possessions.

No thief. Not as such. But the anger swelled again, because *this* was true – he had lost something. Something precious. Something that belonged to him, made by himself for himself.

Grace.

He had lost Grace. And Richard's hand,

reaching for the bottle beside him, fell limp, six inches short of its target.

And now here it was again – the mist, gathering just out of his line of sight, so that he forgot to be angry, and began to tremble instead. A dark not like the dark. White, for one thing. Something quite terrible about it. What? He tried to remember what happened when the mist came down just now. He hadn't been unconscious. He had felt his way to the sofa and lain down, made himself comfortable. So what happened?

Nothing.

Nothing. And that was it. Nothing had happened. Not even Thought. For as long as the mist had settled, Richard had thought about precisely nothing. Not even himself. Especially not himself. He had been empty.

Remembering that, remembering what it was to be empty, Richard's flesh began to crawl and for the first time in his life (since school) he knew terror. And in his terror he murmured a word, a name. Wrenched from the heart of him in spite of himself, in the same way that a dying man, in terror, will call for his mother.

Grace.

Grace.

But having spoken, he held his breath, because he remembered. Every time he had summoned her, she had come. Obedient as a daydream, compliant as a brainchild. He looked around wildly for the phone, ready for the trill. But of course there was no phone. And with that Richard's teeth began to chatter, and the mist moved in a little closer.

And *she* had done this to him. Grace had made herself absent. Taken herself out of the picture, for all the world as if she had a mind of her own. Not obedient, not compliant. Now Richard's teeth chattered so hard they lost contact with each other and began to drive into the soft flesh of his tongue instead. Pain filled his mouth, joined the pain in his head.

Anger as pain. Anger so it could make you sob.

How had she done it? How had she been able to remove herself, when it had all been there, written out for her? Even her words. She didn't even have to think. He had done it all for her, given her an existence other women could only dream about. Flaubert had done no more for Emma, Tolstoy for his Anna.

And what had she done to thank him? Removed herself.

Richard's teeth ground into his tongue, shredding and filling his mouth with blood. Yet still here came the mist, shading out his thoughts. Richard bit his tongue harder still, to keep the mist away, but he couldn't stop it. Settling around him now. He could feel the onset of emptiness. Not even pain could make it go away.

Then he had a thought. A last thought before the mist closed in.

He had made a mistake with Grace. A grave error. And having been the one to make it, he needed to know exactly what it was. He forced himself to sit up. The mist was wavering, giving him a second chance to see, to find his way out of the fog.

He had made a cock-up. An act of mistranslation. A category error. The sort that makes a character go astray, turn into something completely different from what the plot required. He had allowed *Grace* to go astray.

But how?

Simple. He had forgotten what women wanted. All women. Every one of them, Grace included.

He had shown her brilliance. Shown her brilliance when, woman-like, all she had wanted was romance. Love. Lurve. Erotic acts. Rumpy pumpy, the two-backed beast. Rachmaninov played so loud you couldn't hear yourself think. She had wanted night-scented kisses and throbbing goodbyes. She'd wanted hands down her front and poems on the lawn. Torn bodices and sweating bodies.

How could he have forgotten something so easy? He had worked in advertising after all. He knew what women wanted; he knew what sold soap. Yet he'd been so busy with other things, he had forgotten the awful truth. In other words, he had been everything he shouldn't. He had been kind, understanding. He had dried her tears and introduced her to a life less ordinary. He had listened to her endless problems while she snivelled. All but blown her nose for her. And the result? He had acted like he was her fucking uncle.

A fucking uncle.

That was it. Now he knew. Now he understood. Triumphant, he watched the mist disappear, along with all that emptiness. Disappearing back where it belonged – sucking back into the centres of those Godforsaken souls who were not Richard Ortega.

She had gone astray, but he hadn't lost her. You don't lose something that's part of yourself, created for yourself. He groped for the bottle and found it, swilled vodka round his bleeding mouth and swallowed. It tasted like a Bloody Mary. His tongue hurt like buggery, but he felt refreshed, full of what he had to do.

Chapter Twenty

This time Grace was the one to make sure the children were out of the house.

Not the way Simon had done it, causing them to roll their eyes knowingly as they pocketed the money. Besides, Anna would only have stared at her, full of what she still believed she knew. Hostile.

She did it bluntly. 'I need you to find somewhere to go tonight. Stay out and whatever you do, don't come straight home.' And when Rob put on a hurt face she said, 'You know Dad and I have been having problems. Big problems. Well, I want them to end now. But we have to talk. We haven't talked. And for that we need to be by ourselves.'

'Well, why don't *you* go out and do it somewhere else, like a restaurant?' Anna barely tried to hide the insolence in her voice. 'You could talk all you like there.'

'Because I want to be at home. I want us to be somewhere we don't have to behave. I want to be able to shout and swear if I have to. I want to call your father every name under the sun if I need to. And he the same.'

Rob sniggered, 'What you, *swear?*' He saw the look on her face and stopped. 'OK, so

232

what do you want us to do?'

'Do anything you like,' said Grace calmly. 'Just don't come back till late.'

'OK.' Rob nodded. Now he was cunning, like a little boy who thinks he's winning a trick over his parents. 'We'll need money though, won't we, Annie? Probably quite a lot.'

Anna said nothing. She was watching Grace.

'No money,' said Grace. 'You can spend your own. Or do what you would half the time anyway: go to someone else's house. Go to Pete's.'

Anna nodded. It was as if she knew that this was serious. That whatever had happened, whatever Simon had done, or Grace had done, something was going to be decided. Finished.

The house was quiet when Simon came home.

'Kids?' he asked.

'Out,' said Grace.

This time, she had not bathed and dressed and anointed herself. She was as she would always be at the end of the day. Dusty from housework, hot from ironing. Floury from cooking. Busy making a life for others to come home to. Except that this might be the last time she did.

Strange to think that this was all she had

been doing for years, and it was only now she had thought about it. Her friends didn't live like this, within walls. Her friends were outside, in the world; Tamsin with her caseload of lying clients. Even Deborah with her days in the health food shop, teaching yoga to fat ladies. They never waited at home for anyone. Only she was different, and only now did she see how different. More than just different. A throwback, something that had survived every urging of evolution.

Like a dinosaur. The miracle was only that she had lived so long.

Today, for the first time, she had seen herself – clear, every line and plane razor sharp. Herself as a dinosaur, content to amble through a landscape where it took all day to find enough foliage just to keep alive and keep moving. Busy, busy, busy. When all along she could have been something small and inquisitive, equipped to do more than just feed its young. She could have been a creature quick and furry. She could have been a meat-eater. And still have fed her young.

Yet she had been happy to be a dinosaur when all the rest of the dinosaurs had died out. She had cooked and cleaned and mended and tidied. She had kept house, kept *busy*. Lived so there was always time for others – at a time that suited them. Not a bad life, in fact. An easy life, compared with the battle outside.

But she hadn't realised. Every kind of life takes its toll. And what had happened? They had forgotten she was there. Simon hadn't made her invisible. *She* had made her invisible. A dinosaur camouflaged by the foliage that kept it alive; by furniture and flour and shopping lists.

So that's what happened, she thought. I smudged myself out. And once again, she looked back in her mind's eye, to the moment all those months ago, when Simon must have decided to cross the line that divided faithful from unfaithful. The picture stayed the same: Lucy, all sweat and promise, Simon frowning, weighing up the pros and cons.

Except in this new picture he wasn't actually weighing up anything. There was no Grace to decide against. No picture in his mind on which to turn his back. Grace had simply made it so she wasn't there. She had been invisible, still moving aimlessly between trees, perfectly camouflaged, thinking she was busy. Thinking this was all it took to stay alive.

Now, here, tonight, Simon was standing in front of her, seeing her, despite the camouflage – *despite her own best efforts*. In the end, he had made his decision, not in favour of Lucy but Grace. And not because of the woman she had become but because of the woman he remembered. Because of history. And what was that if not love? She saw him now, and said, 'I'm ready.'

'Ready for what?' He looked frightened, afraid of what she had to tell him.

'Ready to come off my high horse. Ready to be with you. Ready for anything.'

He stared at her. Then she saw it, the change in him. Relief, gratitude, love, sweeping through his face, taking the ache out of his shoulders, the stiffness in his back. Making him look like the man she had unsingled at the party all those years ago. Putting himself in her hands.

They moved at the same time, and found each other. Two people suddenly occupying the space of one.

Odd really. There was no shouting after all, no swearing. No name calling. It could have happened anywhere, this meeting – rather, this meeting again. In the road, in a restaurant. But it happened here, at home, better than anywhere else.

Outside in the street, Richard watched a light go on in an upstairs room.

He had found the house without difficulty, although it had unnerved him, having to travel out of London. He had done so in the company of commuters, not trying to hide his contempt for people too timid for a city

236

at night, in flight for the suburbs. Standing in the aisle of the six-thirty from Marylebone (he had been shocked to discover that there was no seat for him) he had automatically surveyed the reading matter around him. And was nauseated to see the same names over and over. Seamus O' Connor, Alicia Milagro. A woman in the corner snivelling over some pathetic paean to self-pity penned by Miriam Rapko. He tried to persuade himself of the humour in it – the fact that not a soul had guessed that in the offing, in the ether, *in their presence* were the seeds of something more wonderful than anything. A work to put these poor efforts to shame.

Sometimes a writer, if he is a true writer...

But of course not here. No writer could actually compose here, crammed in amongst the common throng. Richard shuddered at the thought and retreated into himself, so far as was humanly possible, although still remembering to keep half an eye for the odd recognising glance, the signal from some enlightened soul glancing up and knowing him for what he was.

It didn't happen. Yet it used to happen. Women usually. Well, women always. Not any more. But soon it would again. *Sometimes a writer...* Only there was Grace to be sorted out first.

Now he stood outside their house, an average house with an average amount of Tudor locked into the mock beams. A modest amount of garden running to the pavement. An unassuming front door. Richard's mouth had curled. To think that he had offered an escape from this. Pockets of time when she could leave it all behind...

...But of course, woman-like, she had accepted everything he had offered, and then wanted more. And innocent fool that he was, he had not recognised it.

Leaning against a tree he had watched two people leave the house, shrinking back as he recognised the smaller figure as Anna, the poisonous child who had goaded him with those spiky words. The other was a boy, tall and slouching, reminding him of those boys who came and went at St Olave's. The ones who seemed to shrug the entire experience off their broad shoulders. Happy so long as they had enough to eat.

Of course, never to be heard of again.

Then from behind him, someone else, this time going into the house. A man whose face he couldn't see, tall as the youth who had just gone out. The husband of course. The one who paid for all this ... modesty. Richard had watched the man stop outside his own front door, taking a moment before he entered. Hesitant, collecting himself.

Then, only a few minutes later, there was that light going on in an upstairs room.

Curtains being drawn. And Richard had felt himself affronted. They were shutting him out, these people who briefly, only briefly and for very limited reasons, had become interesting to him, Richard Ortega.

He waited, giving them a second chance. But they stayed in the room, locked against the world. Against him.

Chapter Twenty-One

Grace lay in bed as morning lit up the room, and watched Simon sleep.

She felt as if they had been away, both of them. Journeying into places with no safe passage home. But they had found their way back after all and here they were, together. Happy. This was happiness. As if her gaze had stirred him, Simon opened his eyes. Neither of them spoke. It was enough just to lie and take each other in.

They came downstairs together. Both Rob and Anna were up before them, and Grace remembered she hadn't heard them come home. Rob carried on shovelling Coco Pops into his mouth, unconcerned, but Anna's eyes settled on her parents, travelling from one to the other, suspicious, ready to be disappointed.

Yet there must have been something about them, because a moment passed – then Grace saw the change sweep over her daughter, another version of what she had seen in Simon the night before. Relief. She smiled at her and Anna replied with a small tight smile of her own. A smile that made Grace want to take her in her arms and hold her like when she was a little girl. Her daughter's face, still uncreased, was peachy smooth. She looked grown up, yet she wasn't. Adults could still bewilder her. Her own parents could bewilder her.

Grace made a pot of coffee and Simon sat with the newspaper propped up in front of him. Rob continued to chew with his mouth open and Anna scowled at him. Radio 4 broadcast *Thought for the Day* and, as usual, nobody listened. Grace sat where she always sat. Everything was the same and everything was different.

Half a mile down the road Richard Ortega woke in a cheap hotel, roused by the sound of somebody flushing the lavatory in the room next door. Water rushed inches from his ear, plywood walls no barrier. Made him need to pee. Urgently.

The night before, after the husband had come home, after the light had gone on in that upstairs room, Richard had retreated to a nearby pub and downed three whiskies very quickly, one after the other. Then, drawn by some impulse he couldn't explain, he'd swallowed a fourth and returned to the house. This time, he had shown foresight and brought a whole bottle of whisky from the bar. And needing somewhere more comfortable, he had hopped over the gate and found an old garden chair, which he dragged discreetly to a bush under the hedge. Here he could sit. Here, unseen, he could see everything.

Not that there was much to see. The house stood as it had before, its Tudor beams a bulwark now. Curtains acting like bars against the night – against him! – whilst inside, Grace, his Grace, was moving, eating, sleeping.

Shocking this. The mere fact that she was walking, talking, without any reference to himself. Without permission. The thought threatened to grow large inside him, and made his hand, the one wrapped round the bottle, shake slightly. Then it came to him: the truth – the poetic truth. Grace could walk, talk, do what she had to do, precisely *because* he was here. The truth – the poetic truth – being that she was able to exist only *because* he thought about her. His attention gave rise to her, all the more so because tonight, in his generosity, he was here, closer than she could have expected. Or hoped.

And so he relaxed, now that he knew what

he was doing here, sitting on a plastic chair beneath a bush outside a curtained house. His hand could be steady on the evening's helm. He was here to give life to Grace.

At midnight they came back, the two young ones. The boy was talking, plainly one of those kids who would talk to a wall if he felt like it. Which he might have been doing now for all the good it did him. His sister was ignoring him, eyes trained on the house as she waited for him to negotiate the lock. As if she didn't trust what she would find inside.

The daughter. Richard's eyes closed, then opened. Like the shutter on a lens snapping the evidence. The daughter was what he was up against, as determined to have the mother pinned down as he was determined to free her. A child with a vested interest.

The door closed behind them, and Richard found he didn't want to stay any more. He put it down to the daughter, interfering with the delicate vibrations that trembled between himself and Grace. Destroying his line of influence with a malign influence of her own.

No use hanging around. He had written three letters and pinned them under stones, knowing somehow she would find him. The link was too strong for her not to. Now it had been time to go home, back to his own land.

But at the station everything was dark. The place was shut up. Richard had stared at the deserted building in bewilderment. He banged on the station office door, but no one came. Then hearing a movement behind him, he had whirled round. A man with a dog loomed out of the dark.

'The trains,' cried Richard. 'Where are the trains?'

The man gave a start while the dog growled. A big dog.

'Trains?' he snapped. 'Good God, man. You're not going to find a train at this time of night. Last one to London went about two hours ago.'

He had disappeared into the dark again, leaving Richard to stare after him in disbelief. Unable to imagine a time and a place that would not allow escape, back to London. Back to where the life was. To where the people were.

But it was true, and so he had had to find his way here, to a cheap hotel frequented by travelling salesmen, where they had scanned his credit card and banished him to a small room in which the sound of other people pissing could reach him through the walls.

Richard closed his eyes and blamed Grace.

Arriving back in London, he found Patsy standing outside his front door. There were two policemen beside her, one holding a jemmy.

'Richard!' she said and started to cry.

'I take it this is the gentleman you were worried about,' said one of the officers.

She nodded vehemently through tears. 'Yes, very worried.'

'So I suppose you don't want us to...' he indicated the jemmy.

'No, of course not...'

Richard frowned gently. 'Patsy, whatever is going on?'

'What's going on?' She repeated the question, sounding almost hysterical. 'You were supposed to meet me last night, remember? And Regina. You didn't turn up. Then when we tried to phone, there was no answer. It was just dead. Nothing on your mobile either. Richard, we've been worried sick. I came round first thing to bang on the door and still you didn't answer. I thought ...well, I don't know what I thought. Except I do. So I called the police and demanded that they come and break in. Not that they wanted to, not at first. Then, when I told the story – the *whole* story – they were as anxious as I was. Oh Richard, I was so afraid...'

'Patsy,' he said softly. 'Ah Patsy, Patsy.' He held her close and over the top of her head, smiled at the two policemen, one man appealing to his fellow men. A sobbing woman, a hint of hysteria, they would draw their own conclusions.

Yet instead of smiling back, they merely looked on stolidly. Up till now Patsy must have been doing her sensible woman act, fooling people as she so often did. They waited until Richard had taken all he could stand of tears wetting his neck, then one of them said, 'This lady has told us quite a story. Is it true, sir?'

'Well,' said Richard, 'yes. These have been trying times.' A faint haggard smile to tell the full story. Patsy squeezed his hand.

'Then don't you think you should have brought it to our attention? The lady has mentioned threats to kill...'

'And worse,' interrupted Patsy.

'...Yet you haven't reported any of it to the authorities.'

'No, I haven't. To be honest, there didn't seem any point. You couldn't have done anything. It's a free country. The poor woman could have followed me round till kingdom come and there was nothing to stop her, not in law.'

'On the contrary, sir. There is quite a lot – if it's true she's been making threats. Short of that, we could probably have got her for harassment.'

'See?' cried Patsy, triumphant. 'I told you!' She turned to the officers. '*And* he knows it. He just has this stupid idea he needs to protect this horrible woman from her own actions. He's been ... a ... a saint.'

The officers looked at him. Obviously not willing to see the saint in him just yet. Richard sighed. 'All right, Patsy, I give in. I'll make a full and formal report – alone, mind. Will that make you happy?'

Patsy beamed at him, tears still evident on her cheeks. 'Yes,' she said. 'Very happy.' She began to skip towards her car, turning only to add, 'Mind you tell them everything, Richard. And I mean everything.'

Richard led the policemen into the house. Watched them taking in the tossed furniture, the smeared glasses, the empty bottles.

'As you see,' he said humorously, 'I live alone.'

They didn't smile. One of them said, 'This woman, sir, the one you claim is following you? Let's talk about her.'

'*Claim*, officer?' Richard was wounded. 'I think you'll find it's not me claiming anything. Rather, it's my friends who are doing the claiming.'

'So you have no complaint to make? This woman has not been harassing you, stalking you, making threats or doing anything to cause you to feel at risk?'

'Ah now,' said Richard slowly, sadly. 'That's not what I said either. I repeat – these have been trying times.'

The other policeman stepped in. 'So what do you want, sir? We could have a word with her, caution her – read her *your* rights so to speak. We could advise you to seek an injunction, some kind of restraining order. We might even be able to charge her – if you have the evidence.'

'Oh,' said Richard, 'I have the evidence. Ask anyone who knows me. But...' he sighed heavily, started again. 'You have to understand the situation, officers. I am a writer. This kind of thing happens. Not often, I grant you. One has to be ... special. But those of us who are ... special ... we have a certain influence. We change lives. It seems I changed the life of this poor woman, and now, alas, she wants to change mine.' He shook his head and smiled gently, a man trapped; and yet still able to be amused by his own entrapment. A stoic. 'No, I can't do it to her. No arrests, no charges. Nothing like that.'

'So ... you just want all this to carry on?' The policeman was sounding impatient, irritable. Apparently unable to recognise stoicism if it hit him with his own truncheon.

Richard gasped. 'No! God forbid. Look, how about a compromise? Could you simply make sure it goes on record, what's been happening to me? That way there would be something in writing. Something to call on in an hour of need. Some kind of flag by her name. Could you do that? Is it possible, officer?'

'You'll need more than a flag by her name if she turns really nasty, sir.'

'Nevertheless...'

The policeman nodded, took out his notebook. 'Her name, sir?'

'Grace,' said Richard quietly. 'Grace Waites. I have absolutely no idea where she lives.'

No more dinosaurs. Grace sat down and wrote twenty-seven letters for jobs.

A week went by. Two weeks. Three. She received two replies turning her down without an interview. No one else bothered to answer.

It was going to be hard, finding work – any work – when all this time she had been invisible. Obviously it didn't count for much, being a dinosaur. She pictured people opening her letters and laughing at the temerity of a housewife who thought she had something to offer.

'Forget the stupid jobs,' said Simon. 'Think what you want to do, then work out how you're going to do it. Go back to college. Be a student. You missed all that having the kids, looking after us. Do it now.'

And just like that, the future changed. As if what was there before had simply been a backcloth, a painted horizon made to fool her. Now it lifted to reveal no horizon in sight. No end. It made her dizzy. She sent off for prospectuses, and unlike job offers, they came by return of post.

'There you are,' said Simon. 'There's a message in it. Universities don't ignore you. They want you. Just work out what you want them to teach you, what sort of future you want. And go for it.'

Go for it? Go for what?

What did she want?

These days it was other thoughts that stopped her, right in the middle of something else – sorting the wash, filling the dishwasher, cooking – arriving like a hand pressed against her chest, freezing her to the spot. Thoughts of a future, different futures.

Over meals her children planned careers for her. So eager to get her out of the house she had to wonder if they had ever wanted her there in the first place. Only Simon made no suggestions. He watched and listened until it dawned on Grace that he was leaving it all to her, not interfering. Just waiting.

Language courses, business studies, fashion, philosophy.

The children threw ideas into the ring, serious, as if she could make any one of them a reality. Dentistry, pathology, physiotherapy. Belly dancing, tourism. When she pointed to lack of relevant experience, they shrugged. What was the problem? They didn't have experience either. Not yet. And finally she began to get the point – she was barely two decades older than Rob. There was time to learn everything he could. And more.

It was catching, her children's belief that anything was possible.

Anthropology, archaeology, French polishing.

The phone rang. Grace picked up.

'Yes?'

No answer. And then it came to her, a shiver of warning before...

'Grace.' Faint. Almost a whisper. It should have been unrecognisable, but straight away she knew.

'Richard.' Shocked – the more so because she hadn't thought of him. Not once. Not since the day that Simon had come home.

'I had ... had to phone you, Grace.'

Another long silence.

'I am the beast, Grace.'

'The...?' Grace's voice faltered.

'Beast to your Beauty. Remember how she leaves him, fleeing back to her family. And remember how the Beast repines, laid low by a disease that only she can cure. Alone in his gardens, surrounded by the roses that remind him of her. I am laid low. I am dying, Grace.'

'Dying...? Oh Richard, what are you talking about?'

'Come to me, Grace. I am alone. Come see how it is.'

She wrenched the phone from her ear and stood. Then she brought it back to say, as gently as she could, 'Richard, I'm sorry. My family...'

'Ah yes.' His voice came back to her, also gentle. Unreproaching. 'Your family.'

He sighed and the line went dead.

A real silence now. And Grace, who had always tried to shut out bad thoughts, could not shut out this thought: of Richard, laid low. The man who had helped her, who thought they were friends. So sick of being alone he could call it dying.

She shook her head, trying to dislodge the picture, so she could think of other things. Mathematics, teaching...

...Nothing. The list of futures stalled. She could only see Richard. Alone. Asking for nothing more than to hear her voice.

On his sofa Richard stretched, like the cat he didn't own.

She would be back. He could tell from the tone in her voice. Dismayed, but surely not displeased. Nothing flatters a woman more than a man dying for the lack of her. It's the reason boys jump off tall buildings. It's why they go marching off to war, to impress the womenfolk left behind. Putting their poor numbed skulls above parapets.

But it worked didn't it? They get what they were after, the few that make it back. More girls, more sex than they can shake a stick at. Tell a woman she's killing you and she'll be beating a path to your door. Begging, just begging to come in. Richard yawned, and waited.

Chapter Twenty-Two

Bitch. Stupid ungrateful bitch.

She hadn't phoned. He waited all afternoon and he waited all night.

Night was when he had come to expect her. Imagining her escaping with her mobile to a corner of her modest house, or drawn to the garden and the dark without knowing why, perhaps informed by some higher sense that the same garden, the same dark, had harboured *him*. That was it: in the garden, thoughts and imaginings would finally be set free. He had planted the seed. *Pinned letters under stones*. An erotic growth.

But she didn't phone. He had fallen asleep waiting, and all the night long, tennis balls had punctuated the passing hours. Vicious.

His stomach ached when he woke up. Hunger, rage. He made a pan of porridge, watered and salted, the way they'd made it at St Olave's of the Faint Hearted. Then he saturated it in vodka and sugar and gulped it down. Threw the pan into the back garden.

Hunger gone. Rage still there.

Write. That was the answer. *Sometimes a writer*... He snatched up paper, his favourite pen, and stumbled to the desk by the window where he always sat, knowing that anyone who passed in the street would be able to look up and think: Writer at Work.

The pen hovered, ready to mark the thick white page for ever, virgin snow. And ... nothing, he could think of nothing. Of course he knew the reason – the size, the shape, the exact nature of the obstacle in his way. Grace, simpering Maid Muppet, sat coy on her tuffet, keeping him from his work. Knowing what was expected of her. Doing just the opposite.

He lurched back to the sofa, to wait again.

The phone, a new one, sounded in his ear, more melodic than the old.

It entered his dream so that Grace, dancing naked round a milk pail, suddenly produced a tiny bell from nowhere and tinkled it, smiling at him. Her signal that she was ready, ready for anything he wanted.

The phone trilled again, and Richard awoke and snatched it to his ear.

'Grace!'

'Who? Richard, are you all right?'

Not Grace. Disappointment searing through his veins. Made it difficult to talk.

'Patsy. What do you want?'

'Well ... nothing. I just wondered how you were.'

'Fine, just fine.'

But she wasn't going to let it go. 'Richard, talk to me. Tell me what happened. You spoke to those policemen? You told them everything?'

'Yes.'

'And...?'

He struggled a moment. 'It made things worse,' he said finally. 'Ten times worse. If they were bad before, they're impossible now.'

She gasped. 'Oh my God, why?'

He scowled at the room. He wanted to be asleep still. He wanted to be watching Grace gyrating, small breasts moving. Those curls dancing. And her eyes... Because of course, the eyes had it.

'Richard *why*? Why is it worse?'

He made a supreme effort. 'Because now the bitch never goes away. They can put up all the restraining orders, all the injunctions they like. They could build a fucking wall around me, and she'd still be there.'

He slammed down the phone. And it was true. Every word of it. Close his eyes and she was there. Open them and she was there. The bitch wouldn't leave him. He had done everything he could to help her. Last night he had gone again, into the cold suburbs. Sitting in the garden under the fucking hedge, watching the family come home. Watching the door close behind them all. Like it was some fucking nuclear bunker they had built for themselves.

He had written three letters and pinned them under stones. Fucking Emma Bovary, fucking fucking Anna Karenin would have known to look. They would have known to come out into the garden. Tolstoy never had such troubles.

All she had to do was what she was supposed to. He had made it so she didn't even have to think.

Fucking fuck fuck fuck.

He snatched up the phone again and jabbed in her number. There was no answer. He crashed it down and dialled again. And again. Still no answer. He imagined the phone ringing through her house; imagined Grace smiling, counting every repeated trill as a triumph. He knew what she was doing, the game she was playing. An erotic game of her own. Playing hard to get, thinking she had the advantage.

He knew what she was up to.

In fact, Grace was out of the house. Had been all morning and would be all day. She

255

was in the library, absorbed in reference books that listed all the opportunities for adult learning. History, marine biology, circus skills. Nursery teaching, medicine, accountancy.

Not accountancy.

She had recovered from the phone call, finally remembering that half the charm of Richard had been his urge to exaggerate. He could claim to be alone, but how could it be true, when gathered round him were the women, the ones who made his life so difficult? If ever there was a man less likely to be alone...

Besides, there had been something new in his tone, had threatened to disturb her even more. He had talked to her as though she were a lost love, not a lost friend. Or maybe she was flattering herself. But for a while the thought had refused to go away – the idea that all this time, Richard Ortega had wanted to be something completely different. In spite of herself, it intrigued her, flattered her. Because it had never left her, the shame of those women in the Club, staring at her in distaste. How strange, how *ironic*, that they wanted Richard so very much, when perhaps all he had wanted was her. How wonderful if without even trying she had won what they never had...

But here she had caught the drift of her own thoughts, and stopped. Then and there.

Successful for once. And immediately she felt normal again, all the more convinced that she had done the right thing and resisted the call of Ortega.

Histology, hotel and catering, homeopathy.

Grace's mind had become a litany, her day a recitation.

Chapter Twenty-Three

'Law,' said Tamsin.

'Crystology,' said Deborah.

They were saying goodnight after an evening together, just the three of them. Now they were the last people to leave the restaurant. Behind them the staff were yawning and outside the streets had gone quiet. Even the late night drinkers had gone home.

'Oh dear,' said Grace guiltily, only now realising the time. Tiny Thai waitresses sat on stools, tired out. No one had said a word to make them leave.

On the pavement Deborah took her hand. 'It's wonderful, Grace. Really wonderful. The way you've turned Simon's weakness into a learning experience. It's karma, of course. You're a good person. Things were always going to be all right.'

Tamsin snorted, but said nothing.

Deborah said, 'Did you ever read any more by that writer – the one you met? Richard Ortega I mean?'

Grace paused then shook her head. 'No. The one book was enough.'

Deborah sighed. 'It's such a shame. He has so much to teach. I wish you could have met him again after the ... the bedroom slipper. He must have got completely the wrong impression of you. Poor Grace.'

And Grace smiled.

The women hugged. Tamsin pointed to her car. 'Jump in, I'll drop you both home.'

Deborah prepared to climb in, but Grace hung back. The pavements were quiet as they never were in the day, puddles of light forming beneath the street lamps, inviting as stepping. stones, one leading to the other and on, right into the future.

'You know, I think I'd like to walk.'

Tamsin nodded. 'I'll get you that information on law courses.'

From inside the car, Deborah called out, 'Don't commit to anything, Grace. Not till you've talked to the people at Shambahla.'

They drove off, leaving Grace to breathe in the peace. Behind her, next to the restaurant, was the book shop where she had first encountered Richard Ortega. She turned to gaze at it a moment, its window semi-dark and filled with books, none of them, she noticed, by him. She thought about the bedroom slipper and blushed. Then forgot about it. The litany started up in her head and she began to walk, footsteps falling in time to the lists unfolding in her head.

Financial services, creative writing, cake making...

A nice night, a quiet night. Pools of lamplight drawing her onwards, drawing her home. Engineering, pyramid selling, psychology.

'Psychology.'

She stopped walking, coming to a halt midway between two puddles of light. Yet it seemed anything but dark. She touched her face and discovered she was smiling, beaming, without even knowing why. And then she did know. Because suddenly the future, whose list of possibilities had seemed uncountable, had gathered and stopped at one future.

Psychology.

Why did people – why did Simon, why did she – do the things they did? Why was everything that happened such a *mystery?* Why did understanding so often only come long after, when it was too late? Forty years old, and Grace didn't know. But suddenly she could see how there might be a way to find out. And be useful, make a living. Make a life.

People did mad things. Stupid things. The world needed psychologists more than it ever needed lawyers.

The litany in her head stopped. She pushed open her garden gate into the shadows of her garden. Was only briefly aware of a larger, deeper shadow before...

'Grace!'

The sound she made was so loud and so terrified, he had to clap his hand over her mouth.

'Darling, my darling. It's only me. Your Richard.'

But his words only seemed to make her struggle more. Perhaps, thought Richard, it was the dark that had frightened her. Her own fault, then, for coming home so late, forcing him to wait, here, in the chill shadows of a hedge. Whatever the reason, terror had made her blind and deaf. And struggling. It meant he had to keep the hand where it was, over her mouth, even though she was fighting so hard to scream she was spraying his palm with spit, so on top of everything else he was burdened with the urge to take the hand away and wipe it against the backs of his trousers.

Then he saw her eyes, wide in the moonlight – well, lamplight – and the distaste vanished, leaving him with this surprising realisation: he didn't mind having her mouth wet against his hand. It was like snubbing your hand against a puppy's maw while it struggles to escape.

Delighted, he smiled into those wide eyes. Such terrified eyes, so liquid and blind it made him wonder what Flaubert would have done with them. 'My dearest Grace,' he murmured. 'Look at me. Look who it is. See?'

And slowly, very slowly, she began to recognise him, and he felt some of the terror leave her. Almost disappointed that such a moment had to pass, he loosened the hand against her mouth.

No fear of her shouting now. She had to struggle even to whisper.

'You!'

'Yes, I!'

He found one of her hands and raised it to his lips. 'Frozen' he chuckled fondly. 'Absolutely icy. My poor little Grace, I have frightened you. Can you ever forgive me?'

To his amusement, she shook her head. Not meaning it of course. Already she would be asking herself what he was doing here. Hardly daring to hope that he, Richard Ortega, had come all this way for her, pursuing her as the huntsman pursues his prey. As the lover pursues his love.

Looking into her face he could see it for himself – wild hope pulsating under the skin. Trying to hide it from him. Trying to hide it from herself. How like his Grace, and how touching! More touching even than he could have expected.

He found himself reaching for her other hand.

This time though, she resisted. He tugged, but the hand stayed where it was, clenched against her chest. And it only showed how well his instinct served. The small tussle signalled that everything was true; she was fighting, immersed in a war with herself.

And yet again it touched him, so that he felt softer, more enchanted than ever.

'Don't,' he said tenderly. 'Don't try to fight it, Grace. You know this is meant to be. My darling, my peach, we have been dancing round each other. Too fearful to act. But distance is our teacher, separation the spur. Now we know. We should never have been apart.'

Again she struggled, lips moving to find the words to answer him.

'Darling, don't ... don't say anything. Let me find the words.'

Softly he put a finger to her lips, meaning for it to linger there. Meanwhile, as if on a frolic of its own his other hand rose in search of her breasts and found them, warm under something knitted. Soft. He smiled as he heard her gasp, and under his finger felt her lips begin to part.

Reassuring in its way. It had been a long time, after all, since he'd actually...

Then it was his turn to gasp. Grace's lips had parted only to bite. Not playfully, not by accident, but savagely and with intent – small, well-brushed teeth driving without warning into the soft inky pad of his forefinger, so hard they pierced the skin. Giving him such a shock of pain he couldn't even find the breath to scream.

She released the finger and took a step back.

'Why ... Grace,' he said. His voice was mild, still too surprised for anger. He took a step of his own, towards her.

'Don't... Stay where you are.' Her voice was shaking.

And still he couldn't seem to find a trace of anger towards her. Bewildered, he raised his wounded hand, trying to detect the damage in the dark. Already his finger had begun to swell, with a throbbing rhythm that matched his pulse. Painful – yet not unpleasant. Stranger still, as Richard stood in the dark, he was aware of other parts of him coming to life with an answering throb of their own. Head, heart, chest, throbbing. And not just there. Elsewhere, further down in the pit of his stomach, he had begun to throb. Down, and further down even than that...

Throbbing and swelling. As he hadn't throbbed and swelled in so long.

And Grace had done this to him. With her

sharp little teeth. Grace who was cleverer than she looked. Good at games after all. He sniffed at her perfume in the dark. A steady pulse in his finger and a steadier pulse in his groin. Thoughtful, he put his finger in his mouth and let the blood trickle down his throat.

It was only other people's fluids that bothered him.

'Why Grace,' he said again softly. And moved towards her.

He heard her gasp again, and make as if to bolt. Nothing loath he bolted after her, but as he did, he tripped. Yet his mind, also, was moving fast, and as he began to fall it reminded him of what needed to be done. He flung out his arms and wrapped them round her legs bringing her down with him, under him. One smooth movement which was a piece of poetry in itself. For a fleeting moment it even occurred to him: they couldn't have asked for more on the playing fields of St Olave's.

Then he forgot St Olave's. Grace was struggling beneath him. Like a nymph. Like a dryad caught in the woods. Like Galatea captured at the moment she came to life. As for Richard, he was Zeus himself. Or better, a young Dionysus about to take what was his. Now it was all his blood that throbbed, singing in his veins. Filled with joy, he wanted to raise his head and howl at the lamplight. Half God, half man.

Entirely Richard Ortega.

But then there was the problem with Grace. So clever after all. So clever in many ways. But so stupid in others. Didn't she realise that, sometimes, discretion is the word? If she made half the noise she clearly wanted to, she'd have her husband out, head bowed under the weight of a cuckold's horns. It's why Richard had to lock his hand so carefully about her mouth, while the other hand groped and fumbled with an armoury of clothes.

And here was another problem, the sheer stubbornness of the twenty-first-century curse: panty hose.

Yet despite the obstacles, Richard ploughed on, so happy he could have howled, every part of him alive, throbbing and moving. Happy right up to the moment that...

Chapter Twenty–Four

Grace stood inside her dark house shivering. Shivering all over. Then in a terrible moment of remembering she ran to the door, which she had forgotten to bolt; after that, running from door to window to door, checking every lock and catch.

All closed. Safe. Her house a bulwark against the mad.

Upstairs her family were sleeping. Simon was sleeping. In a minute she would have to go and wake him, tell him there was a man lying in their garden, unconscious but breathing. Although even the breathing hadn't sounded the way it should. When her hand had found the stone from the rockery and brought it down onto the side of his head, he hadn't cried out or gasped. He had merely stopped what he was doing, then rolled off her and begun to snore loudly.

What if he stopped breathing? What if she had killed him?

She stood again, thinking. Not shaking so much now. That was good. When the shaking stopped completely, she would go upstairs. That way she would be calm when she woke Simon and told him about the man lying in the garden. The man she had been seeing in secret for weeks.

She sent her hands over her body, exploring. Her clothes were wet. He had brought her down where the flower beds gave onto lawn, next to the rockery. She could smell the mud and grass trapped in the fibres. But that was all. He had never found his way past her tights, hands tangled in the swathes of her skirt. Snorting and grunting in her ear while he struggled. His body pinning hers where she lay. Later, in bed, she imagined she would feel the weight of him again. Feel his hands, a pair of stupid, blind animals trying to burrow, useless as moles in AstroTurf. Her own hands fell away. What had he left her with? Disgust. Shame. Anger. Fear of repercussion. She waited for the rest.

Waited. And it didn't come. Nothing.

Is that all the effect he had had? Had he even frightened her? Properly frightened her?

It should have been a stupid question. She was standing, shivering as if in fear; teeth chattering as if in fear. But she smelt the mud and it seemed to her that terror, real terror, had come – and then gone. The moment she'd recognised him the fear had melted away, leaving only anger that he had followed her and frightened her. But what about after? He had tried to rape her. Hadn't that terrified her? She thought about the struggle on the ground, tried to remember.

His hands had fumbled and groped and yet she hadn't been afraid. His body had been a vast weight, stronger, heavier. *And yet she hadn't been afraid.* Why? Grace shivered in her dark house and tried to understand.

Then she did understand. Because while he had snorted and grunted and groped, something else had grown inside her – contempt. So strong it had overridden fear, banished helplessness. Contempt had sent her hand reaching for the stone. Rage allowed her to bring it down with all the strength in her arm.

Contempt. Rage. Disgust. She knew why she was shaking now. Rage at herself, at her own stupidity. And blindness. *This* was the man she had kept secret all these weeks, like an accomplice, like a lover. This was the man she would have to wake and tell Simon about. And after Simon, the police.

She would have to tell the police.

Shivering for another reason, too. Because she knew what Simon would say, even if all he said was nothing. She would tell him about the man lying in their garden and they would be back at the beginning, the two of them. As if all these months had counted for nothing. And then what? After Simon knew about Richard Ortega, how long would it be until they slept as they had been sleeping these past weeks, arms around each other? In love with each other.

In trust with each other.

Upstairs she took off her muddy clothes and threw them in the laundry with Rob's rugby kit. On second thoughts, she got them out again and bundled them into the rubbish bin. Then she climbed into bed, lay down beside her husband. Without waking, he rolled over and took her in his arms.

I'll wake him, she told herself. Any minute now I'll wake him and tell him. Then the police. Who would say she had brought it on herself. Would Simon say the same?

The clock with its alarm clicked the minutes and hours, and she didn't wake him.

She lay until the light came back under the curtains. And still she didn't wake him. Half an hour till the alarm. Sliding out from under the duvet, Grace went to the window and looked out. The garden was empty. Only a shallow indentation in the grass beside the rockery to show that anyone had been there.

He had gone. Unable to trust her eyes she ran downstairs and into the garden. But there was nothing, not on the lawn, not on the path. Only an old plastic chair and an empty whisky bottle that someone must have thrown over the hedge.

There came a noise from above, of a window opening. Anna looked out, jet black hair, recently dyed, tumbling round her face.

'What are you doing? Aren't you cold?'

Grace was standing on the dewy dawn grass in nothing but bare feet and a slip.

'No,' Grace said happily. 'Not cold at all. Not even a little bit.'

She blew a kiss at her daughter and ran inside. He had gone. She had seen the last of Richard Ortega. Life could begin again.

Richard slumped into his seat, trying to find

a position to suit the ache in his limbs. He knew people on the 06.45 to Marylebone were staring at him, but he didn't care. His head throbbed. A different kind of throb from last night. Yet even now, thinking of last night, a smile began to spread across his face, mingling with the detritus of mud and blood.

Who would have thought that Grace, little Grace, had such fire in her? Such spirit. But then again, what else should he have expected? He had made her. Moulded her. Never realising in his modesty how well he had moulded her.

He rubbed his aching head and tried again to remember how he had come by it – the throb in his skull. For some reason he couldn't remember. A touch too much firewater. Bacchus nodded. It didn't matter. Everything else about the night was clear. The singing in his blood, her body squirming beneath his body. The smell of mud and crushed grass as though the gods themselves had come down to kiss the good earth.

Above all he remembered Grace. Eyes wide above his quietening hand. Little Grace, with her sharp, clean little teeth. Next time he would have to spank her. He had the feeling she would love it.

Chapter Twenty-Five

He was lying in the bath with a glass in his hand when the doorbell rang. The first two rings he ignored. The third made him sit up. What if it was Grace?

But of course it was Grace. Had to be. Such a flame had passed between them, how could it not be her? Richard Ortega heaved himself out of the water and ran for the door, flinging it open wide.

'My God, Richard...'

Patsy had endured a lot from her authors, but not this – to be greeted by one, dripping wet and naked except for a single beaming smile. Which vanished as he set eyes on her. But then she forgot to be amazed. She had seen the wound on his temple, the scratches on his neck and all over his face. This was a man who had been beaten and mauled, as if by something wild.

Or mad.

'Oh no,' she whispered. 'Oh my dear, what has she done to you?' She could feel the sob rising in her throat.

But Richard seemed incapable of answering. He was staring at her, a look of utter confusion in his face. Frowning as if trying and failing to make the necessary connections in his mind.

'Richard ... it's me, Patsy. Don't you recognise me?'

He gave a start. 'Yes, Patsy. Of course. Patsy.' Then continued to stand in the open door, still naked, still dripping.

'My God,' Patsy said softly. 'You're concussed. My poor Richard. My poor boy.'

She took his arm and guided him back inside the hall, gently, exactly the way she guided her Merlin about their own house, from room to empty room, every day of their lives.

She found a towel and wrapped it around him, and then a blanket. Made him a cup of tea and filled it with sugar. She would have given him brandy, but who knew what was safe when someone has been injured as he had been injured?

She poured herself a brandy though. Setting it beside her as she knelt at his feet, cradling his hands with her own.

'What happened, Richard?'

He shook his head. Touched the wound.

'Are you saying you don't remember?'

He nodded.

'But *she* did this?'

He hesitated then shrugged. And that was all the answer she needed.

She stood up. 'I'm going to phone the police.' Only to sigh as again he shook his head. 'Who then? Someone has to know.'

He considered a moment. 'Regina,' he said finally. 'Friends,' he added by way of explanation.

Patsy sighed again, moved as much as she was frustrated. It always came back to this. Here was the man she had judged so sharply, who turned out to want nothing but his friends. She left him to find the phone. Moments later, he could hear her in another room, speaking to these same friends; to Regina, to Max, to Miriam, keeping her voice low, telling them how finally it had happened, the thing they had always feared. The violence of the mad.

Carefully Richard disengaged one arm from the blanket in which she had swaddled him. When he had flung open the door he had been almost unmanned by disappointment. More than disappointment. For a moment he had had to battle against the urge to throttle her simply for not being Grace.

But needs must. By a superhuman effort of will he had resisted, and let her have her way with him. Not such a bad thing for her to be here. He had almost forgotten the reason for everything. Patsy had made him remember.

Sometimes a writer...

With his free hand he bent to the floor and took a good slug of the brandy, then wrapped himself up, exactly the way Patsy had left him.

She came bustling back into the room. She looked defiant. 'Now don't be cross with me, Richard. I've phoned the police, one of the two who were here. He gave me his number in case something like this happened. He says you have to make a complaint, otherwise all he can do is put it on the record. It's something, but not enough.'

But Richard barely seemed to hear her. Now Patsy had a sense that he was somewhere else entirely, lost in memory. She shivered, imagining a nightmare where madness and pity went head to head. She reached for the glass of brandy and swallowed it, wished she had given herself more.

And indeed Richard had scarcely noticed she was back. He was indeed somewhere else, a better place, smelling of mud and grass. A place where a man could be himself, and howl for sheer joy. A place he wanted, needed, to return to as quickly as possible.

Suddenly he sat bolt upright.

'Patsy,' he said. His voice was normal. 'I need you to go. Now.'

She gasped. 'Go? Why?'

'I have to write something. Have to.'

'Richard, you've just been attacked. You need to rest.' She caught her breath. 'Unless … unless you're going to write about *her?*'

There was a silence. Slowly Richard said: 'Sometimes a writer, if he is a true writer, is compelled to write true...'

There, they were out. Words spoken aloud for the first time. Words that needed to be consigned to the page. And immediately Patsy understood. Already she was scrambling to her feet, hurrying to be out of his way as Richard, wrapping the blanket around him like a toga, made his way to his writing table.

Watching him sit down, Patsy had a sense of history about to be made. Here was a man mired in the madness of another. The same madness that was inflicted on innocent others every day. And now he was about to write about it. Make sense of it. For the first time, all those innocent others might find they had a voice.

Maybe his time had come. Richard Ortega was about to make his mark.

She tiptoed to the door and let herself out, closing it as quietly as she could.

Back at his desk, Richard's hand hovered. The page lay beneath him, white and unstained. A single stroke of the pen and it would bear his mark forever, like a woman's flesh.

Grace's flesh.

He had never seen Grace naked. The fire between them had prevented that. She had fallen and tumbled in the grass – a nymph

yielding to her shepherd. Passion had left no
time for niceties. Yet underneath the mons-
trosity of panty hose, what wonders lay to be
discovered? He allowed himself to imagine
Grace's flesh – white and gleaming as the
page under his hand. Unstained. Never
mind that she was twenty years married.
Grace, *his* Grace, was like a statue, perfectly
formed, but not alive, not yet. Something
else was needed to turn her into a woman.
A divine spark.

The spark of Ortega.

Richard's hand began to shake. He needed
to see Grace naked. See what it was that he
had made for himself, from himself. Like a
New Adam, discover every inch of that unseen flesh and in discovery make it his own.
He wouldn't even want to touch it. Her. Not
immediately. After though, passion, the
singing in the blood, could take flight. Carry
them both away.

First he had to see her.

White flesh. Unstained. His pen hovered
over the page, then slowly came down – but
only to write a letter. Not ready yet, not for
the greater thing.

'Present for you,' said Grace passing something across the breakfast table to Anna.

It was Alicia Milagro's newest book, the
last volume of her autobiography. Anna
thought a moment, then pushed the book

back to Grace.

'You read it first. She would want you to.'

'Who?' asked Simon from behind the newspaper.

'No one,' said Anna automatically. But from under Goth-black hair she smiled at Grace. Meanwhile, from the hall came the sound of mail falling heavily through the letter box.

It was followed by Rob with a pile of envelopes, which he flopped beside Grace's cup.

'Must be your birthday.' He'd been saying the same thing every morning for a fortnight, repetitive as an old man with a single joke.

More information was arriving for her, each batch of mail containing more prospectuses, more opportunities. A week ago, after the assault, she had been frightened that she would lose this new desire to learn. She imagined coming back again and again to the struggle in the garden, the smell of mud and grass; imagined the thoughts hitting her, driving out other thoughts.

But it didn't happen. She hardly thought of him at all. A man had attacked her and yet he seemed to occupy no space in her mind. No purchase there whatsoever.

She might as well have been attacked by a dog. The sort that comes up to you with its tongue hanging out – then tries to carry out gross sexual acts against your leg. The kind of dog that gives dogs a bad name. An old, oversexed dog who shouldn't be let out. You might want to have it put down, but you wouldn't dwell on it.

Grace didn't dwell either, was astonished that she didn't dwell. Richard Ortega flitted in and out of her mind as briefly as a whiff of something rotten. But that was all. He was gone, and life was here – with Simon and Anna and Rob with his single jokes, and now these puddles of envelopes, each offering a possibility of something. A life.

It had turned out she was right. Apparently all the world wanted to train psychologists. All she needed to do was find the fees.

She read through three pages from the Open University, handed them to Simon. More information from Bath. Impossible to get to, unless she actually left home.

She opened another envelope, this one from Oxford Brookes. Closer. Much closer. Grace closed her eyes and weighed the practicality; sitting behind the wheel, headed up the M40. A lone woman in a car with the world ahead of her. How long would it take her – an hour, less?

She handed that to Simon too, without saying anything. But she was beginning to see how it could be, the exact way forward. Up the M40 to a new future.

She came to the final envelope, smaller than the rest, but better quality. Heavy white paper marked in heavy black ink, as if a dean himself had decided to reply. Grace opened it, and began to read. Then she stopped reading and started to stuff the pages back into the envelope.

'Well?' said Simon. 'What's that one offering?'

She forced herself to look at him. 'Nothing. It's junk.' She hesitated. 'Time-shares, that's what it's offering.'

She waited till everyone had taken their eyes off her. Then she went upstairs.

The letter was from Richard. Eight pages of black, flowing script. She sat on her bed and began once more to read, but hearing movement downstairs, she stood up and went to the bathroom, locked the door.

No one must ever be allowed to see this letter.

Richard had spent six days composing it, adding, subtracting, crossing out. Polishing it until it was perfect. Only when he was satisfied did he copy it all out again, remembering to include the odd error with its own line carefully drawn through, making it look like the first and only draft, emerging fully formed from under his hand.

It told her what he would do with her when they met again. An inventory of invention, it employed all his imagination so that nothing need be left to hers; a list of pornographic acts, each one lovingly described. Times. Positions. Locations. Detail within detail of an erotic journey into regions unknown. After the first greeting, he ceased to call her by her name. In the pages that followed she became his belle-buttocked Beatrice, his juicy Justine, his lascivious Laura. He knew that none of the names would mean anything to her (the idea of Grace reading the Marquis de Sade? Laughable). They were there for Posterity, for when others would read these pages.

Let nothing be wasted. As he wrote Richard knew this was a letter that would survive in the cannon, a masterpiece of the erotic. He closed his eyes at the ends of sentences, smiled at his future readers: sweaty-palmed students of literature vibrating at their carrels; aged reverends distracted from their sermons; schoolgirls passing copies round the dorm. Richard wrote and polished and honed, knowing that every anthology which collected this letter would fall open at the page that began 'My darling Grace...'

Grace read it to the end, then lifted the toilet lid on which she was sitting and began to retch.

When she had recovered, she lit the aromatherapy candle at the end of her bath, a present from Deborah. Scents of ylang

ylang mingled with the scorching smell of paper as she gathered up the ashes and flushed them away.

A day went by. Two days. Three.

In Richard's flat the phone had stopped ringing. Word had got round, Patsy had made sure of it. Ortega was writing. No one disturbed him. Once, the doorbell rang while he was on the lavatory but by the time he had pulled up his trousers and run to the door, there was no one there. Only a vast Fortnum and Mason's hamper and a note from Regina:

Dear Richard – to stop the cupboard from going bare while you toil.

Richard dragged the hamper into his hall and opened it. Plunging both hands into a sea of polystyrene nuggets, he came up with a bottle of port and a kilner jar of hare's paté. He prised open both and took them back to his writing desk where he mined the paté with a paper knife and drank the port decanted into a mug. And continued to wait.

The first day he had been patient, understanding that a woman like Grace would hardly know what to do with a letter such as his. Small hands shaking as she read it again and again. The same hands reaching for the family stationery to inscribe some kind of message. Trying and failing to find the right words. Wasting valuable time as she threw away her efforts. Making him wait.

This is what she still had to learn: there was no need for words. Not from her. The script was all written. He had even told her so, in terms, at the end of the letter.

Write to me, my darling. Three words will do. 'I am yours' *are all a lover needs to hear.* That's all she had to say. *I am yours.* Write the fucking words and send them to him. How difficult was that?

Three days now. Richard Ortega stared at the empty page in front of him. *Sometimes a writer...*

Sometimes a writer is beset with obstacles. Kept from his labours by the smallness, the stubbornness of others. By characters who refuse to lie flat on the page. Who don't seem to know what's expected. Some things have to be done for them. Richard swallowed the last of the port, and sighed for the task ahead of him.

The phone rang and straightaway Grace dropped the plate she was holding. It fell with a crash onto the kitchen floor and shattered.

Rob nodded with approval. 'Can I do that or do I have to wash my plate like everyone else?'

But Grace hardly heard him. The phone continued to ring, as if to weave itself into the fabric of her thoughts. Thoughts she didn't own or want, but arrived anyway, occupying her so fully that any sound could make her jump, guilty, as if afraid to be caught thinking...

A man had attacked her physically, and left barely a trace of himself. Now the same man had written to her, and everything had changed. Richard Ortega was smeared across her mind like a trail of mud, permanent as a stain. Words – read only the once then burnt – had survived with a dirty half-life of their own. Thoughts to drive out other thoughts, more powerful than actions, planted like tiny alien seeds that thrived with every attempt to stamp on them.

She listened, briefly distracted as Anna settled into a conversation with a friend, arranging lifts for Rob and herself. But the thoughts came flooding back, returning as they always did – as pictures of herself, the Grace of Richard's imagination. A Grace who cavorted and simpered as though in reels of a film made by an elderly director, one whose fantasies revolved around food and playing fields and bottoms. Frilly knickers and a touch of light spanking. She had stepped into Richard's mind where every scene was made by him. Now she couldn't escape.

Nothing to do but wait for the images to wane. Because surely that was what would happen. Gradually the words would fade and the pictures vanish, the way a book loses its power to disturb. She told herself this was how it would be; all she had to do was wait. Only a question of time.

Surely.

Chapter Twenty-Six

Richard looked around him and sighed at the lengths to which he was forced to go.

He was in a different room from before, and yet it was identical. Wafer thin walls that could barely carry the weight of the framed prints of little boys cuddling puppies and little girls cuddling kittens. Bug-eyed and pointy-eared all of them – animals and children. If they hadn't been stapled in position, he'd have turned them to the wall.

He was back in the hotel.

He cleared the dressing table of the kettle and complimentary biscuits and replaced them with a bottle of sherry and a bottle of champagne, both from the hamper. Positioned a sheaf of paper beside them and a pot-bellied bottle of ink. Now he had everything, except the one thing he needed.

The reason he was here.

He sighed again, and lay down on the bed.

The truth was he was tired. It was taking it out of him, this rolling act of creation. Did Flaubert, did Tolstoy need to breathe so much of themselves into their women, their creatures of the imagination? Richard frowned, ready to be angry with Grace as he so often was angry. Then he remembered the scents of mud and grass and the frown disappeared. Of course it had been easier for Flaubert. What could have been simpler to create than foolish Emma? As for Anna Karenin – the woman had a death wish. All anyone had to do for her was write it down.

But Grace, his Grace, was a more complicated character. More ... rounded. *Nuanced* would have to be the word for her. Richard shifted on the bed, and let his mind wander, moving from the Grace in the garden to the Grace in his letter. The Grace who danced, hot-cheeked and rounded, from one position to the next. Warmer than Anna K, more alive than Emma. Naughtier than both with her small sharp teeth.

Creating Grace was a complicated, glorious, labour of love.

Richard smiled, allowed his head to sink into the all too shallow depths of his hotel pillow. He began to snore. Tennis balls thudded past his ear, but he didn't try to chase them now. Nor did they wake him. Even in his dreams Richard Ortega had greater things on his mind.

When it was dark, he woke, feeling rested and ready for what he had to do. Drank Fortnum and Mason champagne as he showered in the waterproof box they called the bathroom, switching to Fortnum and Mason sherry as he dressed. Before leaving he looked in the mirror, seeing what Grace would see later. Richard Ortega, writer. His eyes hooded yet wise, enquiring yet playful. As for the nail marks raking his cheeks, she would know exactly what had caused those and he imagined the shudder of guilt and pleasure that would shake her as she remembered.

Watching the house, he had a pleasant surprise. In the course of half an hour every person inside it left – except for Grace. The boy and girl (had she always had black hair?) left together, answering the summons of a horn from the road. The husband went clutching a sports bag and some kind of racquet in a cover. Too small for tennis. Badminton? Richard's lip curled.

Grace waved them all off as they went. Richard watched her closely, looking for signs. And there were indeed signs. As the husband closed the gate behind him, she continued to stand in the door, staring at nothing.

Now.

Richard stirred, about to emerge from his

hiding place in the bush, but in the same moment, like a woman waking from a forbidden dream, she gave a start and closed the door.

Richard frowned. Once again she had been swallowed up by the house, set against him now as it had been before. A bulwark against the world. Inside the house, Grace could only be trapped, kept from him, like whatzhername – Rapunzel, that was it – in her fucking tower. Even if he made her come to the door, the house would still exert a tug, holding her back from her true nature, binding her to itself. Ah, the truth of fairy stories.

Then he remembered. He had the key. Rifled from her bag the day she had sat weeping in his room. A visionary act, anticipating such a day as this. He could use the key now, take himself over the threshold. Surprise her, watch her face change as, expecting the husband or the poisonous child, instead she laid eyes on *him*, Richard Ortega. Lover. Suitor. Shock turning to joy as she understood.

He smiled, seeing it all in his mind's eye.

Then once more he frowned. Something not quite right. The instinct of a writer warning of a scene not working the way it should. He looked again, and straightaway he knew what was wrong. The house. The house surrounded her, a cage within a cage. Everything in it a reminder, a tie. The house would smother her natural reactions, muffle the joy so it turned to something else. And worse, having dealt with. Grace, it would turn its attention to him. Every object, every ridiculous photograph, every stick of furniture, becoming aware of him, vibrating like bees waking up to the wasp in their hive. Something to be destroyed.

He shuddered at the thought. A house with a mind, a purpose of its own. A dangerous place.

No. He needed her to come outside.

How? He got up and walked around, confident that here he was safe. Here, in the garden. The garden was where they had found each other. He carried the memory of it in his nostrils. Here he strolled, savouring the tang of mud and grass, and considered how she should join him.

Then from the other side of the house he heard the noise of another door opening, followed by the metal sound of a dustbin lid. Galvanised he raced to follow the noise, but already it was too late. There came the sound of the lid being replaced and the door closing.

He found himself below the kitchen window and ducked. Grace was on the other side of the glass, staring out, hands busy. She was doing the dishes – or supposed to be. But her face gave her away, thoughts scudding across her features, one after the other.

And thinking she was alone, Grace blushed. That blush. It knocked the strength from him. Stamping on his heart what he had always known. She was exquisite. His dairymaid Grace. He would crush strawberries in his mouth and feed them to her.

He needed her. Now. Outside. He forced himself to think. He could bang on the door, front or back; but like an enemy the house was there.

Then it came to him, the solution. A way it could be done. Returning to his place in the hedge he took out his mobile and dialled her number, watching the house as he heard it ring. He could actually see her through the frosted glass of the hall window, a slim figure hurrying to answer the phone.

'Mrs Waites?'

'Yes?'

'Mrs Grace Waites?'

Irish. He'd decided to be Irish, like the nanny who had been kindest to him all those years ago. Kindness being a relative term. He could think of others who...

'Yes?'

'Ah, very good. We were afraid there'd be no answer. We have a situation here, Mrs Waites. Nothing we'd want to frighten you with. That's not what we're here for. But we have a couple of kids in the back.'

'In the back of what?'

'Sorry. In the back of the ambulance.

There's been an accident. The girl's conscious – just – but the boy's not.'

He heard the gasp of shock. 'Ambulance? Why ambulance? Oh my God, what's happened?'

'We'll fill you in when we see you. What's lucky is, according to the young lady, we're just coming to your street, going right past your house. Or we will be in a minute. If you want to be outside and waiting, we'll stop for you. Otherwise you can just follow on in your own time.'

'No!' Grace's voice was wild. 'No, take me with you. Only, won't you please tell me what...'

'Just get yourself outside, Mrs Waites. We're in what's called the golden hour. Got to get to the hospital quick as we can.'

Richard shut off the phone and waited. Seconds later Grace came running out of the house, wearing the same slippers as on that day in the bookshop. Silly Grace, *his* Grace – no more sense now than then. Richard's face was tender as he watched her come to a halt at the pavement, snowmen waggling just as they had all those weeks ago. She had a mobile phone clamped to her ear.

'Simon!' He could hear her. 'Pick up. Pick up the phone.'

But Simon would be busy playing with his toy racquet. Not big enough for tennis. Not there when she needed him. Not like him, Richard. And suddenly he had an idea. Soft-hearted and romantic. Something to make her smile when all had been explained.

He crept out of the hedge and back up the path towards the house. She hadn't even closed the front door. He closed it for her now, knowing that a woman who forgot her shoes would never remember a key to get back in. You might have said Fate was doing his work for him – but Fate had nothing to do with it. This was Grace, *his* Grace, merely acting in the character she was created for.

On the doorstep he laid the present he had brought for her then stood back to wait, hidden by an ornamental bay tree.

Out on the pavement, Grace was sobbing beneath her breath. The street was empty, its silence mocking her. She waited for the sound of sirens, strained for the distant flash of lights and there was nothing. She waited and she waited and still there was nothing. In contrast to the surrounding peace, her mind was a clash of noise and light. A cacophony of brakes, images of children and metal and tarmac.

Where was the ambulance? Where were her children? She punched Simon's number into his phone and still there was no answer.

Ten minutes passed, and she didn't know what to do. Except this: in despair she tried Anna's number. Just as she expected, there was no answer. And then...

'Yeah?'

'Anna?'

'Yeah.'

'*My* Anna?'

'Mum, is that you?'

Grace could hear music in the background, some kind of rap.

'Anna, what's happened? Where are you? Where's Rob?'

'Here.'

'Where's *here?* Darling, tell me. Tell me everything.'

There was a pause. 'Tell you what? Nothing's happened. We're just where we said we would be. At Bar Medee. Remember?'

Grace felt her head begin to swim. 'You're not in an ambulance?'

'No.'

'And you haven't been in an accident?'

'God no.'

'You're safe? Not hurt?'

'No. Mum – what's the matter, why are you talking to me like this?'

'Because someone just told me that you'd been in an accident. Anna, did you get someone to play a trick on me? Or Rob...' she could feel her voice rising. 'Is this Rob's doing?'

'No! Bloody hell, what do you think we are?' Anna snapped. Then she stopped. When she spoke again, her voice was gentle.

'Someone's done something horrible, but it's not us. Never us. Shall I come home? You sound terrible. Frightened.'

Grace let out a sigh and looked around her. The empty street with its quiet pools of light seemed a blessing to her now. They were safe. Her children were safe. No accident. No ambulance. Suddenly she could breathe again. 'No,' she said finally. 'It's all right. Everything's all right. You stay out. Enjoy yourselves.'

Then she sat down on the old garden chair that someone had put under the hedge and began to cry.

For a moment Richard was tempted to go to her there, but stopped himself. These sorts of tears were no good to him. He recognised them for what they were, leakages of pure joy. Not what was required. So he waited where he was, close to the front door. Sooner or later she would need to come back inside.

Ten minutes and Grace wiped her eyes, smiled at the snowmen at the ends of her feet. Everything felt better, washed away. Even the mud trails in her mind. They were safe, her children were safe. Nothing else mattered, not any more.

She stood up and walked briskly to her door – and it was closed, which meant she was locked out, in the dark, in her slippers. But even this didn't matter. Nothing mattered. At the same time, from ground level the snowmen nodded to her, drawing attention to something else, next to the door.

A box of chocolates.

Grace stared. Head still swimming with relief, she couldn't remember if there was a reason for them to be there. She bent to pick them up.

Fortnum and Masons. Immediately she dropped them, as if they had burnt her and stood up straight. Alert now. There was only one person, one person in the world...

She stared up at her house, her empty house. But it was deaf to her, its curtained windows blind. She tried to remember what was behind her. A path, a hedge, a gate. In front of her, a door, still visible to the road. *She* was still visible. And in her hand a phone, its small light a beacon. She raised it to her face...

'No need to phone me, my darling. I am here.'

She didn't turn round, refused to turn round. Yet she could feel him, close to her, his body all but touching hers. She forced the calm into her voice, face still turned to her house as she answered.

'I wasn't about to phone you. I was phoning my husband. Telling him to come home.'

Behind her, Richard laughed gently. 'But my darling, he won't hear you. He's too busy chasing after those shuttle things. Or *says* he is – and we know what that means, alas. Whatever he's doing, he's ignored your phone call twice already.'

And she shuddered, because she knew he'd been there, listening. He knew she was alone.

'Go away,' she said. 'Fuck off.'

'My letter...'

'I burnt your letter.'

He chuckled. 'Sweet Grace of mine. Sweet, dirty, little Grace.' And he moved closer still, hand reaching to close that sweet, clumsy mouth that should never be trusted with words.

Scream. She needed to scream. But when she tried, the noise came from somewhere deep, deep in her throat; revulsion shutting off the noise where terror would have allowed her to scream. She should have screamed before, when she saw the chocolates, when she felt his breath on her neck. She should have screamed for her life. And now it was too late. Richard's hand closed around her face like a lover's. From the road, still visible to anyone passing, they would look like lovers.

Not lovers. Never lovers. But it was too late. She remembered his weight on her body, pressing her into the mud, and knew exactly how it would be. Nothing to save her now...

'What's *he* doing here?'

A voice, young and clear and cold, seemed to cut through the air behind them. Richard's hand dropped away. He despaired. The daughter, always the fucking daughter. Always there, like a leech. The one who would take him on. He turned, already summoning the necessary smile. But seeing the set of that small sharp face, he felt his cheek muscles freeze, and decided not even to try.

Instead he sighed and turned to Grace. '*You're* going to have to deal with this, my dear. There is only so much a man can do, even for Cupid's sake. Perhaps you would like to take the child aside and have a word. The first of many perhaps ... woman to woman.'

There was a silence. In a voice as clear as her daughter's, Grace said, 'Get your phone out, Anna. Dial 999. Tell them it's an emergency. Tell them,' she paused. 'Tell them there's a man here who will not go away. Dangerous. Tell them we need the police. Now.'

Anna nodded and took out her phone. But Richard was keeping his gaze for Grace. Quietly he said, 'You would do this to me, Grace. *To me?*'

'Make sure they know it's not a prank,' Grace continued steadily. 'Make sure they know it's real.'

Slowly Richard shook his head. Generous enough to be patient with her even now, his

296

sweet, foolish maid. 'Grace,' he murmured. 'Grace of my heart.'

And when she wouldn't look at him, he sighed again. 'You must do as you think fit. But have no fear, my sweet girl. Ortega understands. The creatures are not only in our minds. They are real, breathing demons. Flesh of your flesh, they want to suck the life from you, rob you of your youth. But you can fight them, my dear. Even they can be vanquished. And when you have beaten them, Ortega shall be waiting. Together we will live and love...'

'Fuck *off.*' Both women had spoken in unison.

A last sigh and Richard turned, devouring the modest amount of path that led from the modest front door with a weary stride.

Grace looked at Anna. Her daughter's face was expressionless. 'You know I want nothing to do with him. You understand that, don't you...?'

But Anna said nothing. The phone was there in her hand, but she had failed to punch any number. Not knowing what her mother wanted, not even certain she knew who her mother was.

So Grace reached and took the phone out of her hand, and dialled. When the voice answered she told it exactly what she wanted.

'Police. Now. We ... I ... need them now.'

Chapter Twenty-Seven

She might have known it would take a time. An age.

Long before the police arrived, Simon had come home and so had Rob. Time enough for Grace to take Simon into the kitchen and tell him.

Tell him what?

That she had been seeing a man in secret. A man who had listened and comforted. A man whose attentions she had welcomed. Sought out even. A man who called her darling and who had kept her a secret, just the way she had kept him a secret. A man who had nearly, very nearly, raped her. A man she hadn't told anyone about even then. A man who wrote long licentious letters that she hid. A man who...

...Meant nothing to her. It's what she told Simon. But even though the police took so long to arrive, still it was not long enough.

'So you were seeing him all those weeks,' Simon said. 'And you never said.'

'Only because you'd been seeing *her*.'

Her own words came automatically. Words that were inevitable, dragging them back to a past that was meant to be behind them.

Bringing it back to life.

Not enough time for anything. The bell rang and the police arrived, a man and a woman, stepping stiffly over the threshold; sitting down on her sofas, their uniforms making them seem outlandish, removed from real life.

She wanted to tell Simon to leave the room, and not be there when she tried to explain, all over again. She didn't want to see the expression in his eyes as, for a second time, she painted the progress of a friendship that had turned out to be no friendship at all.

What she had not expected was for Simon to stand up without a word, quitting the room scarcely before the officers had sat down, as if he couldn't bear to stay. As if he had already heard enough. Now, suddenly, all she had wanted was for him to stay.

The officers behaved as she expected, took notes as she spoke to them, starting with that first encounter at the bookshop while she skated, red-faced, over the state of mind that took her there. At first she thought it was helpful, the way neither of them interrupted. Then gradually, it struck her that they seemed oddly disengaged. More and more, she needed them to ask questions; without questions, the whole account was too thin, lacking depth. Almost lacking meaning. And when, faltering, she came to the first struggle in the garden, when she had finally understood what he wanted, their faces stayed expressionless. She could have been talking about the weather or state of the nation's roads.

She ground to a halt. Both officers remained silent, watching her.

'Well?' she offered uncertainly. 'What happens now? Are you going to arrest him? Do you need me to identify him or ... or something? I can write this all down,' she added eagerly. 'In fact, maybe it would be easier if I wrote it down. I could describe it all better...'

The woman officer interrupted. 'Could we see the letter? The one you described as obscene.'

Grace flushed. 'I burnt it. I had to. If anyone had seen it...'

The officers exchanged a look.

Something about that look made her feel uncomfortable. More than uncomfortable. She found herself getting to her feet. 'I think I'm going to ask my husband back into the room. He knows the story. He knows that I...' Then the words blurted out of her. '*He* believes me. He knows that man was here. He knows he attacked me once, and would have attacked me again. He believes me, which is good because I'm beginning to think you don't.'

'Mrs Waites.' The policewoman's voice was

300

cold. 'You can call your husband by all means. But you won't like what he'll have to hear.' She watched Grace. 'I think you should sit down again.'

Grace hesitated, then sat.

The male officer flipped back through his notebook. 'You see, it's like this. We've already heard rather a lot about you. We've been getting complaints, Grace. From all sorts of people.'

'Complaints? Who from?'

'Where do I start?' He glanced down at his book. 'Ms Patricia Jenkins, Ms Regina Forbes, Mr Timothy Weatherby – that's to say, Mr Weatherby's lawyers...'

'But I don't know any of these people!' Grace had jumped to her feet again. 'What possible complaint could any of them make about me?'

'...And of course, from Mr Ortega himself...'

'...*Richard?*'

'As it happens, Mr Ortega is the last on the list, the other persons all having made their complaints long before he did. You've been a busy girl, Grace, what with your ambushing, your door stepping, your nuisance calls, not to mention the odd violent attack and threat to kill. We could have arrested you three times over before now. The fact that we haven't is only due to the gentleman himself. Didn't want to make a fuss. He did, however, get the attending officers to flag your name, and that's what they did. The moment we typed it into the police computer – *voil*à.'He closed his notebook, triumphant. 'So you'll understand why we – what's a good way of putting this? – *are one hundred per cent unlikely to believe a single word you want to tell us.*'

He leant back against the sofa, her sofa. 'You're a stalker, Mrs Waites. A bunny boiler. A case for the funny farm. It's lucky for you we haven't come with a warrant for your arrest. Who knows, though? Carry on like you have and we might be back.'

Grace felt her mouth open and close. Like a fish. Like something that has never learnt to talk.

'I don't understand,' she whispered at last. 'What am I supposed to have done?'

And so they explained to her, chapter and verse, exactly what she had done. Places, names and witnesses, so there could be no doubt. And in so doing, they showed her how history can be transformed, simply and by adjustments, only by changing the angle of observation. Adding little or nothing. Taking away even less. Small incremental alterations – that change everything.

She saw how stories are made and characters created for everyone to believe in.

She saw what he had done.

'So what now? Are they going to arrest him?'

Simon's eyes, if not exactly hostile, were wary.

She forced herself to breathe, to answer him. 'No. If they had been going to arrest anyone, it was going to be me.'

'What?'

'He's convinced them I'm the one who's chasing him. No – not chasing – *stalking*, him.'

'You?' There was a silence as he took this in. She watched him steel himself. 'Have you? Is that what you've been doing?'

'For God's sake, Simon! No!'

'Is it a mistake then? A misunderstanding? Something you've done? Something about your behaviour?'

'No.' She could feel him, falling away from her. 'He's lying. Saying things about me and I don't know why. Right from the start, he's...'

'Right from the start, Grace? Right from the start of *what?* What's been going on? Why would he do it? Why make up those lies about you?'

And there it was, the question to which she had no answer. And having no answer, what else did she have to convince him?

Later they lay in bed, neither of them asleep. Hours and hours of not sleeping.

'What are you thinking?' she whispered finally.

For a long time he didn't answer. Perhaps he was never going to answer. Then:

'I'm thinking that you carried that book of his around for weeks. You had it on your lap that night I told you I wanted to stay. I remember wanting you to look at me, so I could tell you the things I needed to say, things I needed you to hear. But you were staring at him. At his face on the cover. I remember it now.'

Suddenly he gave a laugh. Harsh. 'You won't believe this. I actually read it, that book, that *bloody* book. Bought my own copy and everything.'

'You?'

'I thought it would help me know what you were thinking, because God knows, Grace, you weren't telling me. I had an affair, I finished it, I came back to you, and yet you just seemed to carry on like before. You didn't seem to want to know anything – why it had happened, why it was I was even tempted. Why I stayed. We'd been married twenty years, and you didn't seem to want to know a thing.

'Then I read the book. And it was all about a man who could see inside the heads of women. All this stuff about the girl inside, how she becomes invisible. And I thought that must have been what happened. That's what I'd done to you. Somehow trampled the girl inside. Killed you. My fault.'

He sighed. 'That book, it made me look at you, really look at you. It told me I should be looking *for* you – the Grace I remembered, the woman who took me on, all those years ago. I owed you that. It made me look at you. And finally, it made me see – you were still there. You hadn't gone away. People don't die or disappear, not when they're standing in front of you. They will always be the people that they were. But you can lose them, lose sight of them. And I saw how I could lose you. And I didn't want to lose you, Grace.'

'But you didn't,' said Grace softly. 'You didn't lose me.'

'No?' he said flatly. 'That's what's so bloody rich. That book of his, it made me come after you. Find you. At least,' his voice fell back into his pillow. 'At least I thought I'd found you. And all this time you...'

Grace held her breath. When he didn't say any more, she finished the sentence for him '...And all this time I was here, the same Grace. Not even a girl. Definitely not a girl. Just me. And I was so glad you came, that you looked for me. And found me. So happy...'

She stopped. In the dark they lay watching themselves as they had been over the last weeks. Watching themselves being happy. Two small, happy figures, getting smaller all the time, disappearing. Never to be seen again.

In desperation, she turned to him.

'Simon, nothing they say is true. I haven't done any of those things. I never wanted that man. Ever. It was you, only you. Can't you even try to believe me?'

But there was no answer. She had told him everything the police had told her, leaving nothing out. Names, dates, places. He would have tallied up the facts, the reasons for and against, an accounting sheet of evidence. And he didn't believe her. How could he believe her?

Wretched, she turned away. She had lost him. They had lost each other.

But then she felt it, a weight moving across her in the dark. A mouth so close to hers, she could feel the shapes of the words against her skin, as he told her:

'I don't have to try. I believe you. I don't know why he's doing this. I don't fucking know or understand anything about him. But I know you. And I believe you. I believe *you*, Grace. He's the liar. He's fooled everyone else, but he's not going to fool me.'

With that he closed himself around her, the man she had unsingled, who had thrown away his accounting skills and believed her. And the dark became warm again.

Chapter Twenty-Eight

'I don't know. You shouldn't be by yourself. Not today. I'll take the day off, stay home. Damn, we used up all the holiday. Never mind, I'll phone in sick...'

Simon was pacing the room, not dressed. Forgetting to dress. And tired. But most of all, anxious. Worried about her.

'Simon...'

'We could get Anna in on this. She's been there when he's approached you. She could tell them that. She could tell them what he said...'

'Simon...'

'He'll make up some story of course. Twist it round. And of course, with her being so young...'

'Simon.' She stood in front of him as he paced. 'Stop it.'

He looked at her, dazed, as if only now seeing her properly. Then he sighed. 'What can I do, Grace? What the hell can I do? I don't want to leave you by yourself. The man's dangerous. He...' his voice grew rough '...he wants you. He wants *you*.'

They stared at each other until Grace shook her head.

'I don't see how he can be dangerous. Not any more. What can he do? He can't touch me. He'd have to come here, back to the house. In fact, it would be a good thing if he did come – people would know he was a liar then. But he won't do that. He's a clever man. Too clever not to know he can't come back. Not ever. He has to let me go. There's nothing else he can do.'

Simon stared at her. He was trying to think.

She touched his chest. 'Get dressed. Go to work. Come home again. Let's just be normal, go back to the way we were. It's over. It has to be.' She held his gaze with hers. 'It has to be.'

And slowly, he relaxed. Because it was true. It had to be true.

But after he left, Grace sat at her kitchen table, hands crossed in her lap. Waiting. She had convinced Simon, but not herself. Never herself.

So she didn't even jump when it happened, when in the middle of the morning the phone began to ring. Just as she expected.

'Grace! Thank heaven you're there. What lengths have they forced you to? My poor, sweet Grace. How they must have hounded you, gnawed at you.'

'Who?'

'The creatures, the demons. But don't be

308

frightened, I understand. Never think I don't understand. A small lie, a subterfuge, these things are done to survive. Of course you had to call the police. Were they terribly clumsy, did they trample over your soft soul with their great hobnail boots? Was it awful?'

'Yes. Yes it was awful.' She heard her voice shake. 'So I'm asking you – why are you doing this, why did you make it happen? Why have you made people believe I'm some kind of mad woman? Why are you telling these lies?'

This, *this* was the reason she had picked up the phone. To know.

'Lie?' He spoke with wonder. 'Are you saying I have lied about you? Is that what they told you, my sweet, my passionate girl? Then shame on them. Yes, I have boasted of being the object of love, the subject of Cupid's mania. But lied about you? Never! Why should I lie, when I am proud? A woman's love is a precious bind, my Grace. And I am bound to you, as you have bound yourself to me...'

'But I haven't bound myself to you. I'm not in love. Not with you. Leave me alone, Richard.'

He chuckled at her denials. 'Ah Grace.' His voice was tender. 'I do believe I know you better than you know yourself. And we shall be together, you know, when the time is right. Nothing, not even the creatures, will keep us apart...'

She put down the phone. Took it off the hook. Then, feeling the sweat break out of her body, she ran around her house, checking locks, checking doors. Looking for the crack, the chink that would let him in.

Knowing he was already inside, there in her head. Not a door or lock in the world that would keep him out.

She heard the slam of the front door. Simon was home. Early, much earlier than she could have expected him. Almost stumbling in his panic. Relief giving way to anger when he saw her.

'Grace, what the hell happened? I've been ringing and ringing.' His eye fell on the phone, lying beside its cradle. 'You've taken it off the hook! Why? Didn't you realise what it would do to me, not being able to reach you?'

Then he saw her face, and understood. He tore off his jacket and threw it across the room, a man never given to such gestures. They watched it land, then slowly he walked to pick it up and fold it across a chair.

'OK.' He was calm now. 'We'll get the police onto this. Let them know he's coming at you again. We'll get him, Grace, we will.'

'It's no good.' Her voice was dull. 'They won't believe me. They'll say it's all part of the behaviour, the kind of thing we do, people like me. They said if I carried on, they would come back, and this time they would take me with them.'

His hand, already reaching for the phone, fell away.

She had to force him to go to work the next morning.

'I can't leave you.'

'You have to. We've got to keep going, be normal. Otherwise he's won. We can't stop living, shut ourselves up just because of him.'

But *she* could. She was beginning to see how she could. Waving everybody off as usual. Then closing the door and locking it. Finding good reasons to stay at home.

Letting weeds grow on the path.

Shivering as she put the rubbish out.

Every day the same. Days following days. The phone lay off the hook all the time now. *Just keep your mobile with you*, Simon said. *Always have it with you.* And just to be sure, he phoned her every hour, on the hour. She found herself waiting for his calls, longing for them. Like a woman with nothing else to live for. At the same time she told herself it wouldn't go on like this. Richard Ortega was born impatient, intolerant of obstacles. Soon he would have to move on. Have to.

Soon it would end. But the days went by

and sometimes Simon forgot to call or would be busy and then she would have to wait, desperate for him to remember. She was like a creature out of the olden days – a girl shut up at home, for safety's sake. Longing for a man's voice to bring the world to her. Life reduced to this.

It couldn't go on. She told herself this. Made herself repeat it. Soon it would have to end.

One day, she forgot to take the phone off the hook. Mid-morning it rang, making her jump with surprise, so unfamiliar was the sound of it now. Then she felt herself become calm. Two weeks since he was here. It could be anyone. It could be Tamsin, it could be Deborah. Neither of them knew what was happening to her. She had kept Ortega a secret from them. Now she thought about their voices, and longed for them. And picked up the phone.

'*Grace, my sweet Grace, finally! How I have...*'

She slammed it down again.

Then it was the same process as before: running round the house, checking locks, windows, doors. Not once but twice. All set to do it a third time before she stopped herself. She was panting. Sweating, and not just with fear, but disgust. Already searching for a way to punish a Grace who could be so stupid, for picking up a phone, knowing

312

what she knew...

She stood, suddenly aware that the air around her had changed. It carried a taint, an odour, as if an animal had crawled into the room and died there. She had to breathe it in before she understood. It was fear, making her perspiration stink. Acrid and pheremonal, it was like sweat on a man who drives too fast and terrifies himself with a near miss; or beats his children and becomes drenched in it. Animal frenzy. Animal sweat. She didn't even smell of herself. Not any more.

She picked up her mobile and went upstairs. Ran a bath and emptied a bottle of foaming oil into it. Bubbles boiled over the rim, so dense her skin would itch when she got out. But they would take away the stench of animal. When the children came home, when Simon came home, it would be gone. And she could carry on as she had been for two weeks, pretending to be normal.

And it almost worked, lying back, allowing half her Christmas supply of Molton Brown to wash over her, every small bubble expensive. Last Christmas she had never heard of Richard Ortega, or Lucy. Last Christmas she had thought her life was her own, innocent of what was coming her way. Happy as a dinosaur who doesn't know its time is up...

Her mobile blipped.

She picked it up from the floor beside the

bath, carrying it high above the bubbles to her ear, eager to be the one to speak first. 'Darling, you'll think I'm terrible. I'm lying in the bath, with bubbles up to my neck. It's lovely. I should do it every day.'

There was a silence. Then came the voice in reply. Not Simon's voice.

'Lovely? How could it not be lovely? My sweet shimmering girl, naked as a nymph of the streams. Why, I can see you! See the dew glistening on your breasts. Look for me, Grace. I am here on the bank, watching the water play against your...'

Her fingers let go the phone. It fell into the water, disappearing beneath the bubbles. She imagined his voice carrying on, even as it sank, still there, still talking...

She wrenched herself up and out, scrabbling for towels as if to hide herself from greedy, watching eyes. Now she was standing on the bath mat, shaking and swaddled, in a place where she should have been invisible.

No escape. Not even here, in her bathroom where for years it had been understood that no one came. Not Simon, not the children. Even her mother had known better than to enter where her teenage daughter would have lain soaking, a creature of ointments and creams and brushes. The bathroom was her place.

Her. Place.

Now, though, under the towels, under the

scented layer of bubbles still swathing her bare arms, something else was happening. Goose bumps prickling the surface of her skin – up her belly, down her legs, lifting the hairs on her neck, creating warm rough planes of raised flesh, like the hide of an animal on its mettle. Signs. Warnings of sixteen-, eighteen-year-old Grace stirring. Calling on forty-year-old Grace to do the same.

Not frightened, not any more. Just angry, and growing angrier by the second – like when he first came at her in the garden. Furious that he had pursued her even here. The one place...

She threw off the towels and pulled on her clothes. Ran downstairs and unlocked the door. She stared at the modest amount of path leading to the gate. Such a small distance, yet for two weeks it had been too far for her to travel. Already her garden was growing wild through neglect, with rose bushes weighed down by dead heads. Weeds pushing through the crazy paving which she had lain herself, years ago.

And all because of him, Richard Ortega, the reason she had been shut inside, waiting for her family to bring the life back into the house. He might be out there now in the garden, waiting for her, hiding in the laburnum, or camouflaged by lilac.

He might be. But she didn't care. Grace

opened the cupboard by the front door with its shelves of trowels and secateurs and gloves. Weed killer. A small, sharp garden knife that she kept for special jobs. She gathered them all up and marched outside. Laid the knife down on the path beside her in case she needed it. And began to sort out her garden.

She worked all day, until she could smell herself again. But this time the sweat was her own. Proper sweat, the kind that in years gone by would have made Simon burrow closer, half-drunk on musk and warmth, back in the days before she had made herself invisible, scrubbed and undetectable even by sniffer dogs.

She wouldn't be washing again, not today. She had had one bath already. And Simon, he would just have to ... now she was smiling at what he would have to do. Smiling. And hungry. And tired.

Then she remembered Ortega, and the happiness slid away, slipping through her fingers like sand.

She picked up the knife. 'I could kill him.' She said the words loud, fiercely, to strengthen herself. And waited for a sense of shock or amusement. Irony even. Which didn't come. Because the truth was there would never be any peace until he was dead.

And she was Grace, and she couldn't kill anyone.

Now she wasn't happy or hungry. Just tired. Her eye landed wearily on the far corner of the garden, close to where she had brought a stone down on his head. The rockery was Simon's project. She had never really liked it or the small alpine plants that had grown there. Tiny austere growths when she preferred great blousy heads of cabbage roses and dahlias. More like her mother than she cared to admit. Like the path, it needed weeding.

She walked over to it, trying to ignore the other thoughts that threatened to stop her. But already the fear was on its way back. This was the place, the very place where he had caught and felled her. This was where he would have dragged her the last time, if Anna hadn't appeared. Finished what he started.

Now all she wanted was to go inside. Already the chemistry of her sweat was beginning to change, and she would start to smell as she had this morning, of frightened animal. And he would have won again.

She didn't go back inside. She forced herself to stand in the place, the very place. Stop there, where the weeds pushed up through stones. Slowly she bent down, reaching with the small garden fork to deal with them, but the fork was shaking, she was shaking. She wanted to run away, to the safety of walls. But the weeds were still there, mocking her – small tufts of dandelion leaves, sturdier than she was. Ready to take over.

Life was never going to be normal. Not now. Not ever. He'd won.

No.

In desperation she dropped to her knees and started to pull at the leaves, scrabbling, half blind. Knocking aside the rocks to get to the soil that was their anchor. She pushed at one rock, larger than the rest, which rolled, not far, but far enough.

Far enough to reveal what was underneath. Three pages of paper, handwritten. Slowly she picked them up, hands shaking more than ever. The ink had loosened and dispersed with the rain so that parts of what was written amounted to no more than a dirty stain. Which was only appropriate. Because the rest of it – what she could read – threatened to seep into her mind like another kind of stain, bringing with it a tide of nausea.

Which vanished as Grace – belatedly – understood what she was holding.

Three letters from Richard Ortega. Written by him, then pushed under a rock. Three letters to replace the one she had burnt. Proof. All the proof that was needed. She didn't have to kill him.

She gathered them to her breast, smearing them with mud and grass, the way she had been smeared, and ran inside the house.

She used the landline to get hold of Simon, her mobile having drowned. It didn't matter – she wouldn't need it any more. Then she put the phone back on the hook and waited for it to ring. Only a question of time.

Chapter Twenty-Nine

Sometimes a writer...
Richard Ortega put aside the pen. Creation was a delicate process, demanding as an exotic plant. Only when there has been the exact amount of warmth and rain and breeze, only when the sun hangs correctly in the sky and earth teems with the right amount of nutrients – only then can the plant bend itself to the glorious unfurling, its own nod to Creation.

And sometimes the plant will have to wait. Not just days or weeks, but entire years, content to hold its glory inside. Nature seeks its own ideal, like art. Is patient. Sometimes even literature must wait.

Fortunately he, Richard, would not have to wait long. Yesterday she had spoken to him, as he had known she must. He had dialled the number, prepared to wait, as he always did, patient as the plant that waits for rain...

...And she had picked up.

'Grace!'

'Richard.' Her own voice had had a note to it, unmissable. Trembling with what could only be excitement, a sign that the creatures had loosed their hold. Her family had loosed their hold. More to the point, the shock must have worn off, memories of unpleasant encounters with the law losing their sting.

Her own fault, of course, all of that. She would be the first to admit. Next time she would be a cleverer, a wiser Grace. Next time she wouldn't call the police simply to impress a jealous child.

'Darling girl, it's been so long.'

His own voice had trembled. *Darling girl* – he heard the words tumble straight from his heart, his hoary writer's heart – and was content to let them. Let her hear his joy. Let her hear her lover laugh.

'I have been a desert, Grace. Empty and arid. Only you can help me. Only you can water the parched earth so that the words can grow. Only you...'

He was forgetting about the rest, the coarser rub of flesh and heat. Scents of mud and grass. At this moment Richard Ortega was aware of himself as a man alive to the exigencies of art and nothing more. And certainly not less.

'Grace...' He spoke her name again, tenderly. Grateful for her silence. Finally she was learning to leave the words to him.

'Yes, Richard?' So meek she sounded. *Yes, Richard* – words he could listen to all his life.

'Come to me. Come tomorrow, at midday, when the sun is at his zenith. We are creatures of the light, you and I. No more skulking in dank corners.'

'No,' she said. Sweetly, sweetly she was agreeing with him. 'No more skulking.'

Now today, midday, he was waiting for her. Weighing the pen in his hand, savouring the line that would give birth to other lines. Knowing that something else was necessary. Only then would the words flow onto the page and the dam of creation break.

The doorbell sounded and he almost tipped the open bottle of ink in his eagerness to open it, wrenching the door so hard his knuckles met the wall to see...

...Grace, standing on the doorstep with a man, vaguely familiar.

'Hello, Richard.' She was smiling at him. 'This is Simon. I don't believe you've met.'

Richard blinked. And it was as he blinked that the man drew back his fist and punched him, so hard his feet left the floor. A blow that was almost trigonometrical in effect, sending him back so hard he landed, perfectly horizontal, on the floor.

'Simon!' Grace had turned on him, gently chiding. 'You promised you wouldn't do that.'

'I know. Sorry.' He was rubbing his fist as if the knuckles hurt. 'I couldn't help it. Are you angry with me?'

She smiled and he smiled back. Two people with eyes only for each other, forgetting the man laid out on the floor. Until Grace turned.

'I got your letters, Richard. I found them.'

He stared up at her. *Letters, what letters?*

'Remember? The ones you put under the stone. I don't know how you ever thought I'd find them, but I did.'

She opened her bag and waved three pieces of paper. 'I burnt the one that came in the post. But then you knew that. I should have kept it though. If I'd kept it, if I'd been able to show it to the police, they would have known you were lying. They would have come for you and not for me.'

Richard said nothing. He was still on the ground, watching the flap of the letters in her hand. Why, why was she doing this? Had he forced her, the man standing beside her? Had she been brainwashed, hypnotised? *Had she in fact gone mad?*

Now she was standing over him. 'What shall I do with them, Richard?'

He made a small, bewildered gesture. Which she ignored.

322

'I suppose, what I mean is – who shall I show them to? Those women, the ones you told me about? Your agent and publisher. That other one, the writer – Miriam Rapko? Or shall I...' she paused '...or shall I take them straight to the police? Wouldn't that just be simpler?'

And still he had no reply for her. Unwilling even to get to his feet while the husband was there, with all the force of a cuckold in his fist. All he could do was stare at her, his eyes sorrowful and bewildered, searching for a sign, a secret nod that all this was contrived.

The letters though. He watched them flutter in her hand. He might have written them. Bacchus nods. Ah yes, he remembered them now, vaguely. Not his best efforts, nothing he'd want to see in print. Letters for private consumption only. And certainly not for the eyes of Patsy, Regina, or Rapko.

And not for the eyes of the police. Belatedly, as Grace had done the day before, he finally understood what she had in her hand. Three letters. Proof that even he, Richard Ortega, could make a mistake. A huge mistake.

The biggest mistake of his life.

A small sound issued from his throat. Pleading as a baby bird, terrified as a mouse's squeal. But Grace's expression didn't change, her eyes still enquiring, still wondering what to do with the letters. As if she hadn't already made up her mind.

'You know,' she said suddenly – she was addressing not Richard but Simon – 'I'm almost happy not showing them to anyone. I'm happy just to know I have them. It's not every day a famous writer writes to me. The thing is, so long as I had them, I'd know that nothing, absolutely nothing else could happen. That he would never come near me ever again. Because if he did, if he so much as called me on the phone, these letters would go everywhere. One to his agent, one to his publisher. And,' she paused, smiled down at Richard, 'one to the police. What do *you* think?'

It didn't matter what he thought. Grace had decided.

There was a silence. Grace had said all she wanted to, and Richard, he had nothing he could say. Like muggers, like thieves in the night, they had come and robbed him of words. Grace had stood over him and plucked every possible answer from his lips. And her eyes – what had happened to her eyes? They stared down at him now in amused contempt. As if she had been taking lessons, not just from her daughter but others. A whole line of women dedicated to his downfall.

And Grace, his Grace, right there with them.

Grace gazed down at Richard with the eyes of every woman he had ever known. No wonder he had no words.

Out on the street, Simon said, 'I still think you should have gone to the police.' Grace shrugged. She was finding it difficult to walk, simply walk. What she wanted to do was run, overcome with lightness and speed, maybe throw off her shoes while she was about it. She said, 'If I went to the police, I would have to tell them everything. Stuff about you, about me. What we've gone through just to stay together. They'd have had to hear it all. I don't want that. It's private, our stuff. Our lives.' She slipped a hand through his arm. 'It's enough just to get rid of him, never have to see or hear or think about him again.'

He moved his own hand to clasp hers. Now they were walking, arm in arm.

'But what about all those people? What about the police? All of them thinking you're mad or bad. Can you really stand that, Grace?'

She thought. Then nodded. 'All my life long I've tried to be good, did you know that? Always worried about what other people would say, what they would think. Now everyone thinks I'm evil, wicked – and look! Nothing's happened. The sky hasn't fallen on my head. The children like me. My friends are still there.' She looked at him. '*You* are still there.'

Just for a moment they stopped. His hand tightened around her arm. And off they walked, locked together, perfectly in step.

Across the road, Patsy saw them and gasped. Broke out into a run, not stopping until she had reached Richard's door.

Despite the wildness of her knocking, it took an age for him to answer, opening it cautiously, like an old man scared of Tommy Knockers. No less cautious when he saw it was only Patsy. He even tried to close the door again.

'Richard!' Patsy protested and thrust open the door. And gasped again as she saw the bruise growing and deepening on his face. 'My God,' she whispered. 'Someone's attacked you. *She's* attacked you. Again! I saw her just now, walking away. And she was with somebody. He was holding her, tight. Oh Richard!' She clutched his arm. 'What's happened. Who was that man?'

Richard leant against the wall. He needed to answer her, but he was tired, so tired now. And shocked. His whole world had tilted beneath him as if trying to pour him off the edge. Nothing to hold on to. Nothing to anchor him here, where he belonged.

But he made the effort, one last act of creation to draw it all together and bring it to an end. Catch himself before he fell.

'The man?' His voice was weak. 'He was a police officer. CID. Detective Chief Inspector. They've finally arrested her. Had to. Dangerous, too dangerous to be allowed out.'

Patsy stared at him agape. Then she let out a moan of relief.

'Oh my lord. Finally. She's gone then. My dear Richard, thank God. Thank the good God.' She took a moment to blow her nose while Richard flinched and looked the other way. 'There's going to be a trial, of course,' she added soberly. 'We'll all have to give evidence.'

For a moment, Richard seemed not to hear her. 'Trial?' he said at last. 'No. No trial. She's too mad for that. Unfit to plead. They'll simply have to lock her up, for everybody's sake.'

Patsy gave a sigh for pure joy. 'So we'll never see her again. Oh Richard, think! *You'll* never see her again.'

He looked away. It seemed to Patsy that he was a man about to weep. Hardly surprising, she thought. Look what had come to an end – a nightmare from which everyone finally could wake up. Suddenly she had an urge to run home and hug Merlin, no matter that he wouldn't know her. All he would see and feel was a happy woman folding herself around him. And how often did that happen?

Sometimes happiness can be catching, even by the confused and bewildered.

She squeezed Richard's arm one last time and let it go. 'Think of the freedom, darling. You can write the book... Finally.'

She waited for an answer, but there was nothing. She wondered if he had even heard her.

Chapter Thirty

Dark days they had been, the days that came after. Such days he prayed never to see again.

Did he call them dark? That would be misleading. As he'd closed the door on Patsy, the mist had closed in, white, inexorable. Relentless as a slow-moving avalanche that blots out the world. A white into which he had simply merged, melting like a block of ice in water, a lazy dissolution of everything that made him whole and compact.

Terrible, terrible: to be Richard Ortega, and then forget what it meant. This must be the way it feels to be anyone. Anyone at all.

He would rather be dead.

And don't think he hadn't thought about it – the comfort of the Stoic, the solid reassurance of exit. Sometimes, when the gin bottle was almost empty and there was enough concentrated in the dregs to lend him a feeling of himself, the thought had crossed his mind. Better not to live at all. But he had never acted upon it. The moment had passed, to be diluted in the moments that came after.

Days and days of it, of dissolution, of an absence of light. The fading of the hard, steady, diamond-faceted beam that was Richard Ortega.

Ah.

Now he shuddered to think of it. Amnesia would have been preferable. Instead he would be burdened for ever with the memory of that time, that place. Each day of absence stamped indelibly on his mind; every uncentred hour outlined as if by a thick fuzzy pencil. Terrible memories of a terrible place.

A man would kill so as not to return to such a place.

Despite which, one day he had woken to find the fog had lifted. Not altogether, but suddenly thinner, less oppressive. As if whatever malign force was acting against him had forgotten – however briefly – to concentrate its venom. Richard had lain in bed, gauging his strength and the depth of the fog. Careful not to draw attention to himself, knowing it could return at any moment, whiter, denser than ever.

The trick was to be quiet, but quick. And make his escape.

And that's what he had done. Even now, days later, he could thrill to the memory of how he had acted. Stealing through the bars of the mist, swiftly gathering everything he needed, taking nothing he couldn't use. Pens, paper, ink. A key, he needed the key. Bottles, food, even books – his own, of course. He took everything.

Such speed, such efficiency. Such economy of style. Like Raffles the gentleman thief, he had rifled through the most precious objects of a life – his own life – and spirited them away with him, all in a single Fortnum and Masons hamper.

Even so, at the very last, the fog had become wise to him, suddenly aware of what was slipping through its grasp. As he was creeping down the hall, it had gathered itself together, a solid mass of white, rearing up between him and the door. There he had met it, head-on, and now, *now*, was the moment to make a man proud. *He had kept moving*, passing into the centre of the enemy, all but losing consciousness as the mist seeped and bled into the very heart of him, filling every crevice with ... what? Nothing. Yet somehow, with the physical strength that only comes from fighting demons, the creatures that infest us all, Richard Ortega had battled with that same Nothing. He had kept moving, fighting for the door, and freedom.

Stumbling out to the street, using the last of his strength he had hailed a cab. Pressed good money into the man's hand, ordering him to drive and keep driving.

Now he was here. Safe in a safe place. Shuddering to think that he could have been anywhere else.

And it only went to show how adaptable he was. Gracefully lending himself to the contours of his surroundings – so long as they were the right surroundings. He didn't want to think of that first night of exile, the box-like room with its pictures of bug-eyed children and puppies that would not, could not, be turned to the wall. The suffocating smallness of the bathroom with its tiles dimpled like small open pores. The hotel had held him for one night only before catapulting him out on reconnaissance to find a better place, one that could hold him and nurture him. A place in which to incubate the seed that continued to wait inside.

For Richard Ortega was pregnant with creation. He just needed the place in which creation could unfold. And now he was here, high up above the world. Above him sky. Below him, trees. The right place.

And so rich was the irony. For this was a place close to the most dangerous place of all. Here he stayed, skimming the heads of his enemies, like a wasp hovering unseen above the bees as they sleep.

Not his choice of décor, perhaps. Too clean, almost too comfortable. Useless, though, to miss the uneven surfaces, the spikiness of his antique furniture, objects he had grown up with. Sharp corners that over half a century had bruised, abraised or skewered every part of his anatomy. Here the furnishings were softer, sparer. Built and bought to last only for a certain period, a phase. Ten years from now and it would all be jettisoned, having served its purpose.

For now it was serving *his* purpose. And the truth of it was it was giving him everything he needed. A bedroom, a bathroom, a small kitchen, a table that would do for a desk when eventually his time came, when the pains of labour arrived.

Sometimes a writer...

Above all, it was quiet. Richard heard less sound here than he had ever had to endure in other places where the living was similarly arranged in layers. More noise came via the Velux window in the roof than the floor. He guessed at a soundproof system underfoot whilst, on top of that, thick carpets cushioned his every step. He could have danced a foxtrot with an elephant and still not have been heard.

All the same, unwilling to draw attention

to himself, he did his best to move softly as he went about his day. Tiptoed from bed to fridge to sofa to lavatory, even waiting till there was no one else in the building before he flushed, or else ventured out to replenish his supplies, slipping through enemy territory so that nothing woke. He needed so little! Brandy, gin, vodka. Bread, cheese. Fuel for mind and body.

Who would have thought he could have adapted himself to such a place, so small, so bounded by walls?

Maybe not so miraculous. When a man is pregnant with creation, when he carries an entire world within his mind, he does not need to roam. When that man is Richard Ortega, he can wander forever inside himself, a free man.

Besides, the smaller the container, the denser the matter. After the dark days of dissolution, it was time for him to be contained, for the atoms that made up Richard Ortega to condense and come together. Become compact again. Hard again, a carbon durable core of self.

Here, in this place, he could feel himself becoming more condensed every day.

A good place. The right place.

And so convenient. If ever he wanted to know what was going on, he needed only to sit by the window. Wait for the sights and sounds to reach him from outside. Footsteps on the path, the squeaking of the gate. Shouted goodbyes from the pavement. He was learning the timetable of a family, the routine of modest lives, learning it all so well he found he was slipping into the same routine himself!

It made him smile sometimes, gently humorous, this talent he had discovered for being the perfect guest. The sort of guest you would hardly know was there.

Or so he liked to think. The truth was, Richard Ortega was taking too much credit. Anything could have given him away – the coughing fits, the outraged cries in sleep when the tennis balls thudded past his ears. The occasional fart that bellowed like the final trump. Anywhere else and you'd have heard him. Couldn't avoid hearing him.

No – soundproofing was what was making it possible, keeping him invisible. Inaudible. He'd been telling nothing but the truth, that young lad, when he promised Grace all those weeks ago: they could have a herd of baby elephants in that loft and never know they were there.

Beside which, no one ever thought of going up into the loft. Since Ortega had dis-appeared from the scene, no one wanted to be there. Life, when it was home, was where it was always meant to be, down in the heart of the house. A place of comings and goings.

Quite a lot of houses are home to

creatures unknown. Bats in the attic, mice in the cellar. Silverfish, termites, roaches and rats. Wasps under the eaves. Sometimes we don't live alone. Grace and her family had their own pest and didn't know a thing about it.

She might never have noticed anyway. Even without the soundproofing, she might have consigned the creaks and flushings to the noises made by a house grown elderly since its early half-timbered youth. She wasn't home so much in any case. The week after coming away from Richard Ortega she had started the access course that would lead her to the university course that would lead her straight to an understanding of the human mind.

Except she didn't quite believe that now. Reading through her psychology coursework, she could see how rats in mazes or salivating dogs might explain why some people fear spiders; she could see how synapses and ganglia connecting could allow you to remember the name of your wife. All of that. What she couldn't see was how any of it would give her the clue to Richard Ortega.

And she didn't care. He could be a mystery to himself, and stay that way. She was content to understand the understandable. Happy just to have survived with a marriage intact, with her family still there. Living amongst people she could understand.

Right now, right at this moment, she was too happy to care. Happy not to think about him ever again.

Chapter Thirty-One

Simon came into the kitchen.

Grace didn't hear him, not at first. She was reading about a problem in psychology: a true story of a woman attacked in a city street. Her cries had rent the night, bringing all the people in all the neighbouring houses to their windows – and these people had done nothing. Each one waiting for someone else to make the call, afraid of making a fuss.

The woman was attacked so violently she was left for dead. And still nobody did anything. Her assailant came back and finished off the job. The woman died. And *still* nobody did anything. It had led to years and years of experiments, that case, as researchers tried to discover why no one had lifted a finger. Why they had let it happen, all those decent, law-abiding people who could have saved the woman, simply by picking up a phone.

Already Grace was learning that science

can lead to more questions than answers.

'Grace...'

She gave a start, so absorbed had she been, imagining the woman screaming, and the lights going on in all the houses, curtains twitching.

'Grace.' This time he had her attention. There was a look in his face that warned her: something was coming.

He sat down and moved the books out of the way. Which pricked her, for no reason that she could have given; except, perhaps, that she had been reading those books, and now he had just moved them away without so much as a...

'We need to talk about something, Grace.'

She waited.

'It's to do with work. I have to go away, another one of those weeks to be exact. You know the drill. We go to a hotel, we bond, build a few camp fires, that sort of thing.'

He watched her as he spoke. Saw the question already forming on her lips.

'Will *she* be there? Lucy?'

He hesitated, then nodded. 'She's part of the team. But I won't, we won't...'

'Will there be a sweat lodge again?'

'A what?'

'A sweat lodge. You know, hot stones. Company directors pretending they're Iron Brian, or do I mean John? A *sweat lodge*, Simon. All hot and intimate and ... and sweaty.'

He flushed. 'I see. Well ... maybe. It's the same firm of management consultants running it. They did a good job the last time, got people closer. It showed in the results...'

'I'll say it showed,' she laughed. Imagining a team of management consultants working like panders, like pimps, getting people *closer*.

He flushed again, deeper this time. 'Look...'

'I don't want you to go.' The words seemed to come out by themselves. Clipped.

'But...'

'It's all about breaking down inhibitions, beating your chests. Turning you into cavemen. And why? You're accountants, for God's sake.'

There was a silence. Heavily he said, 'I have to go. Have to, Grace. I can't get out of it. Yes, she'll be there, but you should trust me. After all ... I trusted you.'

And what could she reply? She nodded curtly, she even tried to smile. And failed. He waited for her to say something else, but she didn't. The silence stretched until Grace reached for her book and that was it. Discussion over.

She was being unreasonable, she knew that. She tried to jeer herself out of it, and failed. Days went by and still she failed. He was going and there was nothing to be done. She

338

wanted to bend, but she couldn't. This is where everything had started last year.

Things were different now, everything was different. She knew that, yet still she couldn't bend, couldn't be warm. In the nights that followed, she kept to her side of the bed, drawn to the high ground where she knew she shouldn't be. Not so happy now. She lay while Simon slept, and listened to sounds escaping from the sweat lodge. Imagined Lucy flicking all the right switches, like a scientist with a well-conditioned rat. She knew she was being unfair, too much like the Grace who had fallen prey to Ortega, but she couldn't help herself. She lay and listened to her imagination when she should have been listening out for what was real, to the unsuspected life in her house.

Yet how could she have known to listen? She was at home. She should have been safe. Safe as houses.

Now his bags were packed. She peeked inside and noted that all he was taking was tee shirts, nothing else. Hot, where he was going. Hot, what he would be doing. Her lip curled, then trembled. The old Grace still there, just below the surface.

On the point of leaving, Simon took her in his arms, but she couldn't bend. She stood so stiff that his arms fell away. He might as well have embraced a post.

Or hugged a tree. Or Lucy.

Yet as the car pulled out of the drive, Grace pulled herself together. This was Simon, the man she had unsingled, who had thrown every accountancy skill out of the window for her sake. Who had trusted her.

Simon.

She ran out of the house, down the drive and out, chasing after the car. All set to tell him she was wrong; to sweat all he needed to. Too late. His car had sped up and he was gone, leaving her to stand in the middle of the road in her slippers, the snowmen wagging sadly at her feet.

Inside Rob was shovelling his customary industrial quantities of cereal.

'He gone then?' His voice was indistinct.

'Yup.' She picked up a cup of coffee which Simon had made for her, and which she had studiously ignored. Now she drank it, even though it was cold. *When he came back*, she told herself. *When he came back she would be warm again.*

'You weren't very nice to him,' observed Rob. 'Why's that then?'

'Shut *up*.'

She felt like howling.

Rob picked up his schoolbag from the floor – rather, a plastic carrier bag with sheaves of wrinkled bits of paper he claimed was work. 'By the way, I'm staying at Pete's tonight.'

She nodded vaguely. Minutes later he swung down the path with a skinny, rolled-up sleeping bag, which apparently was all he needed for a night away. At least it meant the fridge would be safe from him. Lately their son had taken eating to another dimension, making cartwheels of cheese and whole chickens vanish, then denying he had touched so much as a drumstick. Fibbing, of course. Yet he was still as skinny as his rolled-up bag, skinny as a dog with worms. Maybe that was it. Maybe her son had worms.

'You OK?' This was Anna, running late.

Grace blinked. Two nights ago Anna had bleached her hair so that it was almost white, still so recent it caused her to start, every time she looked at her.

'I should have been nicer to your father.'

Anna shrugged, ate two chocolate biscuits instead of breakfast, expecting her mother to object. Then seeing that Grace was taking no notice, slipped the packet into her bag.

'Oh well. You've got the next forty years to make up for it. Barring accidents.'

And Grace began to feel better.

At the front gate, Anna called back to her. 'Is it all right if I stay at Wendy's?'

'Why do you want to stay at Wendy's?' Grace called back. They should have been having this conversation in the house, instead of here.

'Because Rob gets to stay at Pete's.' She replied as if it was simple, and the connection was obvious. Grace threw up her hands and went back inside. Alone.

Upstairs in his window, Richard didn't hold his breath. He knew the routine by now. And he was right. Minutes after, Grace too left the house, with a carrier bag full of books and a case of sandwiches. More like Rob than anyone could have expected.

Later, though, she would be alone, not just in the day but all through the night. Richard had watched the husband with the cuckold's fist leave with a suitcase. Seen the boy and heard the girl. All of them given permission to be out.

Grace. Grace had done it. Allowed them all to leave. As if she knew what was expected of her. As if she knew how to make it happen. Which of course, deep down, she did.

Grace. His Grace. He had never doubted it for a moment, not once he had battled with the mist. Her mind was a haven for him, the upper reaches of her home a home for him. *She* had prepared a place for him, even though later, shyly, she would swear it wasn't so. Afraid to admit that without him she had no home, no life. No heart, only a barren cell teeming with creatures and demons. Family.

She had made a place for him above them

all, in the eaves. And now, having emptied her house of the demons, the creatures who plagued her, she had made a time.

Grace closed her text book. It was past eleven at night. Simon would be – where?

There, of course, amongst the management consultants. Drumming or chanting, hair falling into his eyes, cross-legged in a teepee, like the very last of the Mohicans, like Hawkeye.

A teepee set right next to a luxury hotel. Isn't this what Rob and Anna used to get up to when they were small? Earnestly set up camp in the garden, ready to stay there all night, only for an owl, or a car backfiring to send them running the ten yards to the back door, falling over themselves to be inside, where it was safe...

She climbed the stairs, aware of her empty house. Anna had rushed in after school and rushed out again with a rucksack. Barely time to exchange a word, a disappearing flash of white hair. No one to say good night to.

As she lay down she had an image, unbidden, of Lucy drumming harder than the rest, her tee shirt beginning to cling. Drumming like one of those bugs that drum branches, leaves – their own back legs – to call a mate. Only a fleeting image. Grace watched her a moment then took the picture and rolled it up, thrust it out of sight. Not the same Grace after all.

She thought of Simon instead. Wishing she could have the last few days again. Wishing he were here for her to tell him she trusted him, wrap her arms around him and lie all night long.

She fell asleep wishing.

Wished so hard she actually dreamt of him, of Simon from an earlier time, in those days and weeks long ago when twenty-year-old Grace had begun to understand she was falling in love. Frightened that she could lose him, or that he wouldn't love her back. Only when he reached for her, only when their bodies came together had she stopped being afraid.

She dreamt of that time now. Of Simon reaching for her, to put body and mind to rest. In her dream he came and lay down beside her. She could feel his breath on her cheek, his hands moving to find her breasts. Confident hands, knowing she would welcome him, show him the way inside.

Her eyes opened. The room was dark, but the dream didn't fade. Simon was still there, a real weight moving across her, ready to fill the space he always filled. She sighed, contented, still drugged with sleep. Her dream had left her warm and wanting. And he was there, a dream come true.

Only then did she remember.

344

He shouldn't be here. He was meant to be a hundred miles away, in a hotel room. Yet he was here. *He had come home to her.* Simon had come home, stealing into their bed like a ghost in the dark. Like a lover, waking her.

She made a small inarticulate cry of happiness. The dream had been no dream at all, merely the way he had chosen to let her know, his hands doing the work, waking the warm, wanting feeling that flooded her. Hands reaching to the parts of her that still lay covered, under the duvet.

No need for words. She wrapped her arms around him in the dark, breathing in the warm familiar accountant smell of her husband...

And it wasn't there. Not even the scent of accountant masked by woodsmoke. Something else. Alcohol and must, as if he had been sitting not in teepees but locked in rooms with mothballs and brandy. It confused her, even while her brain was still too fogged to question it.

'Simon?' Her mouth went to form the words.

At the same time, downstairs, the front door clicked as if in someone's clumsy attempt to be quiet. A sound of footsteps in the hall. Grace woke up all over again. The weight beside her vanished. No Simon, no hands. Nobody. Just a dream. She was alone.

Except she wasn't alone. Someone was in

her house. The footsteps were on the stairs, soft creaks that acted like a drug, pinning her to the bed. Moving upwards, closer. Now they were at her door. She watched the handle moving. Slowly, slowly. Then something snapped, and released she leapt to face the door that was beginning to open. Grace felt her lips part, ready to scream.

And there, silhouetted against the landing light, a shock of bleached white hair.

'Anna!'

Anna inspected her mother swaying on her bedroom floor. 'Who did you think it was?'

'I ... I thought. Never mind.' Grace's teeth had started to chatter. 'What are you doing here? You were supposed to be staying with Wendy.'

Anna looked away. 'We had a row, didn't we? So I came home. Anything wrong with that?'

Grace looked at the clock. It was gone 1 a.m. 'It depends. *How* did you get home? Did someone give you a lift?'

Anna tossed her new white head. 'Walked.'

'What?' Grace almost shrieked. 'Wendy's parents let you walk all the way here, alone, in the dark? Anna, are you serious?'

'They didn't know. And Wendy didn't care. Cow.'

Grace stared at her daughter, helpless. A young girl, alone and in the dark, tramping through the night. Anna scowled. 'Look, I'm all right. I'm home now in case you hadn't noticed. All safe and sound.'

'But Anna...'

'For God's sake, I'm not a child. Look, I've just had the most horrible time with the most complete bitch who ever walked the earth. Scream at me in the morning. I'm going to bed.'

She flounced away to her own room, closing the door firmly behind her.

Slowly, Grace climbed back into bed. She *would* scream at her in the morning. Meanwhile, she watched her daughter walking through the night, long legs pale in the streetlight. She saw the men cruising slowly past in cars, sizing her up, wondering if it was worth the risk.

It was no good; she sat up. She'd never sleep. How could she when what she wanted was to march into Anna's room and shake her? Spank her. Read her a list of all the things that could have happened.

And didn't happen. That was the point. The anger stalled. They didn't happen. Home now. Safe now.

She was almost asleep again when her door opened – again.

'Mum?'

'What?' Grace kept her eyes closed tight.

'Mum, there's a bee in my room.'

'A bee?'

'Well, a wasp then. It won't stop buzzing. It's in the curtains. It's going to be there all night.'

'But Anna...'

'Mum. Don't you remember? When I was little? That wasp that came and stung me on my face? It got on my pillow when I was asleep. It was horrible. Mum, remember...?' Her voice tailed off into the wail of a little girl.

Grace sighed and sat up. She did remember. The shock and pain in Anna's tiny pent up body. Too little to know what had happened. Frightened of wasps for years after. And now here was her tow-haired daughter, looking at her like a little girl again. The same Anna who had just told her she wasn't a child.

'All right. Well, go and sleep in Rob's bed. There are clean sheets. I made him change them yesterday.'

Anna made a face. 'He still slept in them.'

'One night, for goodness' sake.'

'*Mum*, do you know how often he washes?'

'Oh Anna... Well, go into the guest room.'

'No way! You can't see the bed for ironing. It's a tip. Why can't you keep it presentable like normal people?'

Ten past one in the morning and her daughter was nagging her about housework.

'*Anna!*' Grace fell back on her pillows. 'Go upstairs then. There's a bed all made up. Go up into the loft. You'll be all right there.'

'The door's locked,' said Anna flatly. 'I went up there last week, and it was locked. No key or anything.'

'Anna, it was not. Why should it be locked? Just give the door a push.'

And still Anna hesitated. But Grace had had enough. 'For goodness' sakes, just go. Into the loft.' Grace wrenched the pillow from Simon's side of the bed and pulled it over her head, blotting out her stubborn, impossible-to-please daughter, and all the light flooding in from the landing behind her. Kept it there until she was sure Anna had gone.

And didn't notice that the pillow was still faintly warm.

So what made her stay awake? Not any noise from Anna. The soundproofing had taken care of that. In any case, what would there have been to hear? Anna was skinny, wiry as a question mark. The squeakiest of floorboards would be hard put to give her away. Yet she hadn't come back downstairs again so she must, finally, have made herself comfortable.

So why could Grace still not sleep? Lying with eyes barely closed, the way she used to lie when the children were babies and wakeful in the night. Knowing the peace would only last a minute, that there was something

349

they still needed from her. Wondering what that something was. Somehow convinced that Anna needed her now.

A child one moment, adult the next. What else could Anna possibly be needing from her tonight? She had had a row with Wendy. That's what girls did. They rowed. Not these two, though. Anna had known Wendy since she was a little girl, fast friends from the day they started nursery. A row with her would mean an entire world turned upside down. Grace tried to put the idea out of her head, yet still she lay. Unable to think of any other reason why Anna should need her.

Nothing for it. Wearily, Grace tossed away the cover and tramped out of her bedroom, glad she was wearing pyjamas. Knowing that Anna would greet her with irritation, if she would greet her at all. Probably she was already sound asleep. Dreaming.

Chapter Thirty-Two

Richard heard Grace's footsteps on the stairs and felt his heart beat – just a tad – faster.

For two weeks he had lived so close to her, knowing that at any time he could have reached out and touched her. But still he had needed to show restraint, a nod to the creatures who surrounded her. So close and yet so far.

Until tonight. Never would he forget the cry that had issued from her throat in bed when she had known he was there. The clinging eagerness of her arms. A woman with no will beside that of her beloved. And even then they had been interrupted...

Vengeful, he tugged harder at the daughter's hair to warn her not to cry out.

He had had a shock, a series of them. First the exquisite embraces in the dark, ruined by the sound of people, or rather, one person – a trespasser on the scene. Forcing him to take flight, like a god retreating to Olympus. A second shock when his door – which, in his rush, he had forgotten to lock – suddenly opened and there she was, the child with the eyes of every woman who had ever hated him. Staring at him.

At first he'd thought he was hallucinating; that here was some kind of X-ray image of an imp, hair sheet-white when it should have been black. But then, like a man surprised by an idea, he had seized her and closed the door. Thrust her into a chair, so hard it had shaken the flimsy flat-pack joints. And there she had stayed, too frightened to move. Or speak.

He had to give her credit. She had a better talent for silence than Grace. Sitting motionless for ten minutes? half an hour? he had regaled her with what he was going to do with her mother. What he had already done with her mother. Making sure she understood. Sooner or later a child has to grow up.

Freud would have approved.

And finally, finally the eyes had it. Better than Grace's eyes even. He spoke and watched the daughter's eyes grow darker than Grace's could ever hope to be, as one by one he saw them vanish, the women who had stared at him. Finally drawing a line through characters who should never have been given space on the page. All of them, dying now in the eyes of this repugnant child.

A pleasure in itself, watching its eyes change. But Grace was what he had been waiting for. And now she was here. He held his breath as he saw the door handle move. Had she come in search of her daughter? Of course not! Why search for a child in its own house? She had come for him, flesh and spirit drawn to him, always him.

The door opened, and their eyes met. His eyes and Grace's. And yet again, the eyes had it.

No.

No. Grace's mind would not allow it. Unreliable, whispering to her that if she turned and closed the door, he would not be there. Telling her to go back to bed, let the dream end with the rub of the pillow against her cheek.

But Anna's face was turned to hers, terrified. At the same time, infinitely relieved. Thinking everything would be all right now that Grace was here, eyes pleading with her to make it right. The whispers died in her head, and she knew this was no dream.

'Darling!'

Richard's voice gave him away as, for one brief moment, emotion almost broke him. Even the strong can be marked by the weak, betray the fragility that makes a man human.

Besides, if he was moved, what could he say about Grace? He could see her trembling, every fragment of her being in flux. Even now, even after her body had warmed to his, thrilled to his embrace, it was clear she dare not believe it. Ortega was here. Dreams do come true.

He moved and drew her into the room with his right hand. In his left hand he carried something. Sharp, pointed – he had already shown to the daughter, his passport to well-earned silence. Now Grace's fingers lay in his, chilled as dead things.

'Cold, my darling? How is that? Such a short while ago you were hot – sweet, hungry Grace ablaze in my arms.'

'No,' whispered Grace. 'Not you. Not in my bed...'

'Hah!' Richard was impatient and gay at the same time. 'There is no need to lie, not any more. Or is it the child you are worried about? Don't be. See? I have done your work for you. Ortega has told her the truth – great human truths of love and life. About you and me. The child knows the mother as the mother knows the child. I have put you both on an equal footing. Now she can live her life. And you ... *you* can live yours.'

Grace turned to Anna. 'What did he tell you?'

Anna shook her head, averted her face. But not before Grace saw her eyes.

'Anna, he's lying. Everything's a lie. He's making it up, all of it.'

But Anna wasn't looking at her any more. She was gazing at Richard; drawn to him as if only he could convince her. And Richard, seeing this, smiled. It was Anna he spoke to now:

'Why should I lie? What benefit is it to me? Richard Ortega does not throw himself after a lie, no matter how sweet, how erotic, the object. The wise man reaches for the willing peach, and ignores what is beyond his grasp.'

Grace said, 'Anna, get out of here. Get out of the house. It doesn't matter where. Just get away as far as you can.'

But still Anna wouldn't look at her. Eyes trained on Richard with that terrible, rapt expression.

Richard frowned at Grace. 'Is that wise, my darling? What if she runs off to find others who have a claim on you, who will fight to keep you from yourself? Are you sure you are strong enough to withstand them? Sweet Grace, are you?'

As he spoke, he walked to the door. Locked it. Put the key in his pocket. At the same time, the hand that was hiding something from her seemed to glint with a secret of its own. Now, casually, as if he was only noticing it himself, he held it out as if for examination. A small, pointed knife that looked familiar.

She saw the knife, and it was like waking all over again. As if even now she had been asleep.

'Richard.' She had begun to stammer. 'Please let her go. Please. I'm begging you.'

Regretfully, he shook his head. 'Nothing would give me greater pleasure. But we must stifle the lovers' urge to be alone. Where would she go? Where is there that she could not do us harm?'

'She can go to a friend's,' Grace said. 'They won't do anything there. Her father is away. So is her brother. There's no one she can tell.'

Again, Richard shook his head. 'Impossible, my dear. You have such faith in human nature, whereas I...'

A voice interrupted him. Thin, stripped away. A voice like muslin tearing. 'So ... is it true, what he's saying? All you really want is him? Not Dad? Not even us? Tell me, is it true?'

'Anna!' Grace said softly. 'He's lying. Everything he says is a lie.'

Richard sighed tolerantly. But Anna's eyes were wretched. 'Then *why?* If he's lying, then why is he doing this? Why does he speak like you *belong* to him? What is he doing in our house? Why is he here?'

Why? The question hung and shivered between mother and daughter, like a crack, a ripple in everything they thought was true. It rippled through Grace's body, because she had no answer. Happy all these weeks not to think of him, or understand him. Happy not even to try, like a woman asleep. With the result that now she had nothing. No understanding and no explanation. No reason for Anna to believe her. No answer. And no escape.

Except that now, finally, she *was* awake. And thinking.

She made herself look at Richard. He was smiling at the two of them. Fondly, as if he approved every word spoken between them. More than just approving – it was as if he had written the words himself and paid them into their mouths. Now, like a pair of puppets, or people on a page, they were paying them out again.

Words. Something stirred in Grace. What words meant to him. The right words could make him smile, as he was smiling at her now, cheeks soft as cheese, eyes slightly moist. And evidenced by the way he murmured lovingly: 'Grace, my own girl. I know what you are thinking.'

He continued to smile, waiting for the right reply. For the right words. Expecting them.

But what if she – or Anna – said the wrong words? Words not in his script? What would he do? *What would he do to Anna?* She forbade herself to watch the knife, small and sharp and pointed. She was the one who had added it to the drawer of the little kitchen, determined that anyone should be able to live up here, separately, apart from the life downstairs. Outside the circle. Outside everything that mattered.

But the knife gleamed and Grace, who had provided him with it, was beginning to see the result: words could be the death of them. She felt her mind begin to slide, the beginning of the end, as if she was slipping back into a dream.

But Anna. There was Anna. No one to save her except Grace. At which once again Grace came awake, and forced herself to think of words. The right words.

'Richard?'

Somehow she made herself smile. Like when she used to smile at children who bullied her children, or at unkind teachers. Mothers are good at smiles that are not really smiles at all, merely another trick to advance their young. Or save them.

But a smile was all he saw. 'Yes? Yes, Grace of my heart?'

'Do you really know what I'm thinking. Right now? This very moment, as I am standing here?' She allowed a note of wonder in her voice. Awe.

His own smile grew wider, grew positively foolish.

'Why yes, my darling. I have always known what you are thinking. And will always know. Have I not said it before? I know you better than you know yourself.'

'How though?' She looked at him gravely. 'How is it you know me so well?'

'Oh my dear, the sweet stupidity of love! That you even need to ask! I know you because you are mine.'

'Because I am yours...' She repeated the words after him, meekly. Watching him, watching the direction of the mouth, before exclaiming: 'Why ... yes. Yes, I can understand that. But how did it happen? How did I become yours?'

His eyes twinkled, then grew dark. 'Darling, you tell me.'

He was testing her.

Again the words threatened to desert her. But she cast her mind back, through the weeks, to the woman she had been when first they met. Not quite sane. Not the Grace she should have been. An open wound, salted by every passing thought. A woman identifiable only by the insult of injury. Easy, easy for him. She remembered, and the words came after all, slowly, each one judged for its value, for its closeness to the script.

'The first time I met you, I felt as if I was disappearing, vanishing. And somehow you made me visible again. Like I was a girl again. You talked to me as if you could see what no one else could. A girl, even though I had stopped being a girl long ago.'

She stopped. Above the glint of the knife, Richard was nodding.

'After that, every time we met it was as if you took me, and changed me back to the way I'd been. Only better. The sort of woman anyone would want to be. The sort of woman I'd want to read about. Like I was something in one of your books. It's as if you were moulding me, shaping me.'

She paused. But Richard had continued to smile. It was the sight of Grace, his sweet silly Grace, fumbling – struggling, testing each word against the other until she had found the one she could use...

'I changed. Was that you, Richard, turning

me into a different person? Did you take the old Grace and make a new Grace? So that whatever I am now – whatever I do or think or say – it is because of you. Because you made me come alive. Is that how you know what I am thinking? Is that why I am yours?'

She paused, and nodded, answered her own question. Richard held his breath.

'Yes. That's how it is. I *am* yours. You know me because you made me. All this time I've pretended not to know it. Tried to deny it to myself. To everybody.' She looked at him, her eyes steady and humble. 'Not now, though. Not any more. I am yours. How could I not be yours?'

He stared at her, transfixed. Then the smile on his face spread, bursting its banks like a river of treacle. His shoulders began to shake. Finally, Grace – his Grace – had found the right words. The very words he would have chosen for her, and now look: here was the creator brought to tears by what he had created.

And Grace who watched him, knew what she had to do, finally understanding why he was here.

At least, she knew what she had to do to save Anna.

She took a step closer to him, and allowed herself to tremble – simply because he was there, the talented Richard Ortega. Her rock. Her safe place. Her creator.

Chapter Thirty-Three

'I want to be alone, Richard. With you. Now.'

Now. The word pierced him, a sweet wound in his belly, sweeter still in his groin. Reminding him of what emotion – sheer romance – had caused him to forget. This was Grace, *his* Grace, whose teeth had already betrayed the instincts of a small, plump fox. Eyes that suddenly had become inviting as a bitch on heat. How could he have forgotten the throb, the engine of desire?

'Of course, my angel, my love. *Now* indeed.'

He began to shepherd her to the bed, pushing her with the same urgency that propelled him.

'Richard,' she resisted him gently. 'Richard, I couldn't possibly. Not with...'

Anna. She would not look at Anna. If she did, she would be unable to keep to the script. Even without words, she would betray herself. And in that way, betray them both.

Richard stopped. A look, ancient and lascivious, had appeared in his face, as if he had been licked by a satyr. To have the mother, while the daughter looked on... It would have to be worthy of the master, of Sade himself.

Such a violently tempting thought, it made him want to sit suddenly, weighed down by the gravitational pull in his loins. At the same time pictures were rioting for space in his mind, making his heart pound. He sank onto the bed, and would have pulled Grace down beside him. But again she resisted him.

He grunted, about to be irritated, even with her. Yet Cupid bade him try, if only briefly, to persuade. Stabbing at patience he said, 'Sweet Grace. This child has wounded you, stolen your youth – the pleasure, the life that should be yours. Now is the time she can learn that passion is not just for the young.'

But Grace shook her head. Still caught, he could see, by the creatures; still snagged by the demons, for which read *convention*. Useless to argue, not with his mind boiling with images, each more startling than the last. Sometimes actions – the right actions – can be as eloquent as words.

Instead he tugged and Grace fell beside him on the bed, legs akimbo, prettily slut-tish. Across the room the girl looked away.

'No.' Despite the disorder of her limbs, Grace's voice was firm.

'No?' He laughed at the word. Indulgent as only a lover is allowed to be.

'No. Not with her.' Grace sounded impatient. 'How can I when *she's* there. I'll be thinking of *her*, watching *her*. It wouldn't be my fault, even. She's my daughter, my ... my *creature*. That's what creatures do, remember – they steal the attention. She'll try to steal it from you. She'll detract from *you*.' She paused, added softly, 'Don't you see?'

He frowned. The ache in his loins died back a fraction.

Grace touched his arm – then let her hand fall into his lap and left it there. Immediately the throb became unbearable once more.

'Don't you see?' she said again. 'You've won, Richard.'

'There's no need for her to stay. It's better that she goes. I *want* her to go. She can run out into the street, tell anyone she likes. Tell the whole world about us. But it won't change anything. I am yours. You made me who I am.'

Her hand tightened over his trousers, her fingers working, making themselves felt through the thick, dirty writer's twill. In the corner of her eye she saw her daughter shrink into herself, becoming smaller. Older. Grace looked away.

'I'm yours, Richard. I want to be free of them – all of the creatures. I *am* free. That's what you've done. You've set me free.'

There was a silence. 'Then tell her,' he said.

'Tell her?' Her fingers stopped. She looked confused. 'Tell her what you want. Look her in the eye and tell her.'

He spoke, knowing if Grace could look her daughter in the eye and tell her, he would believe her, the man who could see the Grace inside, and the small secret organ where lies are made. Or not.

He watched her; observed the blue shadow of her temple, the delicate twitch of skin. And with infinite regret, he realised that no, he couldn't believe her, even now.

But then the twitch was gone. Grace looked directly at her daughter.

'Anna, you wanted me to tell you the truth. Well, this is the truth. I want to be with Richard ... Mr Ortega. I need to be with him. There's nothing more I can give you. Do you understand?'

She saw Anna quiver. But otherwise she didn't move.

'I want you to go, Anna. Leave us in peace.'

But still Anna didn't move. She was searching Grace's face, not ready to believe, not yet. Then it came, a look to break Grace's heart. Anna's eyes suddenly had become cunning, knowing. They stared at Grace, expecting at any moment to receive a message, a sign. Something to tell her that her mother didn't mean a word. But Grace's expression never changed. Seconds passed and the look of cunning vanished. Behind the smoky, black-rimmed eyes, it seemed to Grace that a fire flared, then died.

'Well,' said Grace. 'What are you waiting for? You don't really want to see what happens next, do you?'

Anna shivered.

'Then you had better go.'

'Where?' Whispering the question.

'Why ... anywhere you like. You're not a child.' She watched her daughter coolly. Said again, 'So what are you waiting for?'

Anna indicated limply to Richard. 'He ... he locked the door.'

Grace looked at Richard. When he said nothing, she leant across his body and slipped her hand in his pocket. Found the key and held it out to Anna. 'Here, take it. Now will you please leave us alone.'

Anna took the key, her fingers grazing her mother's before vanishing. Grace heard footsteps on the stairs, pattering like a child's. Then the door closed and she couldn't hear her any more.

Richard. She was alone with Richard.

No escape. Not for her. But Anna, Anna was...

'Stand up.'

Dully she turned. Next to her on the bed,

365

Richard was staring at her. His eyes seemed to have become glazed suddenly, as if too much had happened too fast. He said, 'I need to look at you. But not with *those.*' With a shudder, he gestured towards the pyjamas. Finding something to frown at, his eyes had cleared. 'Take them off.'

The knife flashed in his hand, yet he didn't seem to be aware of it.

But Grace was. She got to her feet. Now she was beside the window, and eagerly she looked outside. Frightened that even now, Anna might still be in the house. Still in danger. She had to smother the cry of relief as she glimpsed the swing of the gate, the flash of white hair in the dark. Once again, Anna was outside and alone.

Safe.

How strange, though. How strange that all her life, Grace had believed that safety was to be found inside, behind four walls. Thinking the danger was outside, when all the time the danger was here, within these same walls. Not that Anna had understood that. Through the window Grace saw her daughter break out into a run, feet hitting the pavement, and knew exactly what she was running from. Not from danger. Not from Richard Ortega, but her – the mother who told her she wasn't wanted. Not any more.

Anna. She would run all her life now, and still not be able to escape the thoughts planted there by others. Yet Grace had done all she could and Anna, running like a little girl in the dark, was as safe as she could possibly be.

She didn't know that, behind her, Richard was having difficulties of his own. Unlooked for. Not what he had expected. His prize, his reward for so much toil was standing in front of him. He had got what he had come for. Dainty, dirty little Grace had dismissed her daughter. The throb in his groin should be about to transform into a blaze of glory, an explosion of all that is holy...

Instead, unbelievably, the throb was beginning to die off. Something was ebbing away. He could feel it go – blood flowing back into its normal channels, threatening to leave him beached and foolish. No ink in his pen. While Grace – she continued to stand, staring into the dark. He had told her to undress and it was as if she hadn't even heard him.

He needed her to hear him. He needed her to do as she was told. *He needed her to get rid of those fucking pyjamas.*

'Get undressed.' Desperation turned the order into a bark. Grace seemed to wake up out of her trance. She turned from the window and faced him.

'No,' she said between clenched teeth. 'You'll have to kill me first.'

Knowing she meant what she said. Knowing it would have taken fear to save her, fear to be her friend. If a stranger had attacked her, fear would have overcome nausea and disgust. Fear would have made her able to give way.

But Richard was no stranger. Her gorge rose, just to look at him. Disgust and nausea blinding her to the fear. This is what it came to. She would rather die. Knowing that he could make it happen. Wipe her off the page and start again.

She planted her heels, deep into the thick soundproof carpet.

At which Richard's heart nearly burst with love and gratitude. Here was Grace, his Grace, knowing what was needed. Pretending to say 'no', even now. A maid unwilling, inviting the full blown assault of the god. The throb came back, and with it the stiffness in his loins, harder, hotter than ever. He could have howled for happiness.

He launched himself at her, and pushed her to the floor. As she struggled, he laughed, imagining the stars storming drunkenly above, shouting him on and on. Making her struggle even more. Biting and scratching so hard she threatened to wear him out, so that he half wondered how he could make her stop.

But maybe that was it. Maybe she wanted to be hurt, was begging for him to hurt her.

Situations like these, someone has to take control.

Almost without thinking, he took the small pointed knife she had provided for him and held it to her neck, its tip cushioned by soft white flesh. It surprised him, the effect. Instantly she lay still, eyes fixed on his. And that was better, much better; at last he could take purchase of those fucking pyjama bottoms. Passion killers.

Finally she was playing the game. Playing fair. Ready to let him work his way to the centre of her, sweet as a cheap chocolate from a box, better than the expensive kind. Naughty but nice. Nearly there.

Then his hand, working and tunnelling, stopped.

Her eyes, having caught his, now held them. And it shocked him. Grace, *his* Grace, was staring at him with the eyes of every woman who had ever hated him. Grace, of all people. It shocked him so profoundly that, hardly aware of what he was doing, he pressed the knife harder into her neck, so that a snicker of blood welled up. He was aware of it trickling, a fine red thread over white skin. But still he couldn't tear his eyes from her eyes. And all the other eyes.

'Why, Grace,' he murmured. He jiggled the knife slightly, pleading with her. 'Don't look at me like that.'

And that was the moment her eyes changed again. The other women disappeared and now it was only Grace, staring at him.

Staring so that it was almost unimportant that behind him the door to the loft had burst open, to be followed by noise and more noise; in fact, Richard Ortega hardly seemed aware of the hands seizing and pulling him away from the woman on the floor, throwing him against the wall. Absentminded, he opened his mouth to protest, only for a knee to plant itself in his groin, making him double up. And even this he hardly felt, not compared to the other wound, the damage already done.

There was another rush of activity as Grace struggled to her feet. Police everywhere. Yet though there were hands to steady her, no one seemed to want to help her the way she wanted to be helped. Too busy with the wound in her neck, pressing hard to staunch the flow of blood. No one thinking to stop and cover her, so that she had to continue to stand in the middle of them, naked from the waist down.

It was Anna who came to the rescue, pushing through the crowd. Smoky, black-rimmed eyes holding her gaze, so that somehow she didn't feel naked any more.

'Anna,' whispered Grace. For the first time she felt tears. 'You knew. You didn't believe me. You knew.'

Anna rolled her eyes. 'Course I knew.'

'When, when did you know?'

'All the time. All that crap about not

wanting us, not wanting me? Had to be a lie, didn't it? All right – maybe just for a second you made me wonder, but then I knew. No way you couldn't want us any more.' She looked at Grace – five-, ten-, fifteen-year-old Anna – safe with all the knowledge of the years. 'You just love us too much. Couldn't help it if you tried.'

She smiled at the thought of her mother – or anyone at all – being such a fool for love. And burst into tears.

Up against the wall, a policeman – one who had already been to the house – was reading Richard his rights. But it wasn't clear if Richard could even hear him. He stood like a man blind to everything. Deaf. Like a man surrounded by fog.

And it was true. The fog was real, a blanketing monster that could smother a man to death. It had started to descend even before the police came into the room, before Richard even knew they were there. It had appeared at his shoulder when he had pushed the knife into her neck, and the blood had begun to well, and suddenly she had changed the way she looked at him.

Not with fear, not with hate. Not even with contempt. Grace had looked at him simply as if he wasn't there. Even with the weight upon her body and the knife against her neck, it was as if he had simply disappeared. As if he didn't exist. As if he

371

had never existed. Desperate, he looked into Grace's eyes, and finally he understood: *he was nothing but a cloud of particles, abandoned by the laws of gravity. Nothing to hold him together. Nothing to...*

The mist had swirled and settled and blanked him out.

Gone.

Anna turned to Grace.

'Mum...?'

'Mmmm?'

'Did he? I mean did he actually, you know, *do it?*' She blushed as she spoke. Not a child; she had to know.

Grace shook her head. Then, out loud: 'No, he didn't. Just when I thought that he ... that I ... something stopped him, right at the very last.'

'What?'

Grace shook her head again.

'I don't know. I felt the knife in my neck and knew I had lost the fight, that this was it. I'd struggled all I could. And now I was going to die. And suddenly all I could see was us – you, me, Simon, Rob – tramping across a beach, with Daddy and me nagging at you to keep going, like we always do. I could even hear myself saying it – *rest when we get there.* I could *hear* the words. And just for those seconds, I'd forgotten him, the knife, what he was doing. Everything –

except you. I was happy. It seemed that all my life I had been happy. A moment later, they burst in and dragged him off. But the truth is, Anna – he'd already stopped. He'd simply ... stopped. I suppose I'll have to tell them that, tell them he'd stopped. Yet it will only go to make it all so much more complicated.'

She glanced across the room. Richard wasn't looking at her. He wasn't looking at anyone. His eyes stared mildly at ... nothing. Strangely, given the numbers milling about, the crowd itself seemed to have thinned out. As if the main person, the one they were all here for, had simply vanished, leaving nothing but his shoes.

Chapter Thirty-Four

The eyes had it. Eyes bringing him back.

How long after? Months probably. Who knows? The first time it happens, he is sitting in the recreation yard, staring at his feet in prison issue shoes. Aware only that these are indeed his feet. The rest of him is a mass of flesh he barely recognises. Prison food has fattened him up, puffed him out. Not knowing what he was doing, he has accepted every morsel, chewing and swallowing, like an old man eating his sandwiches in a fog, unable to see his own hands in front of him.

But now, at long last, he has noticed the eyes. He looks up, to see who is staring at him.

A kid. Sharp-faced. Bones grinning through a sparsity of flesh. Not actually a kid, he realises after. Probably twenty odd, thirty even. But he will always think of him as a kid, with the premature aged look of a child who's seen too much.

Richard meets the eyes, and the owner smiles, a thin crescent moon of threaded lips. Richard nods. Then the fog comes back and he forgets all about him.

But days later, the fog clears again, and the 'kid' is still there, staring at him. And he is there again, days after that. Richard takes note, despite himself. Observes – dimly – that other men steer clear of the owner of these eyes, as if there's something about him that makes them nervous, like a bunch of elderly schoolmasters afraid of the child who gets away with murder.

Later still he discovers they are right to be afraid. This man (boy?) comes and goes as he pleases, and leaves the scars to prove it. With the result that even in a crowded recreation room, even in the ranks of the prison chapel, he creates a vacuum around him. He has the luxury of space. No one wants to get close.

Richard observes, then forgets. Still buffered by that blanket of fog, too dazed to wonder what he is doing here, in prison issue shoes. Shake him out of sleep in the middle of the night to ask him where he is, and he'll tell you he's at school, back at St Olave's of the Faint Hearted.

Despite that, the Boy/Man/Thing continues to stare, until even Richard feels the attention.

How could he fail to? Wherever Richard happens to be, so is he. Thin shoulders twitching beside him in the dinner queue; staring into the mirrors of the urinal as Richard steps out of a cubicle. Always there. In between the stacks of the library; standing next to him in the tuck shop where Richard likes to spend his pocket money on KitKats and Lion Bars. Sweet, cheap chocolate he never used to have a taste for, but does now. The only thing he can taste in the fog.

Eyes gradually, little by little, waking him up, threatening to pierce the mist.

Eyes waiting to make contact, choosing their moment.

And finally it happens. Richard is in the library. They gave him a job here when he arrived, assuming he would know about books, that he would at least have an interest. He has carried piles of them around for months, shifting them from one place to another, without ever bothering to check a title. He doesn't read. Every now and then, a name might give him pause, seed the beginnings of a frown. Seamus O'Connor, Alicia Milagro. But it passes. It always passes.

Today he has been sitting motionless at a table. Books everywhere. None of them his own. Sitting while the library clock moves without any urging from him. Time has no meaning for Richard Ortega.

A thin hand steals across his field of vision, a spider crab appeared from nowhere, scuttling across the table. Then it's gone, leaving behind a Special Edition for Limited Period Only cherry-flavoured KitKat. Richard stares at it.

'G'wan. It's for you. I know you like them. I seen you scoffing them down.'

Slowly, Richard picks it up.

'Get fat, though. Fat*ter*.'

Richard's hand hovers then puts the chocolate bar down again.

'Makes no odds, though. People like you, you can be anything you like. Fat, thin. Ugly. You can look like a monster, but who gives a fuck – if you write like a sodding angel?'

Richard looks up, and meets the steady gaze of the Boy/Man/Thing. Who says, his voice reedy as a blow pipe, 'See, I know who you are. Not like the other cunts here who don't know fuck. I've read your books. All of them. Fucking fucking fucking brilliant they are. Specially this one.' He pushes something else across the table – *The Hierophant*, a prison copy.

Richard blinks.

'Have to tell you – when my mum killed my dad, I thought the fucking world had come to an end. I thought I'd have to end up ordinary. Go work in a car phone warehouse, meet a girl, do the lottery like all the rest of the poor fuckers in the world. See, something like that, it eats away at your certainties. Then I read your book and it all made sense. *Ordinary* is for losers. *Ordinary* is for people prepared to be, invisible. *Ordinary* is for people who have never come across the genius of Richard Ortega.' He pauses. 'Troy,' he says almost shyly. 'The name's Troy.'

He reaches out his hand. But Richard only stares at it, never occurs to him to take it. Yet somehow this only makes Troy nod and he puts the hand away.

He says, 'Didn't recognise you at first, did I? Then one day I'm looking at a photo, then I'm looking at you, then I'm looking at the photo again, and what do you know, it's the same fucking face. It's your fucking face. Fatter, of course. You should watch your diet, you know. Couldn't believe it. *What the fuck*, I ask myself, *what the fuck is a man who writes like this, doing here? Pure fucking genius, and not even dead...'*

He grins at Richard, who wonders dimly if Troy is waiting for him to tell him why he's here. The trouble is, he can hardly recall himself the exact reason he is here. His own suspicion is that he has wandered in by mistake, lost in a fog, and simply hasn't got round to wandering out again.

But he doesn't have to worry. Troy doesn't need an explanation. He already has one.

'...Then it comes to me. It's Fate. Destiny. Divine chance. You're here because I'm here. The one man in the world I want to meet. Here. In my prison. On my patch.'

Is it Richard's imagination or are there tears in this boy's eyes, making him think briefly of a face held under water.

'Waiting all this time to tell you, I have. Choosing my moment. Now it's come. So here we fucking go. You were my rock, Mr Ortega. My safe place. Honest to fucking God.'

Until now he has been standing, as if keeping the last vestige of distance between them. Now though, he comes and sits down next to Richard. Who instantly can detect the internal friction of skin and bone working away inside this Boy/Man/Thing; smells the hot acrid exhalations of internal combustion on his breath. The watery look has evaporated. Troy lowers his voice.

'Know what I did last week? My sentence was coming to an end, which is a laugh in itself. You'd think they'd want to keep me in longer, have the power of their own convictions. "Sheer motiveless violence", the judge called it, me doing over that old lady. As if he'd know! See, not so much of the motiveless. Do you know what she had at the top of her shopping bag?'

Richard shakes his head.

'A fucking supermarket copy of Miriam Rapko's *Quilt Making For The Soul*. Well, that was it as far as I was concerned. Ran out of patience, didn't I? Not only had the old bitch refused to give me her purse, she was reading that kind of shit. I saw stars then, I tell you. Had to give it to her, a kicking simply to make her see sense. It's like my feet had a duty, God-given.'

His face, which had lit up like an explosion of marsh gas at the memory, grew dark again. 'But then, last week, they were going to ship me out. *For good behaviour*, they said. One-third of my sentence duly served. One-third of fucking nothing. Makes you wonder what the country's coming too. So you know what I did?'

Again Richard shakes his head. Not quite so dazed now. Fog less dense. That mention of Rapko has centred him. Finally he is beginning to wake up.

'I tell you what I did. I went up to D wing

379

and grazed The Old Fart with a steak knife. Put him in hospital for three days. Now they can't do nothing. I'm in for the duration.'

He watches Richard, curious to know if he understands what he's hearing. The Old Fart is the oldest man in the prison. Seventy-nine years old, with incipient Parkinson's that no one wants to pick up on. Slowly, patiently, Troy goes on to explain:

'So you see, no one's sending me anywhere, not now. I'm staying with you, Mister Ortega. Wherever you go, I'll go. Wherever you are, I'll be there too. That all right with you?'

The question is purely rhetorical. Troy edges closer.

'Genius like you, he should have the right people round him. I'm going to make sure that happens. I'm not going to let you be alone, not in a place like this. A man of your calibre needs friends, people who understand him.' His eyes, so sharp a moment ago, grow almost dreamy. 'Know what? I'm even going to get the screws to change the cells. They do anything I tell them here. Couple of weeks from now, and I'll be there, day and night, waking and sleeping. We'll have a cell all to ourselves. We'll never be apart. Like the sound of that do you, do you, Mr Ortega?'

Richard stares at him. Fog finally shredding. Mind coming clear as a bell.

A mind that wants to know only one thing.

'Who ... who else do you like – apart from me? Who else do you read?'

The boy stares at him in joy. Does he know these are the first words Richard Ortega has volunteered in six months?

'Who do I read? Fucking everybody. Every fucking body there is. But they're shit, all of them, and that's the truth.'

'Who? Who are you talking about?' says Richard urgently. 'Seamus O'Connor?'

'Shit.'

'Alicia Milagro?'

'Lesbian shit.'

'Marcia Coyote?'

Troy's eyes roll in his head like pellets of mercury. 'Oh Mister Ortega, that you even have to ask.' He leans back in his chair. The hollows in his cheeks are full of dark deeds, real and imagined. 'The only one who's up there, with you, Mister Ortega, is the mighty Amis himself. Magnificent Martin – hand on heart, he's the only man fit to lick your boots. Fuck the rest.'

Richard Ortega hears him. And with these words, the last traces of fog have vanished. No more than a memory, never to be thought of again. Ever. For a moment Richard sits, feeling the hard, diamond-centred beam of his self, back again. Slowly he gets to his feet.

'Where you going, Mister Ortega?' Already the boy is there, muscles twitching, at the ready.

'To my room, of course. My ... cell.'

'To do what, Mister O?'

'Why, to work, what else?'

'Fucking ace. Fucking brilliant, I say. Pardon me for saying it, but you're looking more like your back cover already.'

Richard nods. Because it's true. He makes his way to the door, back to his cell, his familiar at his heels. Not Flaubert now, but Faust. Ready to make his mark on the page, at long last ready to begin.

Sometimes a writer, if he is a true writer...

The publishers hope that this book has given you enjoyable reading. Large Print Books are especially designed to be as easy to see and hold as possible. If you wish a complete list of our books please ask at your local library or write directly to:

Magna Large Print Books
Magna House, Long Preston,
Skipton, North Yorkshire.
BD23 4ND

This Large Print Book, for people
who cannot read normal print,
is published under the auspices of

THE ULVERSCROFT FOUNDATION